blue ridge sunrise

Center Point
Large Print

Also by Denise Hunter and available from Center Point Large Print:

Barefoot Summer
Falling Like Snowflakes
The Goodbye Bride
Just a Kiss
Married 'til Monday
Sweetbriar Cottage
The Wishing Season

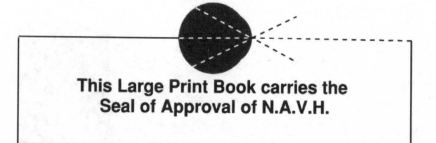

This Large Print Book carries the Seal of Approval of N.A.V.H.

blue ridge sunrise

Denise Hunter

CENTER POINT LARGE PRINT
THORNDIKE, MAINE

This Center Point Large Print edition
is published in the year 2017 by arrangement with
Thomas Nelson.

The text of this Large Print edition is unabridged.
In other aspects, this book may vary
from the original edition.
Printed in the United States of America
on permanent paper.
Set in 16-point Times New Roman type.

ISBN: 978-1-68324-612-1

Library of Congress Cataloging-in-Publication Data

Names: Hunter, Denise, 1968- author.
Title: Blue Ridge sunrise / Denise Hunter.
Description: Center Point Large Print edition. | Thorndike, Maine :
    Center Point Large Print, 2017. | Series: A Blue Ridge romance
Identifiers: LCCN 2017040158 | ISBN 9781683246121
    (hardcover : alk. paper)
Subjects: LCSH: Large type books. | GSAFD: Christian fiction. |
    Love stories.
Classification: LCC PS3608.U5925 B58 2017b | DDC 813/.6—dc23
LC record available at https://lccn.loc.gov/2017040158

part one

chapter one

Zoe Collins never expected to step foot in Copper Creek again. But the one thing that could bring her back had happened.

She stepped out of the dark sedan, a little wobbly on her heels. Brady, her brother, quietly took her elbow as they followed their father across the manicured cemetery that would become Granny's new earthly home.

She drew deeply of the early spring air, fixing her eyes on the surrounding mountains and pine forests. Copper Creek was nestled down in the foothills of the north Georgia mountains. Some might say the town was a throwback to simpler days, but for Zoe the memories of home were a conflicting cocktail of bliss and misery. Heavy on the misery.

Her boyfriend, Kyle, had stayed at the hotel with her daughter, Gracie. Zoe's long-buried grief and guilt warred with an intense feeling of relief at finally being alone. She would focus on the latter, she decided, filling her lungs with the familiar sweet smells of home: hyacinths, sunshine, and freedom.

As they neared the tent, Zoe's best friend came toward her. Hope Daniels hadn't changed a bit— still a natural beauty with that dark, wavy hair

7

and those sparkling green eyes. When she smiled she was the spitting image of Rachel McAdams. But today that wide grin was nowhere to be seen.

Zoe slipped off to intercept her and found herself swallowed in a hug like only Hope could give. One part love, two parts boa constrictor.

"Zoe."

"Hey girl," Zoe squeezed out.

"I'm so sorry I couldn't make the funeral."

"No worries. It's so good to see you."

Though Hope only managed the Rusty Nail on the weekend, a round of spring flu had taken out some of the waitstaff so she'd had to fill in. Radio was her true love. She hosted a daily call-in program called "Living with Hope" on a local station, using that psychology degree she'd worked on so hard.

"How are you holding up?"

"All right, I suppose."

Hope released her, allowing Zoe to draw a full breath.

"Oh, I've missed you," her friend said. "Five years is too long—and hardly a phone call," she scolded. "Never mind. I'll chastise you later at a more appropriate time."

"Good job. Your filter's come a long way."

"Not really. Stick around a minute." Hope's gaze flitted toward the tent. "Now where's that sweet little angel I've been dying to get my hands on? It's a sad state of affairs when I have to make do with Facebook and Instagram."

"I thought the funeral might be a bit confusing for a four-year-old, and I didn't really want her to meet Dad here, so I left her with Kyle."

"I can't believe you're still with him."

Zoe tilted a look at Hope. "And you wonder why I never call. Kyle's been there for us, Hope."

"We'll talk about it later. Appropriate time and all that."

"I can hardly wait." Zoe's eyes swung to the tent. "I hate that I wasn't here to lend a hand with arrangements. We just couldn't get away from Nashville any sooner."

Hope pressed her lips together, obviously suppressing another thought. "Well . . . you know your grandmother. She had everything in place, God rest her soul. There wasn't much to do. How's Brady holding up today? He was kind of a mess the day she died."

Zoe glanced at her brother, now under the tent. The black suit made the best of his tall, sturdy frame and short dark hair. He was chatting with their dad, and she tried not to be jealous of the easy relationship they shared. Zoe'd had only sporadic contact with Brady—or anyone else for that matter—since she'd left.

Granny. It was too late now. Guilt pinched hard. But she shook off the feeling.

"How's Brady been doing since the divorce?" Zoe asked.

Hope shrugged. "As expected, I guess. I don't know how he ever put up with that woman, but he sure loves baby Sam. He gets him every other weekend, you know."

Audrey had left Brady, no doubt breaking his heart, while Zoe had been AWOL. Yet another person she'd let down.

"He wanted custody, but Audrey fought him and won. I swear she just did it out of spite."

From what Zoe knew of Audrey, that was probably about right. But she didn't want to think about her brother anymore. It was too close to the topic she was avoiding.

"How's the orchard faring in Granny's absence?" she asked.

"Last few years she barely even oversaw it. She dealt with the retailers, but otherwise it's practically run itself, what with all the help." Hope opened her mouth as if she had something else to say, then bit her lip instead.

Zoe closed her eyes and could almost smell the peaches, ripe to harvest. Feel the fuzzy skin and taste the sweet juicy flesh. She'd spent every spare hour at the orchard, growing up. It had been better than home, especially after her mama died. She'd have liked to spend a couple quiet hours there. Too bad Kyle was in such a rush to get back to Nashville.

"I never thought it would be her heart, of all things," Zoe said.

"I know, right? She seemed fit as a fiddle. Just last week I walked in on her perched at the top of a sixteen-foot ladder. I said, 'Granny Nel, what are you doing?' and she said, 'Changing a lightbulb.' I said, 'Get on down from there! You're twelve feet off the ground!' And she said, 'Which is the perfect height to change this bulb.' "

Zoe gave a wistful smile. "Sounds like her."

Regret raged inside like spring floodwaters. Zoe had left because she thought she'd let down Granny and everyone else. She hadn't realized that leaving would be the ultimate disappointment to them. The regret threatened to pull her under, but she fought to the surface. She was doing that a lot lately. One day soon she was going to lose the battle.

Hope squeezed Zoe's forearm. "Hey. Enough with the sad eyes. Granny Nel wouldn't want you crying in your soup."

Zoe blinked back tears, looking past Hope at the cars still pulling up to the curb. She scanned the crowd, hope and dread duking it out for the lead. She quickly turned back to her friend.

"You're right. Tell me about what's going on around here. With you? What'd I miss?"

"Oh, you know Copper Creek. Nothing much changes around here. I'm still doing my radio program and working at the Rusty Nail on weekends."

"You're being too modest. I saw that snippet online about the rising popularity of 'Living with Hope.' You won an award, right?"

Hope shrugged. "I love what I do. But it's just a local program."

"Not for long. You're on your way, girl."

"We'll see about that. But how about you?" Hope nudged her. "Opening for cool bands and all that."

Kyle's band, Brevity, had opened for some well-known artists. It was a rush, performing for a large audience.

"Well, I'm only a backup singer."

"Please. Your vocals are amazing. You know, Last Chance is playing at the Rusty Nail tomorrow night. You should sing a couple songs with them."

"Oh, we won't be around that long. We're leaving after the interment."

Hope's face fell. "Are you kidding me? You just got here last night. I waited almost five years for you to come back."

"Sorry. There's a gig we need to get back for." And as nice as it was to catch up with Hope, there were other people she was less keen on seeing.

The stragglers were making their way toward the tent, a small wave of darkly clothed humanity. It was almost time to begin.

She squeezed Hope's hand. "I'd better go. We'll catch up later."

She turned toward the tent, making her way

over the bumpy ground, and nearly stumbled as her eyes caught on the person she'd been watching for.

Cruz Huntley had never looked better. His crisp white shirt contrasted with his Puerto Rican skin, and the suit coat accentuated his broad shoulders. He looked up just then, and his dark eyes pierced hers.

Her heart was like a kick drum in her chest as she got caught in his gaze for a long, painful moment. Was he remembering the last funeral they'd attended? And everything that had happened that day?

His lips curved in a thin smile.

She tore her eyes away. Fixed them on the white casket propped under the tent. On the spray of colorful flowers arranged over the top. She shook Cruz from her thoughts. She wasn't going there today. Never mind that she hadn't set eyes on him in forever. Never mind that he'd once stolen her heart—then broken it so thoroughly.

You're a stupid girl, Zoe.

Under the tent she took a seat between her brother and dad, trying to ignore the coldness that radiated from Daddy in waves. She'd tried to hug him when she'd seen him at the funeral home, but he'd only stiffened in her arms. She'd drawn away, the sting of rejection burrowing deep.

He'd never been Granny's biggest fan. His mother-in-law had been too spirited for his liking, and she'd only encouraged Zoe's independence. It had been a sticking point among the three of them that only grew worse when Zoe's mom died.

But she wasn't going to dwell on her relationship with her dad. Today was about Granny. About laying her to rest.

Zoe emptied her lungs, letting that thought sink in. Letting the ache swell in her chest until it spread outward. As if sensing the sudden rush of pain, Brady squeezed her hand. She squeezed back.

Granny's gone.

The thought hit her like a sledgehammer as Pastor Jack stepped forward to say a few final words. Her grandma was gone. And with her, all the love that had sustained Zoe even from afar.

Somehow it didn't feel real. Somehow she'd thought Granny would outlast them all. But nothing lasted forever. Not even love.

chapter two

It had been less than five years since Zoe had walked away from him, but Cruz wasn't sure he would've recognized her on the street. She sat graveside, under the tent between her brother and dad, her shoulders rolled in on themselves. Her hair, auburn then, was now blond, and her natural curls had been tamed into sleek locks that fluttered in the late March breeze.

Cruz skirted the headstones, joining the gathering crowd. He'd slipped in late to the funeral and sat in the very back of the church, work having kept him longer than he planned. He hadn't offered his condolences yet.

A moment later Pastor Jack began the graveside service, speaking loudly enough for his voice to carry to the back of the large crowd. Nellie Russell had been a town favorite. A feisty woman with a keen sense of justice. She'd given *him* a chance, hadn't she? When others thought he was just another loser from the wrong side of the tracks. He'd loved her as though she were his own grandmother.

The service was short but heartfelt, and when it ended Cruz stood on the outskirts, waiting his turn to approach the family. His best friend, Brady, seemed to be holding up well, accepting condolences with a stoic smile and a firm handshake. This was a big blow on the heels of his divorce from Audrey.

It was Zoe, though, that his eyes kept returning to. Chin tucked, eyes turned down. *Meek* was the word that came to mind. No, he wouldn't have recognized her on the street. What had happened to his lioness? His *leona?* He had a bad feeling he knew.

She knuckled a tear from the corner of her eye, and a wave of protectiveness swept over him. Where was Kyle now? He should be here holding her hand. The trio had arrived in town yesterday in a red Mustang. That bit of news was too juicy for the grapevine to miss: return of the hometown boy and girl made good gossip.

He eased to the front of the line as people slipped away, his heart going like a jackhammer. Almost five years since she'd swapped him for a dream. Since she'd left and broken his pathetic schoolboy heart.

She was still a beauty, with her flawless skin and lean build. Still had those long legs, though she'd grown into them now. She was no longer the gangly colt.

Her lashes swept up just then, her green eyes landing on him. A direct hit. Her face softened for the briefest of moments, her lips parting.

His heart seized up as a dozen images flooded into his mind. Zoe hanging out his passenger

16

window, red hair snapping behind her like a proud flag. Leaping from the high bank of Sutter's Bend, her squeal carrying on the sultry breeze. Hopping onto his back as they ran through the orchard, her laughter ringing out like the most beautiful melody.

He blinked away the memories, feeling disoriented as Zoe came back into focus.

Her eyes were shuttered now, and her lashes swept the tops of her cheeks, a tight smile forming on her lips. She received condolences and made small talk. And then it was his turn.

She turned toward him. Her eyes sparked, and her chin tilted up. "Hello, Cruz."

Ah, there was his leona. Though why on earth she was peeved at him, he didn't know. He brushed the past aside as he clasped her hand. "Sorry for your loss, Zoe. She sure was a special woman."

"Yes, she was." Her voice was like velvet, soft and quiet, her drawl all but gone. Her eyes everywhere but on him.

She pulled her hand from his.

"Granny Nel loved you an awful lot, you know. Talked about you all the time. She was very proud of you." He didn't mention how much it hurt to hear Zoe's name spoken so often—or in tandem with Kyle's.

Zoe blinked rapidly and folded her arms over her stomach. "Thank you for saying so."

"Brady didn't tell me you were coming."

"He didn't know for sure."

Cruz felt the sting of guilt. She and her brother had been so close once upon a time. It was Cruz's fault the wedge was there. His fault there'd been a wedge between him and Brady too. It had taken months to restore their friendship after Zoe left.

The moment stretched on, awkward and uncomfortable, the words they'd said before she left a messy pile on the ground between them.

❧••❦

Zoe had been dreading seeing Cruz again since the second she'd left him. Which didn't explain why her heart squeezed tight at the sight of him or the way his touch sent a shiver racing up her arm.

"How've you been, Zoe?"

She'd forgotten the low scrape of his voice and the way it made her insides hum.

"Good. Just fine." She wanted to see those amber flecks in his brown eyes again, but she'd gotten good at avoiding eye contact with men. "You? How've you been?"

"Not bad. Not bad."

"Glad to hear it."

If there was an award for most boring conversation of the year, they were a shoo-in.

"Congrats on all your success," he said.

She didn't feel like a success. Whatever she'd achieved had come at a high price. And she was no longer sure it was worth it. "Thank you."

She wondered if he ever Googled her or checked the band's social media pages. God knew she'd had to stop herself from keeping tabs on him. Kyle would've found out, and there would've been hell to pay.

"What have you been doing with yourself?" she asked.

"Excuse me, Zoe," Joe Connelly said as he stepped closer.

She released a pent-up breath at the welcome interruption.

"I'm sorry to intrude, but I have a two o'clock appointment." Joe looked every inch the attorney in his pressed suit and sideswept hair. "We need to schedule a meeting to go over the will."

"Oh," Zoe said. "I'm afraid I'm leaving today. I have an event to get back for. I thought Brady could just handle everything?"

Joe made a face, then checked his watch. "You should really be there for this. Listen, I have an opening at four o'clock. Would that rush you too much? I know you must want time with your family."

She'd planned to introduce Gracie to her dad—not that he'd asked. "Suits me fine. I'll let Brady know. Thank you, Joe."

He took her hand. "Your grandmother loved you very much, Zoe. She made no bones about that."

Too bad Zoe had all but thrown that love back in her face. A burn started at the back of her eyes, and her throat tightened. "Thank you."

With a final nod he was gone.

And it was only then that she realized Cruz had left too. Had slipped away as quickly and silently as his love.

chapter three

Connelly Law Offices was about as homey a place as such a business could be. The lobby and halls were painted a warm taupe, the walls sported Georgia landscapes, and the air smelled of freshly printed documents and new carpet.

Joe ushered Zoe and Gracie into a room, Kyle on their heels, and said, "I'll be right in."

An oblong mahogany conference table dominated the space, its surface bearing a few battle scars.

Zoe tugged Gracie along as they joined her brother at the table. Zoe was conscious of Kyle's looming presence and the tension he'd hauled into the room with him.

Brady's gaze lit on Kyle, probably noting his long tousled hair and careless style of dress that actually took longer than one might think to achieve.

Her brother's jaw went rock-hard. "What's he doing here?"

Kyle set a hand at the small of her back. "Somebody has to look out for Zoe's best interests."

"Am I supposed to think that's you?" Brady's eyes slid to Gracie, his face softening.

Zoe approached her brother, who'd stood to meet his niece. "This is your Uncle Brady, Gracie."

"Hey, sweetheart."

Gracie turned her cherub face into Zoe's leg.

"She's a little shy," Zoe said.

"That's all right. We'll get acquainted afterwards." Brady looked at Zoe. "She looks just like you did. Those red curls and pale skin."

"Remember me telling you about Uncle Brady, honey? About how we used to dig for worms and go fishing in the creek?"

Gracie peeked out, blinking up at Brady.

His eyes softened. "Hey, squirt. You're getting so big."

Before Zoe could respond she felt the pressure of Kyle's hand on her shoulder. She let him guide her to the opposite side of the table, where they took their seats.

The air conditioning kicked on, and Gracie shivered. Zoe wrapped her arms around her daughter. She should've brought her girl a sweater. Why on earth couldn't she do anything right?

Silence stretched out, and tension closed in like a spring valley fog as Brady and Kyle eyed each other across the table.

"Nice you decided to join us for the will portion of the day, Kyle," Brady said. "Where were you two hours ago when Zoe was weeping graveside?"

Zoe winced. "Brady."

Kyle stiffened, almost imperceptibly. "Watching Gracie so Zoe could grieve in peace. Don't you

22

judge me. You don't know anything about us or our lives."

"And whose fault is that?"

"I'm guessing it's yours."

"Zoe always answered my calls before you took her away."

Kyle smiled smugly. "I didn't kidnap her. She came of her own free will. Maybe she just doesn't want to hear from you. That ever occur to you?"

"Guys, come on," Zoe said. "This isn't the time."

"All right." Joe blew into the office like a welcome breeze and sat at the head of the table beside Zoe.

She breathed a sigh of relief as all heads swung his way. Blood had rushed into her cheeks, making her warm. The air seemed stuffy and thick now.

"So here we go," Joe said. "Thank you for making it last-minute like this, and on such a sad day. Your grandma was a special lady, and it was my privilege to help her get her affairs in order. She loved the two of you so much."

He shuffled the papers and set them flat. "She begins with the normal preliminaries, naming the two of you as her beneficiaries. I won't bore you with the details, but my secretary is making copies for you."

He nudged his glasses up high on his nose and began reading.

Zoe was already having difficulty focusing,

with Kyle bristling at her side and Brady glaring at him. The legalese jumbled anything of value she did manage to hear.

She was relieved when Brady spoke up. "Joe, would you mind just cutting to the chase? No offense, but you attorneys sure know how to muddle up the simplest of things."

Joe's lips twitched. "Not at all. Is that okay with you, Zoe?"

"Of course."

Joe folded his hands over the document. "The gist of it is, your grandmother wanted the two of you to share equally in her worldly goods. But she was keenly aware of your different needs and passions."

He looked at Brady. "Brady, to you she left her various stocks and bonds and mutual funds."

"Granny played the stock market?" Brady asked.

Joe chuckled. "Like a pro. She started investing early, and she's grown quite the portfolio. It's substantial."

"Go, Granny," Brady said.

"I can go over the details with you later, but she knew how you like working on high-performance cars, and she was aware of how the divorce left you financially. She wanted you to continue your work and be able to take care of your son. There's plenty here to do all that and get your boy through college someday, if he's of a mind to go."

Brady nodded, his jaw tightening, his eyes finding the tabletop.

"As I said, she loved you immensely."

"I never dreamed she had all that money," Zoe said. "She lived so simply."

"It was never about things with Granny," Brady said.

He was so right. Granny'd always had time for her. Always had an ear to lend, a hug for the taking.

Zoe dabbed the corners of her eyes. "It was about love."

"And being independent," Brady said. "She taught us to stand on our own two feet. Just last week I caught her mowing that hill by the road with the old push mower."

Zoe snorted. "Sounds about right."

Joe looked at Zoe. "Your grandma ran the 5K last spring. The one benefitting cancer survivors? She didn't finish last either."

"Came in somewhere in the middle, actually." Brady smiled wistfully. "She buzzed right past Mayor Walters. Embarrassed the daylights out of him."

A longing rose up in Zoe. To see Granny one more time. Walk the orchard. Snap green beans with her on the porch. How was it possible she was gone?

She set her cheek against her daughter's head, regret flooding through her. Gracie had only known Granny's love from a distance. Zoe had cheated her daughter of so much.

Kyle shifted beside her, checking his watch. Boredom practically rolled off him in waves. Zoe knew he was eager to get back on the road. Get back to the studio where he was in charge and important.

"That leaves you, Zoe." Joe's eyes softened on her. "Your grandmother had such fond memories of walking the orchard with you. She felt you had an affinity with the land, and an insatiable curiosity about the process that reminded her of her husband."

A terrible dread rose in Zoe even as the words left Joe's mouth.

"She left the orchard to you, Zoe. The orchard and the farmhouse, minus a few personal things you'll read about later. She hoped you'd return home and run the place."

"What?" Her exclamation was more breath than word.

Kyle bristled beside her. "That's ridiculous."

"Nonetheless," Joe said. "Nellie was adamant that the orchard go to Zoe."

"She'll have to sell it then," Kyle said. "She has a career and life away from here."

Brady nailed him with a look. "This is none of your affair. You shouldn't even be here."

"The heck it ain't."

"Let's just simmer down," Joe said. "Decisions

don't need to be made today. Let's just take some time to let this sink in."

Kyle stood. "There's nothing to sink in. She's selling it. Come on, Zoe."

"Is there . . . is there anything else, Joe?"

"Nothing of consequence. Sheila will have your copy of the will ready at the front desk."

Kyle was already at the door, a dark look on his face. Aimed at her.

Zoe rose, taking Gracie's hand.

Brady looked as if he were about to come out of his chair. Joe had his hand on Brady's arm as if holding him there.

Zoe gave Brady an apologetic look. "I'll call you later."

⇒•⇐

"I can't leave tomorrow, Kyle. I have responsibilities." Zoe stood between the two hotel beds, her purse still hanging from her shoulder. He'd only agreed to one more night, but tomorrow was Saturday. She needed at least a few days.

Somehow being back home—near Brady and Hope and the people who loved her—had given her courage.

Or maybe it was only stupidity.

Gracie had fallen asleep in the car, and Kyle had hardly said a word since they'd left the law office. They'd secured another night at the hotel and lugged their suitcase back inside. Kyle had plopped on the bed, and now he surfed through the channels, his jaw tight. The longish brown hair his female fans were so enamored with flopped over one eye.

He was giving her the silent treatment. It was his most effective form of punishment. Zoe couldn't stand being shut out, so she sucked up to Kyle and soon gave him his way. Anything was better than his cold shoulder.

Her grandma's will had thrown a wrench into everything, but Brady hadn't helped matters either. At least Kyle hadn't come face-to-face with Cruz today. She didn't see that going well. Thank God Kyle hadn't attended the funeral. He never would've let her go alone if he'd known Cruz would be there.

She hated this side of him. The stubborn, angry side that made her feel so alone and helpless.

But he had a good side too, she thought, remembering the gentle way he'd laid Gracie on the double bed, tucking the covers around her as if she were his. And he was generous. He'd donated the profits from their last concert to his bandmate's son who was fighting leukemia.

It was his compassion and generosity that had attracted her in the beginning. He'd taken her under his wing and provided stability at a time when she had nothing to offer. When the foundation of her life was crumbling. When she'd felt stuck and afraid.

He treated Gracie as his own, and his tenderness toward her daughter had endeared him to Zoe. But as their relationship shifted into more, his possessiveness and manipulations had become more apparent. She'd been blind in the beginning to his faults. But she was blind no longer.

She looked at him now. At the tightened skin at the corners of his eyes. If she pushed him it would only make things worse. But they had some decisions to make.

"Kyle, we have to talk about this."

He calmly punched the channel button on the remote.

"It'll only take a few days to tie this up."

Although she didn't know how, exactly, it was going to get "tied up." She now owned an orchard, for crying out loud. What was she going to do with it? The thought of selling it about broke her heart.

Her grandma and grandpa had built that business with their own two hands. Grandpa died when Zoe was young, and Granny had spent the rest of her life growing it into a successful operation.

Zoe couldn't sell the orchard. She owed her grandma so much.

But she couldn't run it either. She had a life. One that included a lot of traveling and a boyfriend who was never going to stick around Copper Creek. Especially not for a bunch of peach trees.

Would Brady want it? He'd never expressed much interest in the family business. His passion revolved around cars. There wasn't the room or desire in his life for farming.

Or in hers for that matter.

That wasn't exactly true. Farming was in her blood. She'd always loved the orchard. Her grandma had been right about that. Even now she woke up sometimes in the dead of night missing the loamy scent of earth, the smell of morning dew on the grass, the sweet tang of a ripe peach, still warm from the sun.

It was almost April. Harvest season would arrive mid-May. Even if the orchard "almost ran itself" as Hope said, someone would have to be there to make decisions and oversee operations.

For a moment she let herself imagine she was that person. She closed her eyes as her breath left her body in a long, weight-shedding exhale.

"Kyle . . . I'm going to need more than one day to sort this out. If you need to leave, you can go ahead. I can join you in a few days."

He'd never agree to that. But maybe the thought of her sticking around without him would inspire some flexibility. Talking to Kyle was sometimes like playing a game of chess.

He flipped to the next channel. And the next.

He didn't have to say what he expected her to do. Call a Realtor and list the place. Handle matters from afar. Distance herself from Copper Creek and everyone in it. Just getting him to come back for the funeral had been like moving a mountain.

But suddenly she knew she wouldn't do what he wanted. She couldn't leave with all this unsettled. She'd already let Granny down. She was going to do right by her this time—whatever that meant.

Zoe sank onto the bed beside him, wishing he'd at least look at her. "The Realtor's offices are closed now anyhow and will be for the rest of the weekend. We need to stay put at least through Monday."

His eyes darted to hers, then back to the TV, a shadow flickering as his jaw twitched.

"We can leave Tuesday and still be back in plenty of time to get ready for Summer Fest. You'll have more time with your friends here." She still had no idea what she was going to do, but she had to buy some time.

"I didn't ask for this, Kyle, but I have to handle it." She put a hand over his, stroking the back of his hand with her thumb. It always softened him. "Be patient with me?"

His eyes turned to hers, sticking this time. Those eyes that could burn like blue fire or grow as cold as a glacier. Right now they were somewhere in between, and she knew her efforts were working.

He sighed. "Fine. But we leave Tuesday morning."

It was a major concession. She squeezed his hand. "Thanks, Kyle."

But later she lay awake for hours, the night slowly ticking away. She remembered the sound of Granny humming in the orchard. Remembered the way she'd sat on the floor playing games with her and Brady, never too busy for them. The way she'd encouraged Zoe when algebra had her in tears.

And then, as always when she remembered those days, her thoughts turned to Cruz. To the strength she'd once found in his sturdy embrace. The love she'd seen in his deep brown eyes. Then she remembered the way his gaze had felt on her today, warm and wistful, and tears melted silently into her pillow.

chapter four

Zoe didn't know how Kyle had talked her into coming tonight. The Rusty Nail was packed with locals, every seat taken, and a crowd milled around the bar. The smell of grilled burgers hung heavily in the air, making her stomach turn. Rawley Watkins, the lead singer of Last Chance, belted out the chorus of a country tune about a girl that got away.

Zoe pushed back her plate and helped Gracie reach her cup of juice. Kyle was at the next table, talking with Axel Brown and Garret Morgan. His chest was puffed out as they quizzed him about his rock star life.

She blocked out the conversation, glancing at the entrance for the hundredth time. A few stragglers entered, no one she recognized.

She turned her attention to the band onstage as one of the musicians broke into a rousing solo on his violin. The crowd applauded when the solo ended, and the chorus kicked up again.

"Mama!" Gracie held her arms out. "Pick me up."

Zoe lifted her daughter from the booster seat. "You all full, sweetie pie?"

"Yes." Gracie rubbed her eyes with her pudgy fingers, which Zoe had, thankfully, just wiped clean.

The band would break soon, and Zoe hoped Kyle would be ready to leave. They'd only played one set, but Gracie needed to get to bed. But seeing as how a fan club had formed around Kyle, she was going to have a hard time getting him out of here.

Brady returned to the table with their drinks as the band announced their first break. Hope skirted the other tables, stopping to check on customers along the way.

"Want me to take her?" Brady asked, nodding toward Gracie, who'd settled against her shoulder.

"I'm fine."

"Break time." Hope plopped down at the table, arching a brow at Brady as her gaze raked over him. "Nice shirt, Collins."

Brady looked down, scowling as he wetted a napkin. "That may or may not be spit-up."

"Color looks good on you. Brings out your tan."

"That was my goal."

"Where is little Sammy?" Hope said. "I want my cuddle time."

"My weekend with him got cut short. Long story."

"That was a phenomenal set," Zoe said. "The band's even better than I remembered."

"We have got to get you up there, girl. Next set. Come on, pleeaase?"

"You should do it, Zoe," her brother said.

"Oh, no. I'm on vacation this week." The thought of singing in front of all these familiar faces made her mouth go dry. Plus Kyle wouldn't like it, and there was already enough tension arcing between them to zap a grown elephant dead.

"You should ask Kyle to sing, though," Zoe said. "He'd probably do it."

"Seriously? The band would sooner quit than let him on that stage." Hope propped her arms on the table, leaning closer. "Zoe, when are you going to leave that loser? He's no good for you."

Brady held his Coke aloft. "Preach it, sister."

It was nothing Zoe hadn't told herself a hundred times. She and Kyle had started as only friends, but now her life, her livelihood, was entwined with his. And she didn't have the gumption to untangle it.

Hope set her hand on Zoe's arm. "Come back home. Run the orchard. You'll have a place to stay—a stable home for Gracie, close to family."

"You'd make a good living," Brady said. "And we'd be here for you all the way."

Zoe refused to admit it was the very thing that had been spinning in her mind all day. "Stop ganging up on me."

"We care about you, Zoe," Hope said. "And we don't like the way he treats you."

Zoe's eyes darted to the next table, only to find Kyle's gaze fixed on her. She knew he couldn't hear their conversation, but the way his eyes

35

narrowed made her wonder if he had telepathic abilities.

A chill raced down her spine. She tore her eyes away from him and dug through her purse with her free hand. For what, she didn't know.

"You're different, Zoe," Brady said.

"He's isolated you from your family. Can't you see that?"

"What is this, an intervention?" Her face flushed as she rooted through her purse and came up with a Chap Stick. She rubbed it on Gracie's lips, her hand trembling.

"You don't need him," Hope said. "If you're staying on account of the band, Last Chance would take you in a heartbeat. I know they're not as big as Brevity, but the genre is more up your alley. Please consider it."

"You know why Granny left you that orchard. It's where you belong. Where you've always belonged. You can't sell it. Do you really want to see it leave the family?"

Suddenly Zoe was tired of being told what to do. What to think. How to feel. "Stop pressuring me!"

Brady and Hope traded looks.

"We're not trying to pressure you, honey," Hope said, squeezing her hand. "We just want what's best for you."

Zoe felt, more than saw, the entrance door swing open. Her heart gave a sturdy punch as

36

Cruz crossed the threshold, scanning the crowd. He looked like every country girl's dream in his plaid button-down and worn blue jeans.

Zoe jerked her eyes away and pushed back from the table. "I'm taking Gracie to the bathroom." Tugging the startled little girl by the hand, Zoe skirted the tables, headed down the short hall, and ducked into the restroom, her heart keeping pace with the up-tempo song blaring from the speakers.

⇒••⇐

Cruz's eyes flittered over the crowded restaurant. The place was jammed tonight, as it always was when Last Chance played. His friends had promised to save him a seat, but he stepped up to the crowded bar, knowing table service was probably running slow.

His eyes caught on a woman walking the opposite direction. It took him a moment to recognize Zoe's slender form. At the sight of the child close beside her, a fist tightened in his gut. He looked away.

Those last weeks before she left began playing out in his mind in vivid Technicolor. That familiar ache in his chest returned, making it hard to breathe. He had to stop thinking about her. She'd soon be gone, just like last time, and he was done nursing that sore spot.

When he got to the front of the line he ordered

a drink and withdrew bills from his wallet. He was just stuffing it back into his pocket when the hairs on his arms bristled.

Surprise, surprise. He found Kyle an arm's-length away, staring at him, his cold blue eyes gloating.

The song ended, the energetic sound of the crowd taking over for a few long beats.

Kyle's lips curled up at one corner. "Huntley. Still hanging around this Podunk town, I see."

It was supposed to be a greeting, but the mocking sound of his voice and the smug look on his face made Cruz want to slug him in the jaw.

"Jimmerson." He feigned indifference, but he couldn't help antagonizing. "How's my girl?"

Kyle's lips fell, flattening into a hard line. His nostrils flared. Muscles, probably honed at some fancy hotel gym, bunched up as his spine lengthened.

Cruz was glad for the extra few inches he had on Kyle and hoped like heck the idiot would throw the first punch. It was a long time coming.

But Kyle must've been worried about messing up his face. As the next song started up, he slowly relaxed, that smug look returning.

"She hasn't been yours for a long time, Huntley." His eyes lit with something spiteful and cruel. "It's my bed she's sleeping in now."

The arrow hit its target, the words simultaneously making his flesh crawl and his blood boil. His fists clenched.

Just one hit, God. That's all I'm asking.

Before Cruz could think of a response, Kyle reached for his beer, winking at the attractive bartender. He lifted it in salute to Cruz just before he sauntered away, and Cruz was left gritting his teeth.

❧•❦

This was the longest night in all eternity, Zoe thought as she shifted Gracie on her lap. Her daughter had fallen asleep almost an hour ago, and Zoe's arm was going numb. Her own eyes were getting heavy, but Kyle wasn't going anywhere now.

He'd planted himself at her side as soon as she'd returned from the restroom, and he hadn't left since. His arm tightened around her, and he pressed another alcohol-laced kiss to her forehead. It sure wasn't the "redneck music" keeping him here. He was going to rub their relationship in Cruz's face as long as he could.

Heat rolled off her, and her left eye began twitching. Cruz had no doubt gotten over her long ago, but she hated being a pawn in Kyle's little mind games. With every day, every hour she spent in Copper Creek she wondered more and more what she was doing with him.

She pulled in a lungful of air, her tightened

chest feeling the stretch. The familiar spicy smell of Kyle's cologne assaulted her senses, making her stomach turn.

Her eyes wandered a few tables over where her brother sat with his friends Jack and Noah, and Noah's wife, Josephine. And Cruz. He was part of the group as well.

Realizing her gaze had fixed on him, she tore it away, focusing on the lead singer as he belted out the lyrics.

She remembered when Saturday nights at the Rusty Nail were the highlight of her week. When it was just a bunch of friends, talking and laughing and being real. Nothing seemed real anymore. And she couldn't even remember the last time she'd laughed.

What kind of example is that for Gracie? She set her cheek on her daughter's downy-soft curls.

The song came to a bold close, the audience applauding and whistling loudly.

Hope stepped up to the mic, and the noise died down. "Thank you so much! Y'all are awesome, and the band appreciates your support. All right now, we have a special treat for you tonight. I want you to put two hands together for the gorgeous . . . and talented . . . sweet friend of mine . . ."

Oh no.

"Zoe Collins!"

Zoe straightened, her face heating as every head turned her way. Kyle stiffened beside her.

40

She was somehow frozen to her seat, the weight of her daughter holding her there.

But then Brady was lifting Gracie from her arms. "Go on, sis. Your fans await."

"Come on up here, girl. Show 'em what you're all about. Help me out, y'all! She needs a little encouragement."

The crowd applauded louder, whistles piercing the space.

Zoe's heart thudded against her chest, and her smile felt as tight as a fiddle string. She had to go up there. What else could she do?

She stood, avoiding Kyle's eyes. The audience showed their approval, growing even louder as she approached the stage.

"It's been a few years," Hope said into the mic, "but I think this one's gonna come right back to ya, friend!"

The band struck up the rousing intro to "Country Girl." Zoe took the mic from Hope, then her friend slipped off the stage.

Zoe shared a smile with the lead singer. Her hands trembled, but she tapped her foot, keeping time with the four-on-the-floor beat. She made eye contact with the drummer, an old classmate, and he nodded his encouragement.

Rawley started the first verse, and Zoe found her body moving in time to the catchy tune. The stage lights weren't as bright as they were at the gigs she usually played. She could see familiar faces, friends she hadn't seen in years. They smiled, clapping along. The dance floor filled until there was hardly room for the crowd to move.

When the chorus began, Zoe lifted the mic and began singing harmony, trading looks with Rawley and playing it up good. It was a fun song, the words quick, the beat snappy, and Zoe couldn't help but fall right in.

When the chorus ended, Rawley gestured to her, and she lifted the mic and started into the second verse. Her heart was thudding, her skin flushed with heat. But the words came back like they'd never been lost, and an exhilaration she hadn't felt in years flooded her to overflowing.

The crowd was loving it, loving her, and though she was getting out of breath, the mood was contagious.

When the chorus came around again she slipped into the harmony, her voice blending with Rawley's like they'd rehearsed it a hundred times. She shimmied and waggled her head, giving herself over to the playful lyrics.

The guitarist started his solo, and Rawley spun her around until she was dizzy. The violinist's bow flew across the strings, and the drummer executed a well-timed fill. The lead guitarist's fingers worked the neck of his guitar, leaning back, and the bass player turned her way, nodding in time to the beat.

She was used to singing in a band, but she'd

never felt so much a part of one before. They belted out the chorus for the last time, and Zoe found herself wishing the song could go on all night.

But like all good things, it came to an end, the drummer and other musicians building up to the last dynamic beats. And then it was over. A cheer, almost deafening, rose up to fill the sudden silence.

"Thank you!" Zoe was flushed with pleasure as she handed the mic back to Hope and stepped off the stage.

"What'd I tell you?" Hope said. "Let's hear it for our hometown girl . . . Zoe Collins!"

Zoe's legs trembled with excitement, and she beamed at her friends and neighbors as she navigated through the crowd, accepting high fives and hugs.

As she approached her table, her gaze connected with Kyle's. He was standing, waiting for her with his trademark smile, but the look in his eyes made her blood slow to a cold crawl.

Her mood deflated as quickly as a punctured party balloon, and she worked hard to keep her smile in place.

He pulled her into a hug that must've seemed celebratory to the onlookers. But the too-tight squeeze and the growl in her ear made his real mood crystal clear.

"Get Gracie. We're leaving."

She pulled away, trembling for a different reason now, and turned to Brady.

"That was sweet, sis," Brady said over the music.

"Thanks." She held out her arms for Gracie, and he handed over the sleeping girl.

"You're not leaving . . . ?" he asked.

"Um, yeah. Need to get her to bed. Good night, y'all." She didn't dare make eye contact with Cruz.

The smile on her face felt plastic as she made her way to the exit. Kyle's hand on the small of her back felt hot and suffocating somehow.

The rapid shift in her mood had left her suddenly exhausted and confused and angry all at once. The door slapped shut behind them, the music dropping a dozen decibels. Enough that she could hear the pebbles shifting under their feet and the crickets chirping nearby as they made their way back to the grassy lot where Kyle's Mustang was parked.

He moved to her side, his hand dropping. "What was that, Zoe?" His words were clipped.

She shifted Gracie, trying to work up some remorse. But she felt no regret. She'd felt more alive in those three minutes than she'd felt in years. She'd remembered, just for a few minutes, who she used to be.

And, man, did she miss that girl.

"It was just a song, Kyle."

"You were flirting with Rawley. Right there on stage for everyone to see!"

He did the very same thing with Lindsay, the keyboardist in their band. "It was just part of the show."

He grabbed her elbow, jerking her to a stop.

Gracie slipped, and Zoe tightened her grip to keep her from falling.

"You made a fool of me!"

"I was just performing."

"Were you performing when you were staring at Huntley all night too? Do you think I didn't notice the way you followed him with your eyes?"

"That's not true."

Something flashed in his eyes. "You've been talking to him!"

"No, I haven't."

His fingers dug into the flesh of her arm. "Don't you lie to me."

"You're hurting me." Unable to keep hold of Gracie, she let the girl slide down her leg. Gracie whimpered in her sleep as she settled in the grass.

Zoe tried to step away from her, but Kyle grabbed both her arms, sinking his fingers deep until she winced. His breath bathed her face with the stench of beer and fury.

"I never should've agreed to stay. We're leaving right now." His eyes shot daggers at her. His face was twisted.

She should be afraid.

But instead heat flowed up her neck, and her hands clenched. She didn't know if it was the country air or the moment she'd had on stage or having the people she loved nearby. Whatever it was, she found courage she hadn't felt in years.

"You know what, Kyle? It's not always about *you* and what *you* want."

Surprise flashed in his eyes a moment before his hand tightened painfully on her elbow. "What did you just say?"

Her heart was ready to explode from her chest, and her mouth was as dry as a cotton ball.

But somehow she pushed out the words. "You heard me. And I'm not going anywhere. I'm staying here."

Was she talking about the Rusty Nail or Copper Creek? Staying temporarily or forever?

Even as his lips twisted in that way she'd always hated, even as his cold eyes narrowed on her, she couldn't bring herself to take back the words.

chapter five

Cruz shifted in his chair, his eyes drifting to the door for the tenth time since Zoe and Kyle had exited less than a minute ago. Conversation continued at the table, but he heard none of it.

Something wasn't right. It was odd that they'd left so quickly after Zoe's performance. And he was troubled by the look in Kyle's eyes as he'd ushered her from the building.

Cruz thought of all the changes he'd noticed in Zoe and the cruelty in Kyle's tone during their confrontation earlier. He didn't like it. Didn't like it one bit.

He pushed to his feet.

"Where you going?" Brady asked.

"Just . . . I'm going to check on something."

Now that he'd decided, Cruz couldn't get outside fast enough. He skirted the tables, his long legs making quick work of the space. He pushed through the crowd milling near the door, worry building with each step.

The parking lot was dark except for puddles of light from the overhead lamps. It was crowded, the gravel lot full and spilling onto the neighboring grass lot. He had no idea where they'd parked. They could even be gone by now.

He stopped, scanning the area, listening. The

heavy bass leaked through the restaurant's walls, and night sounds mingled in. A metal clip pinged on a nearby flagpole in the cool wind.

Then he heard something else. A shuffle and a grunt. Cruz's feet were moving before his mind kicked into gear. His adrenaline pumping, he skirted cars as he scanned the crowded lot. The music grew louder as he neared the back of the restaurant, but his eyes had adjusted to the darkness, catching on shadowed figures two rows away.

He heard Kyle's voice, a low growl. "Get in the car!"

Cruz was already running as Kyle's shadow meshed with Zoe's. And then there was another grunt, and she was on the ground.

Something red and hot rose inside him. He raced toward Kyle, unable to think past the roar in his ears.

Kyle lunged toward Zoe.

"Hey!"

Kyle turned just in time for Cruz to plow a fist into his face. The man stumbled backward, tripping over something, and went down with a grunt.

"Zoe." Cruz started toward her, but she was scrambling for her daughter, and from the corner of his eye he saw Kyle pushing to his feet.

Oh, no he didn't.

Cruz's punch landed in the guy's gut with a

48

satisfying *whomp*. But Kyle recovered quickly and came across with a jab to his face.

Before Cruz could recover, someone grabbed him from behind and a voice said, "Back off, Kyle!"

Brady. Cruz fought, but the arms were like bands of steel.

"That's enough, both of you!" Brady said.

Kyle wiped his mouth with the back of his hand.

"Zoe!" Hope was there too, crouching at Zoe's side.

It took Cruz a moment to realize the little girl was crying. She must've been what Kyle had tripped over. Zoe was soothing the child in her arms. A dark spot of blood trickled from the corner of Zoe's mouth.

A dark cloud of anger flooded him, and he surged forward, breaking free. He nearly got away, but Brady grabbed him again, and someone else blocked his path, arms extended.

"The sheriff's on his way," Brady said. "Come on, settle down. Let's not make this any worse."

⇨•⇦

Hope helped Zoe to her feet. Her arms tightened around her daughter, whose cries had diminished to a sniffle. They'd done a quick check and found only a scrape on Gracie's leg.

Zoe became aware of the gathering crowd, of

Cruz, held back by her brother, staring daggers at Kyle.

A rush of heat filled her face until she felt woozy.

"This is the thanks I get?" Kyle's voice grated across the few feet separating them, his eyes narrowing on hers. "For keeping you around, for taking on your . . ." His eyes dropped meaningfully to Gracie, rising to hers in a cruel threat.

Zoe's heart stuttered to a stop. Her arms tightened around Gracie. He wouldn't say it. He'd rather die than admit the truth. The secret had allowed him to own her. To control her. And now it allowed him to lord his position over Cruz, up close and personal.

The moment dragged on, time ticking away slowly.

Finally Kyle's lips pressed together, curling at the corners. He started toward her, but a couple guys jumped into his path, and someone grabbed him from behind.

"The sheriff's on his way, Kyle," someone said. "Best you get on out of here before he arrives. Don't want to get hauled off to jail now, do you?"

"He's not going anywhere," Brady said. "Jail's exactly what he's going to get."

Judging by the look on Cruz's face, that was exactly what *he* wanted.

"No," Zoe said. "Please . . . I just want him to go. There's been enough drama for one night."

"You'd better leave then, Kyle," someone said.

Kyle nailed Zoe with a look and called her a name that made her face grow ten degrees warmer.

"That's enough, Kyle!" Brady said, struggling to hold Cruz.

"You're nothing without me!" he shouted.

The fog cleared from Zoe's mind. She saw the scene, heard Kyle's words with a clarity she hadn't felt in a long time. Remembered all the ways he'd manipulated her, all the ways he'd cut her down, held her back.

Her back straightened as she met his heated gaze head on. She was done bowing to his will. Done tucking all her feelings away. Being someone she didn't even recognize anymore.

"Just leave, Kyle," she said.

Kyle jabbed a finger at her. "We're done! Don't call me. Don't text me. You hear me, Zoe? You're finished!"

He jerked the car door open and got inside. A second later the tires spun, shooting grass behind, and the car peeled out of the lot.

"I'm finished with you," she whispered.

chapter six

Zoe sat in Hope's office inside the Rusty Nail, the reality of the situation beginning to wash over her. The sheriff had shown up shortly after Kyle left. She hadn't pressed charges, despite everyone's encouragement to do so. She just wanted this night to be over. A medic in attendance had checked over Gracie and her. They were both going to be fine.

Physically at least.

After the sheriff left, the small crowd dispersed, going back inside to their friends and conversation. A whole new topic on the menu now. The gossip would be all over town by morning.

The music played on, the bass thumping outside the manager's office.

Hope dabbed gently at Zoe's lip with a paper towel. "Sorry if it hurts."

"It's fine."

Brady was washing Gracie's leg in the adjoining bathroom, and Cruz stood just inside the office door like a guardian angel, looking formidable with his tight jaw and dark, piercing eyes. One of those eyes was swelling. He was going to have a real shiner in the morning. His arms were folded, his biceps bulging under his sleeves. He hadn't spoken to her once.

Zoe was only now becoming aware of the pain in her jaw. She was going to have a whopper of a bruise. But the injury was nothing compared to the dawning realization of her circumstances.

Kyle was gone. He'd taken off with Gracie's booster seat—with their car! *His* car, she reminded herself. It was in his name. As was everything else she'd just said good-bye to. He was probably swinging by the hotel on his way out of town and taking everything they'd brought.

"What have I done?" She clutched her purse— her lone possession—with trembling fingers.

"What you should've done a long time ago," Hope said firmly.

"You don't understand."

"He hit you, Zoe. That's not okay."

"I know."

Zoe winced as Hope dabbed at her cut. But the injury didn't hurt near as bad as her pride. How had she sunk so low?

"Sorry." Hope's touch gentled. "Has he done this before?"

"No."

Hope gave her a look, her eyebrows lifting over her green eyes.

"He hasn't." Maybe he'd shoved her a time or two. But only when she'd made him really upset. And he'd never been anything but gentle with Gracie.

Gracie.

She didn't even have a change of clothes for her girl. Or a place to stay. She closed her eyes as worry flooded like a spring creek.

"It's going to be okay," Hope said. "You'll see."

"I don't have a car or a job," she said quietly, not wanting Cruz or Brady to hear. "I only have twenty dollars in my purse! My credit card is in his name, and he'll cancel it."

Hope grabbed her restless hands. "You have family, and we'll take care of you."

Zoe jerked away. "I don't want to be taken care of!"

She was sick and tired of being taken care of. Of letting someone else make all the decisions. How had she let this happen? She used to be so independent and bold and fierce. Just like Granny. Everyone had said so.

"You've got the farmhouse and the orchard. Let's just take one day at a time. Do you want to stay there tonight or come home with me?"

"She's not staying alone."

Zoe glared at Cruz.

"He could come back."

"That's true," Hope said, looking back at Zoe. "Do you think he will?"

She hated to admit he was right. As much as she wanted to assert her neglected independence, she had Gracie to think of. Kyle had sounded pretty done with her, but he was unpredictable. He might feel differently about all the time and

54

effort he'd put into her and their relationship. Not to mention the band.

Funny how love didn't even come to mind. "I don't know."

"He's not going to just let his daughter go." This from Cruz.

Zoe pressed her lips together, her eyes meeting Hope's. They both knew Kyle had no legal claim to Gracie, but she wasn't about to tell Cruz that.

"Why don't you stay with me tonight?" Hope said. "We can swing by Walmart on the way home and grab a few necessities."

Gracie entered the room, her red curls bouncing, Brady on her heels. Her daughter looked none the worse for wear. Zoe hoped she'd been too sleepy to realize what had happened.

She climbed onto Zoe's lap and showed off her Band-Aid. "Look, Mama! Uncle Bwady fixed my boo-boo."

Zoe forced a smile. "I see that, baby. Did he give it kisses?"

"No." She frowned at Brady. "Uncle Bwady, you didn't kiss my boo-boo!"

"Sorry squirt. I'm a rookie."

"What's a wookie?"

Zoe gave the Band-Aid a big smack. "There. All better."

Gracie held her mom's cheeks in both hands, frowning. "Mama, you have a boo-boo too!"

"I know, honey, but it's all better now."

55

Gracie leaned forward, kissing the corner of her mouth. "Now it's all better."

❯•❮

Cruz's eyes sharpened on Zoe. Her lower lip was swelling, the cut at the corner red and angry looking. Her jaw was bruising up, his mood darkening along with it.

He wished he'd gotten in a few more swings before Brady had come along. Wished he'd seen Kyle hauled off to jail where he belonged. What was he doing, hitting a woman? A woman he was supposed to care about? And what else had he done to Zoe and her daughter in the years they'd been gone?

No wonder she was just a shadow of her former self.

And yet the first thing Cruz had done when he'd come face-to-face with Kyle was provoke him. He winced, guilt flooding in deep and overwhelming. He watched Zoe waver as Hope helped her to her feet, and he called himself ten kinds of fool.

Brady took the little girl, and Hope grabbed Zoe's purse.

"She's staying with you?" Cruz asked Hope as they neared him.

"Yeah, but we're running to the store first."

"She should go to the clinic and get checked."

Zoe met his gaze head on. "Stop talking about me like I'm not here."

He was glad to see a spark of anger in those green eyes, even if it was aimed at him. "Sorry."

He was sorry for a lot more than that. His eyes narrowed on her swelling jaw, and he reached out to touch it. But just as quickly he let his hand drop. He had no right to touch her.

"Might want to get some ice on that ASAP," he said. "It's swelling pretty bad."

"Right back at you." Her eyes softened on his before they dropped to the floor. She cleared her throat. "Thanks for your help tonight."

He waited a beat, but she didn't look at him again.

"Anytime, Zoe."

He'd fight all her dragons, every last one of them, and she didn't even have to ask. It had been true then, and it was true now. For the first time in years he allowed their long and complicated history to rise to the surface of his mind. Allowed himself to remember the way it had all begun and the way it had ended.

part two

chapter seven

Cruz remembered the exact day Zoe Collins came into his life.

He and his mom had only been in Copper Creek a couple months, but already Brady Collins was like the brother he'd never had. On the first day of school Brady had invited Cruz to sit at his lunch table. It was there they discovered their shared passions for cars, fishing, and girls—in no particular order.

Brady was open about the fact that his birth mom was a drug addict and his aunt and uncle had adopted him as a baby. Mr. and Mrs. Collins were his mom and dad as far as everyone was concerned, but Cruz could tell Brady felt a little out of place sometimes.

Brady's family had a nice house, but he preferred to spend time at Cruz's dumpy old rental. In fact, that seemed to be where they hung out the most. Maybe it was the appeal of Cruz's mom—even at seventeen, he had to admit she was pretty cool. She worked two jobs, but now that Cruz had gotten hired at the hardware store he was hoping she'd quit the Wash 'n' Spin.

It was going on midnight, and he and Brady had just started playing PlayStation in his upstairs bedroom when Cruz heard a noise outside the window. He frowned and went to shut off the lights. Copper Creek seemed like a safe place, but he'd learned back in Atlanta how to take care of his mom and himself.

"What are you doing?" Brady's fingers were jabbing the controller buttons as he blasted away aliens.

"Thought I heard something." Cruz moved to the window.

A final blast sounded from the TV, then it went quiet. "I'm going to the bathroom," Brady said.

Cruz barely heard his friend leave the room. He eased away the curtain and reared back at the face staring right at him.

It was a girl. Her hair blazed like a lion's mane in the moonlight and fluttered against her creamy skin. It was her eyes, though, that held him captive. Eyes that lit mischievously as if they harbored some amusing secret.

His heart gave a heavy thud, and his body flooded with warmth, fogging his brain. Cruz's olive skin and black hair made him popular with the ladies—he could thank his mother for that. But if he'd ever thought to wish for any girl to appear at his bedroom window, he'd have wished for this one.

Cruz gathered himself enough to tug up the stubborn sash. But once he had it open his words dried up like a puddle in July.

Her lips curled upward. "You wanna let me in? I'm fixing to fall, you know."

He pushed the windowpane all the way open and helped her through. Her skin was the softest thing he'd ever touched. She squeezed through the opening, all long-limbed and nimble-bodied in her filmy white shirt and cutoffs.

She plopped onto his twin bed, brushing off her legs.

He blinked at her, finally finding his voice. "Who are you—how did you—?"

"I'm Zoe. Your rose trellis needs some fixing. It's rotted in places. I almost fell twice. Sorry about the mess."

Zoe. Brady's fifteen-year-old sister. The one he was so protective of.

Cruz wanted to turn on the light and get a better look at her, but he was afraid it would somehow break the spell. Or maybe he was dreaming, and if he was, he sure didn't want to wake up.

Her eyes sparkled in the light of the TV screen as she returned her gaze to him. "Why are you looking at me like that?"

"Like what?"

"Like I'm a ghost."

"Are you?"

"There's no such thing, silly."

"How do you know?"

She arched a playful brow. "Have you ever seen one?"

"Maybe."

She reached for his hand, squeezing it softly. "See? One hundred percent real."

He felt the zing at the top of his head, at the tip of his bare toes, and every place in between. He wanted to hold her hand forever.

But she pulled it back, crossed her arms, and tilted her head. Her eyes raked over him, and he felt the look like a touch. A shiver ran down his torso, reminding him he was only wearing jeans.

"Do you play sports? You must work out a lot. You have lots of muscles."

He suddenly wanted to be one of those jocks who squeezed out reps on a machine instead of a kid who got his workout stocking shelves at the hardware store.

"Who are you talking—" Brady stopped just inside the door, his gaze narrowing on the girl sitting on the bed. "Zoe. What are you doing here?"

She lifted an impertinent shoulder. "You should check your back seat before you take off, big brother. Never know who might be stowed away back there."

"Daggonit, Zoe, now I'm going to have to take you home, and I just got here."

"Oh, relax. I'm just having a little fun. What game are you playing? Oh, I love this one." She grabbed for the controller.

Brady took her elbow. "Oh no you don't. You're going right home."

"You're worse than Mother and Daddy. I'm not a baby."

"It's after midnight."

She gave a look of mock horror. "Oh no! Midnight. I might turn into a pumpkin."

"You've got to stop sneaking out, Zoe. It's not safe."

She rolled her eyes. "This is Copper Creek. I couldn't find danger around here if I dialed it up on my phone."

"I'm telling Mom and Dad this time. Let's go."

Zoe evaded his grasp, giving him a saucy look. "You won't tell them. Because I know who was parking with Bridgette Malloy at Sutter's Bend last Friday when he was supposed to still be at work."

Brady's lips flattened. "How did you—never mind. Come on, you're going home."

Zoe's face lit up. "Oh, I know. Let's go swimming. Or set off some fireworks. We can go down by the bridge where we won't get caught."

"The only place you're going is home."

"Ugh! You're such a bore! Fine. I'll go home, but I'm walking."

She marched past Cruz, leaving a wake of the sweetest perfume he'd ever smelled.

Brady was on her heels. "Oh no you're not."

She turned at the door and gave Cruz an impish wink. And just like that he was smitten.

chapter eight

Zoe slipped inside her parents' dank barn, the familiar smells of hay and horseflesh assaulting her senses. Her eyes fell on Cruz over by the stalls. The brush in his hand was gliding down Buttercup's withers.

"Whatcha doing?"

His head snapped toward her, then turned back to Buttercup. "Waiting for Brady."

Cruz had been coming around for a couple years, hanging out with her brother. He was so handsome, with his beautiful skin and guarded brown eyes. Just looking at him put butterflies in her stomach.

But he ignored her to the point of rudeness. To him, she was just Brady's pesky little sister.

She stepped up beside him and leaned on the stall door, close enough that her arm brushed his.

He stiffened but didn't pull away.

She bit the corner of her lip. She couldn't have picked a worse boy to have a crush on. But now, with the hardened flesh of his arm touching hers and his subtle woodsy scent invading her senses, relentless hope took hold. She'd never been one to lack for courage.

"Are you going riding?"

"If he gets here before dark."

"I could take you if he doesn't. I know all the best spots."

His Adam's apple bobbed, calling attention to his unshaved neck and jaw. He looked older than other boys his age. It was the five o'clock shadow, she thought. Or the world-weary look in the depths of his eyes.

He set down the brush and stepped away, shoving his hands into his front pockets. "No thanks."

Zoe's hand trembled as it glided down Buttercup's nose. "You don't have to be so mean. I was just trying to be nice."

"I'm not being mean. I'm just waiting for Brady."

She gave him a haughty look. "You ignore me all the time."

A shadow flickered in his jaw. "No, I don't."

"Yes, you do."

He gave her a look.

"Well, you do."

"I'm Brady's friend. I'm here to see him, not you."

"There you go being mean again." She batted her eyelashes, a trick she'd learned from Marci Allen. "Anyway, I'm only two years younger than you."

He sighed hard and mumbled something in Spanish.

"What does that mean?"

His eyes twinkled. "I was praying to God for patience."

Humph. She narrowed her eyes and pursed her lips.

He glanced down to her mouth, and her breath caught in her throat. Had something besides indifference just flickered in his eyes?

But an instant later he was pacing away as if he were bored to death with her and their conversation.

She sighed. Try, try again. "When are you going to college?" Brady started in the fall, and Cruz was a whole year older. He was still working at the hardware store.

"Who said I'm going to college?"

"Then what are you going to do?"

"I'll figure it out." He looked away, a beam of light cutting across his face, making his features harsh.

She was suddenly aware of the differences in their upbringings. Her parents were paying for Brady's schooling, and they'd pay for hers too if they could talk her into going. She wondered if Cruz had to stick around and help his mama make ends meet.

"You could go to trade school around here. What do you want to do?"

"You're very meddlesome."

She tilted her chin. "You're very evasive."

The corner of his lip tucked in, calling attention

to his plump lower lip. "Big word for such a little girl. Maybe I don't even know what that means."

She rolled her eyes. "Brady told me you graduated fifth in your class. You could get a scholarship if you wanted."

He stopped and held a hand out to Buttercup, who nuzzled his palm. When he didn't answer, Zoe continued.

"Brady's probably working late. I can saddle up a horse for you if you want."

He spared her a look. "I know how to saddle a horse."

"I was just trying to be friendly. You should try it sometime."

Her heart was stuttering in her chest. No other boy had ever made her so nervous, and she didn't like it one iota. Plenty of boys were sweet on her; she wasn't going to beg for scraps from someone who couldn't stand the sight of her.

His feet shuffled to a stop nearby. She hadn't even heard his approach.

Her eyes cut to his, and she caught him staring at her hair. Heat flooded her cheeks. She lifted a hand, pushing back the untamed mass of curls. She wished she'd taken the time to tie it back. Her hair was the one thing she'd inherited from her beautiful mother—it couldn't have been her curvy figure or pretty blue eyes.

"Stop staring. It's rude." She picked up the grooming brush and ran it down Buttercup's withers. "I already know I have ugly hair. I don't need you confirming it."

"It's not ugly."

She snorted.

He mumbled something in Spanish again.

She scowled at him. "If you're going to insult me, do it in English."

He looked at her long and hard, until her knees grew wobbly and her chest was so tight she could hardly breathe.

The brush slowed to a stop. He confused her. He was mean to her and yet sometimes he looked at her like . . .

She rested her fists on her hips. "What?"

"I said . . . it's the color of a lion's mane." The rough texture of his voice made her insides hum.

She blinked. The roots of her hair tingled as if he'd just touched it. Heat spread into the tips of her ears, and she couldn't look away from him. Couldn't find a single thing to say. Or even string two thoughts together.

He suddenly tugged the brim of his ball cap and turned toward the doorway. "I gotta go. Tell your brother I couldn't wait around anymore."

And then he was gone, taking a little piece of her heart with him.

chapter nine

It was well into fall by the time Cruz saw Zoe again. He was making his last lumber delivery of the day. He pulled the truck to a stop beside the orchard's farmhouse.

As he exited the truck he spotted Zoe coming out onto her grandma's porch in a pair of cutoffs and a red shirt tied at her waist. A sliver of creamy skin drew his eyes. He gritted his teeth as he began unloading the deck lumber, reminding himself of the promise he'd made to Brady to look out for Zoe while he was away at college.

Seeing as it had been months since Cruz had even seen her, he wasn't doing such a good job. Word was she'd gotten her second speeding ticket, and her license had been suspended. Maybe that would slow her down.

"Watcha doing?" she asked.

"Unloading your grandma's deck lumber."

His eyes flickered off her slim form. She had her hair down today, a curly mass flowing over her shoulders. The sunlight glinted off it, turning it copper. At first it had only been her looks that had reminded him of a beautiful lioness. But now he also knew her to have the spirit of one.

Mi leona. He shook his head at the fanciful thought. She wasn't *his* anything.

He grabbed an armful of wood and skirted her, noticing her Nissan in the drive as he headed toward the back of the house. "I thought you couldn't drive anymore."

She dumped an armload of boards down beside his. "It's just down the road. I won't get caught."

"You're going to lose your license 'til you're sixty if you're not careful."

"I already have one big brother, Cruz. I don't need another."

Her tone was uncharacteristically snappish, and he wondered what he'd done wrong. Maybe she was missing Brady. As much as they fussed, they were close.

She was quiet as she helped him with the rest of the load. The sun was over the hills by the time he snapped the tailgate shut. He sent the papers inside with Zoe, and she returned with the clipboard and her grandma's signature.

"Go for a ride with me," she said.

"You're not supposed to be driving."

"Then you drive."

"Zoe . . ."

"Are you done for the day?"

His lips pressed together, more tempted than he had a right to be. *You'll be keeping your promise to Brady,* one side of his brain said. *Brady'd kill you if he knew the thoughts you have about his sister,* said the other.

"Well, you can stand around sucking up all

72

the oxygen. I'm going for a spin." Zoe whirled around, hair flying over her shoulder as she got into her car.

"Zoe, stop."

She started the engine and looked up at him through the open window with that sassy smile. "Whatcha gonna do about it?"

"*Pequeño mocosa*," he mumbled, rubbing his forehead.

"Did you just call me a little brat? I took Spanish this year, you know."

"Wow, a whole year. I'll never be able to get anything by you again."

She narrowed her eyes at him and slid the gearshift into drive. "*Adios, amiga.*"

"Ami*go*. I'm a man."

"Are you? Hadn't noticed." She eased off the gas. "*Hasta la vista*, amigo."

"Wait." He grabbed the door handle, heaving a sigh. "Move over."

A satisfied smile formed on her lips as she slipped the gearshift into park and hopped over the narrow console.

"What about my truck?"

"It'll be fine."

"Shouldn't you tell your grandma you're leaving with me?"

She gave a saucy smile. "I already did."

Was he that predictable? He spared her a look as he pulled down the gravel drive. It was a small

73

car, and their shoulders nearly touched. The sweet flowery smell of her wove around him like a spell, making his heart thud in his chest.

When he came to the end of the drive he braked. "Where are we going, since you seem to know everything."

She reached into her pocket and pulled out a coin. "Pick a number between one and fifty."

"Why?"

"Just do it."

He rolled his eyes. "Five."

She flipped the coin. "Tails. That means first turn we go left."

He shook his head but did what she said. "You must be bored if this is what you do for fun."

He wished he had time to be bored. His mom had gotten laid off, and now he was the sole earner in the family. He was working six days a week, sometimes ten hours a day.

At the next intersection she flipped the coin again. "Heads, go right."

He slowed the car and turned. It was a country road with rolling farmland on both sides. A creek ran parallel to the lane. The leaves shimmered, gold and red, and the scent of fall hung heavily in the air.

"We're going to end up in the middle of nowhere. What's the point of this anyway?"

"Are you always such a Debby Downer?"

He braked as he came to an intersection. "Let's

go right here. It'll take us back to town." And back toward her grandma's house where he could drop her off and put her out of his mind.

Right.

"That's cheating." She flipped the coin. "Go left."

He sighed and indulged her.

"Have you heard from Brady?" she asked.

"He called yesterday." His friend wasn't liking college much. Cruz had a feeling he was only trying to please his parents by getting a business degree. All Brady had ever wanted to do was work on cars.

"He didn't call me."

He glanced over at Zoe in time to catch the hurt in her eyes.

"Well, he asked about you. You should call him. He misses you."

At the next intersection she flipped the coin again. "Go right."

"What are you going to do after you graduate?" he asked.

Her chin tipped up. "I'm going to Nashville. I'm going to be a singer and become famous, and they're going to play my songs all over the radio."

She probably would too. She had a voice like an angel. She sometimes sang at church, and her silvery voice practically hypnotized him. "What do your parents think about that?"

She snorted. "Like I've told *them*. They think I'm going to study law at University of Georgia, and then come back here and take over Daddy's practice."

"Well, you are real good at arguing."

"Maybe Brady's doing things their way, but not me. I don't want to be stuck in this hick town for the rest of my life. I'm going to go do things. Big things."

The thought of her leaving put a knot in his chest. He tried to tell himself she was still a while off from that decision. It'd be better if she left anyway. Maybe then he could get her out from under his skin. Maybe then he could actually go out with other girls and stop wishing they had red hair and creamy skin and tiny freckles on their noses.

"What?" she asked. "You don't believe me?"

"You can do anything you set your mind to." Heaven knew she had all the resources she needed. He wasn't sure she appreciated the leg up she'd been given the way Brady did.

He felt her perusal for a long beat. "That's probably the nicest thing you ever said to me."

He glanced over at her and took in her hair, blowing in the wind. The way her green eyes had softened on him. By a sheer miracle he kept his gaze from falling to her lips.

He looked away, swallowing hard. "You're a good kid, Zoe."

He could almost feel her bristling beside him and knew he'd said the wrong thing.

"Well, Kyle Jimmerson doesn't think I'm a 'kid.' He asked me to sing with his band next month, and I'm going to. Brevity gets gigs in Atlanta. Well . . . they got one gig."

His gut clenched at the thought of Zoe getting taken in by that guy. He didn't come from the best of families, and from what Cruz had seen, he was as arrogant as his father.

"You should watch out for him," Cruz said. "He's a player."

"There you go again, being my big brother."

"Well . . . Brady's gone so . . ."

"I don't need a babysitter. Kyle actually believes in me. He thinks I'll be the perfect backup singer for him someday, after my voice has matured."

Cruz pressed his lips together. He hoped Kyle realized her voice wasn't the only thing that needed to mature. Zoe might be spirited, but she was innocent. And she was seventeen now. Old enough to get into plenty of trouble, and Kyle Jimmerson wouldn't help matters.

Cruz tried to tell himself he wasn't jealous. But the thought of Kyle being anywhere near Zoe made him want to slug the guy in the face.

Zoe flipped the coin and slapped it onto the back of her hand. "Heads. Make a right up there."

He braked, turning onto an old gravel drive

that led into the woods of the foothills. Basically leading nowhere.

"Now you have to stop," she said.

He eased the car to a stop and put it into park. "Now what?"

"We're here. Turn it off."

He rolled his eyes at her bossiness but did as she said.

The overhead canopy of leaves blocked the sun, darkening the car's interior. The road was one lane and more dirt than gravel, now that he was looking at it. There were steep banks going upward on either side. Outside the window a squirrel nattered, and a thrasher chirped from a nearby tree. The smell of pine suffused the car.

He leaned back in the seat. "And where exactly is 'here'?"

"We flipped five times, so this is our final destination. Now you have to think of something for us to do." She gazed out the window, no doubt scoping out the hilly landscape, winding gravel road, and thick woods.

But he couldn't take his eyes off Zoe. Off her creamy skin, her pert little nose, and that hair, all wild and windblown around her shoulders. His head felt like it was filled with helium, and his heart punched his ribs like a prize-fighter.

As she contemplated the scenery she bit her lip.

Her lower lip was plump, and the natural pink color needed no lipstick.

He could think of something to do all right.

Her lips tugged upward as she turned toward him. "You've sure got your work cut out for . . ." The smile slid from her lips. Something shifted in her eyes.

He couldn't look away if he tried. Did she know she made his heart stutter in his chest? That he thought about her every night as he lay in bed? That he dreamed of sifting her hair with his fingers, caressing her lips with his own?

He hadn't realized how close they were. He could almost feel her breath on his lips. And suddenly almost wasn't enough. Drawn by some magnetic force, he leaned closer, touching his lips to hers. Soft. Impossibly soft.

Impossibly unsure. Was he her first? He could hardly breathe at the thought. Could hardly think past the emotions rolling through him. A niggle of guilt surfaced but he pushed it back, sweeping his lips over hers again.

She responded more boldly this time. She cupped his jaw, a feather-light touch that shook him to the core.

Her response made him heady with want of her. He couldn't stop his fingers from threading into her hair. It was as soft as he'd dreamed. Like fine silk. Her scent wrapped around him like a warm embrace, pulling him closer.

His blood buzzed in his veins. It grew louder until the sound pulled him from his dream. Until he realized it wasn't his blood buzzing, but her phone.

Reality calling.

The reality that included her brother and their gap in ages and walks of life. An image of her dad surfaced, disapproval in his eyes as he looked down his nose at Cruz. Zoe was destined for big things. He was not.

He eased away, watching, mesmerized, as her eyes fluttered open. As raw emotions flickered in those hooded green depths. As the stirrings of want—for *him*—faded into wonder, then confusion.

He'd done the impossible: rendered her speechless.

What had he been thinking? She was still Brady's little sister. The one he'd been entrusted to look out for. Oh, he was looking all right.

Idiot.

He eased away, putting much-needed space between them. Pressed his back to the seat and knotted his hands before he could do something stupid like touch her again.

He cleared his throat. "I'm sorry."

She looked into his eyes for a long moment, warmth leaching from her expression. "Sorry?"

The phone was still buzzing, and he latched onto the distraction like a drowning victim to a life preserver. "You should answer that."

She blinked at him, then pulled her phone from her pocket and checked the screen.

Before she could answer, it stopped ringing. Her hand fell to her lap, the phone in it. "What . . . what was that, Cruz? Why did you kiss me?"

He gave a wry laugh. Oh, the answers to that question. They'd knock her on her backside so fast she wouldn't know what hit her.

"It was a mistake. I'm sorry."

Hurt flashed in her eyes, followed quickly by a sheen of tears.

A vise tightened around his heart.

"Quit saying that," she said.

He looked away, couldn't stand to see the hurt he'd put there. Needed to put an end to what he'd started.

¡Estúpido!

He swallowed hard, tried for a casual tone. "You're a cute girl, that's all. I shouldn't have done it."

He thought he might die in the long stretch of silence that followed. He ran his palms down the length of his thighs and made a study of the view out the windshield.

"A cute girl," she repeated.

He steeled himself against the tightness in her voice and drove in the final nail. "That's the thing about guys, Zoe. We're pretty much a bunch of jerks. You should learn it now while you're still young."

A flush bloomed on her cheeks, and her shoulders stiffened as she nailed him with a look. "Finally, something we agree on."

After a weighted moment he reached for the key and turned it. The engine was loud in the quiet of the car. Heart beating up into his throat, he backed out to the road into the glaring sunlight.

He wished he could turn back time. Maybe then he wouldn't know the sweetness of Zoe's lips. The impossible thrill of her response. The heavy burden of her pain.

But the moment *had* happened, and now he'd spend a lifetime trying to forget.

chapter ten

Zoe didn't like waking before dawn, especially during summer, but it was picking season, and picking was best done in the cool of the morning.

A fog was hanging over the trees when she arrived at the orchard, and the air smelled of dew and earth. Toward the east the mountains rose majestically from the mist, and swaths of periwinkle and pink striped the sky. There was nothing like sunrise at Blue Ridge Farms.

Granny was already at work with her crew. She perched on a ladder, wearing faded jeans and work boots, her upper body all but swallowed by the tree.

The flatbed truck was parked in the middle, the plastic bins there waiting to be filled. Zoe greeted some of the crew—the ones she knew. The low murmur of voices and soft thump of the peaches as they were tossed into the bins broke the morning's silence.

Granny was humming her favorite song, "Sunday Sunrise," as Zoe approached. The old Anne Murray song reminded her grandma of her late husband, and she hummed it often.

"Morning, Granny."

Her grandma smiled over her shoulder. "Morning, sugar. Grab a bag and join the fun. The peaches are ripe unto harvest."

Zoe fetched a bag from the flatbed and slid the strap over her head, then joined Granny at the freestone tree where a ladder waited. She climbed up, reached for a peach, and twisted carefully, lifting it to her nose. She inhaled the sweet, familiar fragrance.

"Aren't they beautiful? Look at that nice rosy blush. It's a good crop this year."

"They smell yummy." Zoe bagged the peach and reached for another. "Can I come over Saturday to make a cobbler with you?" Nobody made a cobbler like her grandmother. Zoe could almost taste the sweet, plump peaches and buttery crust right now. Her stomach gave a twist.

"If it's all right with your folks."

"I'll ask Mama to come too. It'll be a girls' day."

"Sounds fun."

"Morning, ma'am."

Zoe nearly tumbled from the ladder at the familiar deep voice. She turned to see Cruz Huntley standing there, his hands pressed deep into his pockets.

"Morning," Granny said. "You're right on time. Just grab a bag over on the truck and join us. You need a refresher course?"

"No, ma'am. I remember."

His eyes flickered off hers. He didn't look very happy to see her. "Morning, Zoe."

She notched up her chin. "Morning."

Zoe watched him walk away, her heart thumping at a ridiculous rate. She looked back at her grandma, who'd already resumed picking as if she hadn't just set Zoe's world spinning.

Granny was the only one who knew about her confusing feelings for Cruz. Who knew about the way he'd kissed her last fall, apologized, then gone on to ignore her for months. Zoe couldn't help but feel a little betrayed.

"What's *he* doing here?" she whispered through the tree's leafy branches.

Granny didn't even spare her a glance. "He needed the work, sugar."

"He works at the hardware store."

"Well, I guess he needed some pocket change then. He came to me a few weeks ago."

"You didn't think to warn me?"

"It's a big orchard, dumpling."

She stared wide-eyed at her grandma, but before she could respond, Cruz approached, pulling a ladder up to the tree beside them. Right beside them!

She gave Granny a flinty look, which the woman missed entirely.

They picked in silence for a while, but Cruz's presence had changed everything. Instead of enjoying the peaceful waking of the day, the sights and smells and sounds of the orchard, Zoe was battling her thumping heart, spinning thoughts, and trembling hands.

"Looks like a good crop this year, ma'am," Cruz said as the sun was peeking over the distant hills.

She hated that the very sound of his deep voice set her heart racing.

"Oh, it is. This is the kind of crop that keeps me going." Granny adjusted the weight of her strap. "How's things going for you over at the hardware store?"

"Pretty good. Working toward a promotion, in fact."

"That so. Well good for you."

"What about you, Zoe?" Cruz asked. "You going off to college in the fall?"

She snapped a peach from the limb and placed it in her bag. "I don't know yet."

She was in an epic fight with her dad over it. She wanted to pursue her music, and he wanted her in college studying prelaw. Her grandma was the only one who seemed to trust her with her own future, but that only put Granny at odds with Daddy too.

When she didn't expand on her answer, Granny stepped in. "She wants to run off and become a big star—and she could do it with that God-given voice of hers."

"No doubt. It's a hard life though, Zoe. Why

would you run off when you have all this?" Cruz held out his hands, palms up. "Good town, good roots, all this beautiful land . . ."

Granny chuckled. "You're a smart boy. Stick around a little longer, and I just might hire you right out from under Bud."

Zoe shot Granny a look as she descended the ladder. Her bag wasn't quite full, but suddenly she couldn't wait to empty it and find another tree to pick clean.

chapter eleven

It was three weeks before Zoe spoke to Cruz again. Oh, she saw him around the orchard, but she made sure she was picking far away from him. She saw him at the gas pump. She saw him across the church sanctuary. She saw him in the crowd at the Rusty Nail when she got to fill in as backup singer with Brevity. Saw him scowling up at her from his corner table.

She managed to put him from her mind most of the time. She'd finally talked her parents into letting her take a year off school. They weren't happy about it, but she mollified them by interning at her dad's law office during the afternoons. On the weekends she volunteered at the animal shelter.

It was there she met Brownley, an old coonhound someone had dumped on the side of the road. He had droopy brown ears and soulful eyes that lit up when Zoe reached for him. It was love at first sight. She talked her parents into letting her keep him, then took him to the vet only to find that Brownley had a gastrointestinal condition that would be fatal if he didn't have surgery soon.

But Zoe only had 220 dollars to her name, and her dad refused to help no matter how much she pleaded. He was on a mission to convince her she needed a college education, and apparently he thought this was a good time to make his case.

So with Peach Fest just days away, Zoe hatched a plan to raise the money for Brownley's surgery. She didn't have anything to sell or enough time to bake a bunch of pies, and people weren't going to pay her to sing. So she decided to open a kissing booth. Just a little peck for a good cause.

On Saturday she set up among all the craft and game booths. She plastered her *Save Brownley!* sign to her booth façade and leashed the dog nearby in the shade for visual incentive. She hung her *Kissing Booth* sign and set her collection jar on the ledge. She was open for business.

The smells of peach confections filled the air, making her stomach rumble. People milled about, visiting with neighbors and stopping to let their children play games that featured plastic rings, balls, and water-shooting guns. Down the alley carnival rides spun round and round, making riders shriek and laugh.

She leaned on the window's wooden ledge, trying to look enticing. The festival drew folks from all over the state, which was good, as she hoped not to kiss anyone she'd actually set eyes on again.

At five dollars a kiss, it was going to take a lot of customers. And considering how little experience she'd had, it was probably a rip-off. It would all be worth it, though, if she could just raise enough money for Brownley's surgery.

⋙•⋘

Cruz was strolling down junk food alley when he saw her. He must have some kind of Zoe radar, because he always *felt* it when she was nearby. Nadine Morgan, who'd sidled up to him fifteen minutes ago and hadn't left, casually brushed his hand again—probably hoping he'd take it. But she wasn't his type, and he wasn't about to lead her on.

He tore his eyes from Zoe an instant before his brain registered the sign. They cut back, narrowing on the bold letters above her. He peered around the people blocking his vision—a line for her booth, he realized.

What the . . .

His jaw clenched as his feet halted in their tracks. Through the crowd he caught sight of some guy pushing a bill into the jar and leaning close to Zoe.

His heart thrashed about in his chest, and the whoosh of pumping blood filled his ears. His feet cut a path through the crowd.

"Wait up, Cruz . . ." He barely heard Nadine's whiny voice.

He was too busy grabbing the shirt of the guy who had his lips all over Zoe's.

"Hey . . . !" The guy stumbled backward.

Cruz glared at Zoe, whose eyes had gone wide. Her lip color was smeared and her mouth was still damp from the kiss. He barely stopped himself from dragging his hand across her mouth. From wiping this guy and all the others away too.

"I paid for that kiss," the guy complained. He looked to be Cruz's age, though he was a good four inches shorter.

Cruz nailed him with a look. "And you got one. Now move along."

The guy slowly wilted under Cruz's glare, then he straightened his shirt and sauntered off.

Zoe planted her fists on her hips. "Get away from my booth."

It was bad enough he'd had to watch her make eyes at Kyle Jimmerson onstage. Bad enough he'd had to watch her go off to senior prom with Roland Henry. Now he was supposed to watch every randy guy in Murray County plaster his lips all over hers?

"A kissing booth, Zoe? Really?"

She narrowed her eyes on him. "You're scaring my customers away," she hissed.

"Good! Does your family know you're doing this?"

"I'm a legal adult. I don't have to ask my parents' permission to have a booth at the fair."

"I'll take that as a no."

"You can take that as a none of your darned business!"

"Did the festival committee approve this?"

"Of course. I'm not stupid."

"Close up, Zoe. Now."

"You're not the boss of me, Cruz Huntley."

"Hey . . . ," someone behind him said. "We ain't got all day. We want our turn."

Cruz shot the first guy in line a look meant to fry him on the spot. He looked away but didn't leave the line.

When Cruz looked back at Zoe, something had shifted in her eyes. She arched a brow. "Careful, Cruz. I might just start thinking you're jealous."

"Don't flatter yourself."

"If you're not going to kiss her, buddy, move along."

"Yeah, Cruz, are you going to kiss me?"

His teeth locked together until his jaws hurt.

Zoe looked over his shoulder, then crossed her arms and tilted her head at him. "Your date's getting bored."

"She's not my—" He huffed, deciding not to waste his breath. "I'm calling Brady."

She tipped her chin. "Go ahead. He's working in Ellijay today. And I'm not closing shop till I raise the funds, so you can just mosey along."

He tore his gaze from her, and his eyes caught on a sign. *Save Brownley!* He scanned the paragraph below the header.

A dog. She was selling her kisses for some

stupid mutt. He saw said dog under a shade tree behind the booth, lying there all innocent-like, tongue lolling out, ears drooping practically to the ground.

"Move along, Cruz."

He noted the stubborn set of her jaw and the determination in her eyes. He knew that look. She wasn't leaving unless he threw her over his shoulder. And as tempted as he was to do just that, he couldn't babysit her all day. He had to be at work in an hour.

He swore in Spanish and jerked the brim of his hat down, fixing her with a stony look.

She watched him, eyes stubborn and wary at the same time until he turned on his heel and left.

⇒•⇐

Her mind was on Cruz as she kissed her way through the short line. Sometimes the guys tried to deepen the kiss, but she just pressed her hands to their chests and gave them a gentle shove. "Your five dollars are up, bubba."

Overall her customers had been well behaved, the donations from the community generous. If she kept it up, she'd have what she needed by the end of tomorrow. She wilted a little at the thought of two days' worth of kisses. Turned out these were nothing like the one she'd shared with Cruz. It was like comparing apples and oranges. Melba toast and warm peach cobbler.

She forced a smile as her customer strutted away, glancing back with a wink.

"Next!"

A palm smacked the shelf.

She jumped at the sudden sound and vibration.

Cruz was in front of her, struggling to stuff a fat wad of bills through the jar's slotted top, his eyes pinning her in place.

"What are you doing?"

His jaw was set, frown lines separating his dark brows, a thunderstorm brewing in his eyes as he glared at her without a word. He gave the wad a final shove and the bills fell through, fluttering open inside the jar.

He grabbed her face in both hands and pulled her close, mashing their lips together.

It was over before she could even close her eyes. She blinked against a wave of dizziness as she stared into his flinty eyes.

"There. You've earned your money," he said in a clipped tone she hardly recognized. "Now close up shop and go home."

Without looking away, he jerked the signs from her booth.

Zoe blinked dazedly, watching him walk away with the signs. Her pulse skittered, and something unfurled inside her. Something warm and pleasant. Something that made her smile from the inside out.

She should be cross at him. He'd been

high-handed and bossy, and she never tolerated either. But he'd just given up what must amount to a couple weeks' pay, and he'd done it to keep her from kissing anyone else.

She touched her lips with trembling fingertips. The kiss had been hard and angry. But darned if it wasn't the best one she'd had all day long.

chapter twelve

Cruz never should've lost his temper at the kissing booth. It had taken Zoe about two seconds to figure him out. When he ran into her at church the next Sunday there was a knowing look in her eyes. In the sardonic brow she arched, in the curl of her lip. Yes siree. She was on to him. But instead of facing it head on as he might expect, she took a different approach.

She drove him downright crazy.

When he ran into her on the street she tossed him coy looks, put an extra wiggle in her walk, winked at him. When she sang love songs with Brevity she sidled up to Kyle, gazing up at him like he was her salvation. She ran the backs of her fingers down his face as she sang until Cruz was ready to lock her in her room. Oh, yeah. The little minx knew what she was doing.

On nights she didn't sing she danced with other guys. Lots of guys, snuggling up close while giving Cruz *Watcha gonna do about it?* looks over their shoulders.

He'd stop going to the Rusty Nail, that's what he was going to do. A man could only take so much. But he swore she must be privy to his schedule, because he was always running into her when she was on a date. He tried not to let her behavior get to him, but seeing her with other guys made him want to put a fist through a wall.

In the fall Brady went back to school for his sophomore year, leaving Cruz a little bereft. Cruz's mom had gotten on at the Blue Moon Grill and was making good tips. She was also dating a nice businessman from Atlanta and seemed to be on her way to an engagement.

In the winter Cruz got a promotion, along with a raise, at the hardware store, and at twenty-one he was finally able to get his own place. It was only an apartment above the Mitchell Construction office, across the street from the Rusty Nail, but it was his. With his mom finally settling into a secure life, his first taste of independence was sweet.

He'd been looking forward to having Brady over when spring break came, but the Collins family decided it was the perfect time to take Granny out to California to visit her brother and his grown kids. Zoe stayed behind because Brevity had a gig in Atlanta, and their regular backup singer had just had a baby.

Tonight the band was playing at the Rusty Nail, so Cruz found himself alone in his apartment. He rinsed off his lone dish from supper and stuck it in the dishwasher. Hiding from a little slip of a girl, that's what he was doing.

Idiota.

He was shoving the dishwasher closed when

his phone buzzed in his pocket. He checked the screen and saw Brady's name.

"Hey, buddy. How's California?"

"Where are you?" Brady's voice was raw and tense.

"At my new place. What's wrong?"

"It's Mom." The last word sounded squeezed from his throat.

"What happened?" Cruz waited, heart stuttering, for Brady to collect himself.

"There was a-an accident. We were riding bikes. Someone ran a red light and hit Mom. She's—" Brady broke down.

The sound of his sobs about ripped Cruz's heart out. "Take a breath, amigo," he said a minute later. "It's going to be all right. We'll get through this."

"She didn't make it, Cruz." His voice broke. "She's gone."

The words made him freeze. *Oh, no. Oh, man. Zoe.* She was going to be destroyed. She and her mom were close, often allied against her father.

But what kind of a friend was he, thinking about Zoe when his friend was weeping on the other end of the line?

Cruz grabbed the hair at his nape. "Oh, buddy, I'm sorry. I'm so sorry."

He pictured Mrs. Collins with her regal posture and kind blue eyes. She wasn't the warmest mother, especially not when he compared her

98

to his own mama, but she'd always been good-natured and fair.

"Are you all right? I mean, did anyone else get hurt?"

"Just minor stuff. Scratches and bruises, that's all. Dad's a mess. And Granny . . ."

"Aw, man." Nellie Russell only had one other daughter, Brady's birth mom. But she was who-knew-where, strung out on drugs. He couldn't even imagine what the woman was feeling. Didn't want to.

Brady sniffled and seemed to be making an effort to pull himself together. "You . . . you have to go find Zoe."

His heart sank as his breath left his lungs. "She's at the Rusty Nail. Brevity is playing tonight." He checked his watch. They didn't start till nine, and it was quarter till now.

"Can you go get her?"

"Yeah, yeah, of course. You . . . you want me to tell her?" *Please, no.* He could hardly bear the thought of breaking her heart.

"She should hear it from me. But I don't want her to be alone when I tell her, and with all our family out here . . ."

"Okay. All right. I'll go get her and I'll call you back."

He jabbed off his phone, slid on his shoes, and moved toward the door. He was in a desperate fog as he took the outdoor stairs.

Dios ayudarles. Help her.

The muggy air pressed against his skin, and his breaths came short and fast. He crossed the deserted street, following the thumping bass that carried through the night air.

Once inside the Rusty Nail he pushed his way through the pressing crowd. The band hadn't gone on yet, and "Don't Stop Believing" blared from the speakers. But over all the heads he saw that the group was mingling side-stage. His eyes skimmed for Zoe, and he found her chatting with the drummer. She tossed her head back, laughing, and his heart squeezed tight at the wreckage this news would cause.

"Hey!" someone said as Cruz jostled him aside, but he didn't stop. He didn't make eye contact with anyone or respond to greetings he barely even heard. His eyes were laser-focused on Zoe.

And then he was behind her. "Zoe." His throat closed up, tightening around her name.

He cleared his throat, touched her shoulder, and raised his voice over the music. "Zoe."

She turned, surprise flickering in her eyes before she remembered how things were between them.

She lifted a brow and tilted her head.

"You have to come with me."

She gave a sharp laugh. "Yeah, right. I'm about to go on, Cruz." She turned around to resume her conversation.

He took her elbow and leaned forward. "I

know, but you'll have to excuse yourself. I need to talk to you. It's important."

"Now? You need to talk to me now?"

Kyle planted a palm on Cruz's shoulder and shoved. "Get lost, pal. She doesn't want you. Come on, Zoe. It's time."

She turned toward the stage.

"Zoe, something's happened. You have to talk to Brady. It can't wait."

Her brow puckered, and worry flashed in her eyes. "Brady is . . . Brady's in California—"

"I know. He just called me."

She looked into his eyes for a long, painful moment. Must've seen the dread and the pity that twisted his gut, because the worry in her eyes morphed into fear.

"I have to go," she called to Kyle.

Cruz ushered her through the crowd, his hand on the small of her back. He was vaguely aware of Kyle pitching a fit behind them. The music soon swallowed his protests. Cruz pushed open the door, and they spilled out into the night.

The instant they were outside, Zoe spun toward him. "Cruz, what happened?"

Dread beat up into his throat. He took her elbow and pulled her across the street. "Let's go to my place. Brady wants you to call him."

He pulled her forward.

"Tell me!"

They were almost to the stairs leading up the

side of his building when she stopped, her feet planted on the ground. She folded her arms across her chest. "I'm not going anywhere until you tell me what's going on."

Her eyes clashed with his in a battle he couldn't fight with her. Not tonight.

She fished in her pockets. For her phone, he realized. But she must've left it back at the restaurant, because she gave a little growl. "Tell me!"

Now she'd have to come up to his place. "Come on, Zoe," he said gently.

He started up the steps, leaving her little choice but to follow.

She grabbed his arm, halting him on the first step. "Tell me what happened, Cruz Huntley! Why are you being so cruel?"

It was the way her voice wobbled on the last word. The way tears made her green eyes liquid. The way her bottom lip trembled ever so slightly.

The air spilled from him in a slow breath. He'd left his own phone in the apartment, and he wasn't about to torture her another second. Not when she was looking at him like that.

He eased down the step, and her hand fell away.

"Honey . . ." He made himself say the words. "It's your mama."

"Wh-what about her?"

He'd rather throw himself off a cliff than say the next words. He set his fingers on her arm, needing to touch her, ground her. "There's been an accident. She was riding a bike, and she was hit. I'm so sorry. She didn't make it."

She froze for a long moment, the tears glittering in the moonlight. "No . . . You-you're making it up."

His thumb swept her hot skin. "I'm not, honey. I'm so sorry."

"You're making it up!"

His throat tightened. "Let's go upstairs and call Brady."

"You're making it up . . ." This time her words crumbled like wadded-up newspaper. Her knees buckled.

He caught her around the waist. Swept her up into his arms.

"No!" She pushed against his shoulder, squirmed and twisted as he took the stairs. He tightened his grip.

"Let me go! Why are you doing this? It's not true!" She hit him on the back. "It's not true!"

His throat burned. "It's going to be okay, Zoe. I promise."

At the top of the steps he pushed through the door and let her squirm from his arms.

She gave him a final shove, nailing him with a glare.

He retrieved his phone and dialed.

"Give me the phone!"

Brady picked up right away. "Is she there?"

"She already knows. I had to tell her. I'm sorry."

Brady sighed, from relief, Cruz hoped. "All right. Let me talk to her."

Some of the anger was draining from Zoe's face and something worse was taking its place. She held out her hand, and it trembled in the space between them.

He gave her the phone, and she lifted it to her ear, barely breathing as she listened.

"No . . . ," she whimpered. Tears fell down her face, and her body wavered until Cruz feared she was going down.

He tugged her gently into the oversize chair with him and put his arm around her as if he could shield her from the pain.

"Okay," she said to Brady a moment later, then passed the phone to Cruz.

Cruz put it to his ear. "It's me."

"Stay with her, okay?" Brady's voice cracked.

"I will. I will. Don't worry."

A moment later as he hung up, sobs began tearing through Zoe. The shock was wearing off.

"It can't be true. It can't be."

He pulled her closer. "Come here, honey."

She turned, melting into his chest.

Her sobs shook him. His heart cracked open, and he tightened his arms as if he could absorb her pain.

"Mama," she wailed into his chest.

His eye sockets burned. "I know. I know, honey. I'm so sorry." It was all he could say. He couldn't even imagine losing his own mom. The whole family had to be reeling, and the coming days were going to be rough. To say nothing of now.

He murmured useless words, smoothed her beautiful hair, knuckled away her relentless tears. Time seemed to trickle past as the ache inside him grew. Was there anything worse than this helpless feeling?

He had no idea how long she cried. Longer than he dreamed possible. But sometime later the sobs subsided to an occasional shudder.

Still he held on. Her warm body had sunk into his chest. There was nothing he could do to relieve her pain. Nothing he could do to bring back her mom. But he could hold her. He could be here for her when her family was not.

As her breathing evened out he slid deeper into the chair and pressed a kiss to her damp curls.

chapter thirteen

The funeral was almost a week later. Gentry Memorial Home was located in an old rambling Victorian with the high ceilings and narrow windows and doors of a bygone era. The floors creaked with age as people milled around.

Zoe tried to focus on the elaborate cherry molding and fussy wallpaper. On the ornamental chandeliers and woolen rugs. Anything to keep from looking at the open casket at the front of the room where her mama lay, looking nothing like herself.

People pressed around her saying things that were meant to comfort. But nothing would fill the giant aching hole inside, and Zoe, who normally loved a room full of people, wanted nothing more than to bury herself under her covers.

She nodded and tried to smile as her grandma's friend Ruby Brown murmured and patted her arm. But all she could think about was her mama's last moments. And how she hadn't been there. She'd been on a stage pursuing some stupid childhood dream while her mama died. She'd missed her mother's last precious days. Her throat tightened. She didn't know if she'd ever be able to sing again.

A wave of heat swept over her despite the air

conditioning pumping through the vents. Her chest tightened, and her breathing quickened to accommodate. Her head spun dizzily even as she felt desperate to escape this room. This crowd.

"I—Excuse me, Miss Ruby, there's something I need to see to."

She didn't wait around for a response, but turned and quickly walked away. Was she going to pass out? She'd always laughed at those silly girls who fainted. It wasn't so funny now that it was her head spinning, her lungs gasping.

She ducked through a door off one of the parlors and found herself in a large empty closet. She closed the door behind her and flipped on a light, a barren bulb with all of fifteen watts.

She leaned against the wall which, she noticed absentmindedly, was also covered in floral wallpaper. She closed her eyes and breathed deeply until her heart rate began to slow and her head stopped spinning. She'd never had a panic attack, but this must be what one felt like. She could live the rest of her days and never do this again.

Or the whole week for that matter. Her emotions were all over the map. She could scarcely believe Mama was gone. The house seemed so empty without her. Her dad had returned from California too lost in his own pain to comfort anyone else. Brady seemed to think she needed an extra parent now and had nominated himself for the role.

Zoe had scrubbed the house from floor to ceiling, trying to stay busy. The freezer was stacked with casseroles no one had an appetite for. Her dad returned to work, and the home phone rang endlessly with neighbors offering to help. She'd made decisions about caskets and flowers and pallbearers—decisions no nineteen-year-old should have to make.

Through it all she ached for her mother and replayed their hasty good-bye over and over. She hadn't even told Mama she loved her.

Her throat went tight, and tears prickled behind her eyes. She shoved her palms into her eye sockets. Not yet. Not yet. If she gave in to the flood of emotions she was afraid she'd never stop.

The doorknob rattled and she straightened, her shoulder muscles tightening. Why couldn't everyone just leave her be? Was that too much to ask? Bad enough she had to get through an exhausting service and host a hundred of their closest friends at the house.

The door opened and Cruz slipped through, shutting it behind him.

Her shoulders sank in relief. He looked so handsome. His skin was dark against the crisp whiteness of his shirt, and his hair was slightly tousled as if he'd recently run a hand through it.

Her annoyance drained away even as her feet rushed toward him.

And then she was in his arms and he was holding her, and she took the first full breath she'd taken all week.

She hadn't seen him since the morning she'd awakened in his apartment. She'd barely had the time to enjoy the steely security of his embrace before he was untangling their limbs, a flush crawling up his neck. But then the night before came flooding back, and she felt the crushing loss of her mom all over again, a concrete block lying heavily on her stomach.

His absence ever since had been like a nagging loss in the back of her mind. But now that he was here, she realized it was all she'd needed. She clutched at his shirt, probably wrinkling it beyond repair, but she couldn't bring herself to care.

His hand cradled the back of her head, and he pressed his cheek to the top of her head.

"What can I do?" he whispered. His fingers dug into her hair, making every follicle come to life.

She tightened her arms around him. "Just this."

⇒••⇐

Cruz had seen Zoe slip from the crowd, her skin pale against her pink lips. It had been so hard to stay away from her this week. But her family was home now. It wasn't his place to comfort her.

"I missed you this week." Her words were muffled in his shirt.

109

He wondered if she noticed the way his heart accelerated. "I was trying to give your family some space."

"You saw Brady."

"He's my best friend."

"And what am I?"

My girl. Mi leona. Mi amor. Cruz closed his eyes. Clenched his jaw against the words. *Be strong, Huntley.*

At his silence she pushed away, her swollen eyes narrowing. "No answer, Cruz? Nothing?"

"This isn't the time, Zoe."

"It's never the time. When are you going to admit you have feelings for me?"

He pressed his teeth together, steeling himself against the longing in her eyes. He forced himself to remember his best friend. Her dad. To remember how young she was. Not just in years. But in *life.*

"You're young, Zoe, you have your whole life—"

She shoved him. "Don't you dare patronize me. I'm nineteen—a grown adult."

"Brady would never understand." Neither would her father. But saying that would only make her want to be with him more.

"My brother can't tell me who to be with."

"I want to be here for you, Zoe, but you'll be off to college soon, and you have a bright future ahead of you. You're smart and talented, and you don't need someone like me dragging you down." His voice had gone all raspy. He swallowed against the dull ache that had lodged there.

Zoe had gone uncharacteristically quiet. She stared at one of his shirt buttons, a sheen of tears making her green eyes sparkle. There were dark half-circles under them, making him wonder if she'd slept at all this week. Who was going to take care of her after Brady went back to college? Who was going to make sure she was eating? Sleeping? Surely not her dad.

She lifted her eyes, and he saw so much there. Fear. Pain. Longing.

"But I need you," she said.

The words were a sucker punch to his gut, and he was helpless against them. When she rose on tiptoe there wasn't a reason in the world that could stop him from tasting her lips, so sweetly offered.

I give up, he thought as his lips swept hers, the feeling of coming home so strong it all but engulfed him. *Can't do this anymore.*

He gathered her close, loving the feel of her against him. Her fingers threaded through the hairs at his nape, raising gooseflesh on his arms.

He pushed his fingers into the luxurious silk of her hair. It was just as soft as he remembered.

She's vulnerable, his conscience cried. *You're taking advantage.*

When she tried to deepen the kiss, he gave her lips one last brush and forced himself to draw back until he could meet her gaze. Her sleepy eyes were almost his undoing.

"This is a terrible idea," he whispered, but there was no conviction behind his words. He was weak. So weak.

"This is a wonderful idea."

"You're grieving. You're not thinking straight."

"I know my own mind, Cruz," she said vehemently.

It was true, he was forced to admit to himself. Zoe was the most opinionated person he'd ever known. He could think of ten times right off the top of his head that her crazy, stubborn opinions had gotten her in trouble. With her parents. Her teachers. Her friends. It had been all too entertaining to watch from the sidelines.

Her shoulders went rigid under his hands. "You're laughing at me."

"No . . . I'm not."

His affection for her must've been all over his face, because she relaxed in his arms one muscle at a time.

Her eyes searched his. "I want to be with you, Cruz. Surely you know that."

He thought back over the last year. The kissing booth, the boys trailing in and out of her life. The way his heart ached with yearning every time he saw her with someone else.

He was tired of hurting. Tired of wanting.

Maybe it could work. She was nineteen now. Brady would understand—eventually. And maybe he could prove himself to her dad, prove what a hard worker he was, how well he'd treat his daughter if only the man would give Cruz a chance.

Zoe cupped his jaw. Her breath fanned across his chin. Her eyes said things he'd been wanting to hear for so long.

"I need you," she whispered.

His chest tightened at the words. And finally he let himself say what he'd been holding back for so long. "I need you too, mi leona."

Her gaze raked over his face. "What does that mean?"

Heat suffused his neck at the admission. "My lioness."

Her mouth turned up just before he brushed her lips in a slow, sweet kiss. A moment later he set his forehead against hers. His heart was pounding like a jackhammer. He'd never had so much to live for. So much to lose.

"I have to tell Brady," he said.

"Let's wait a while. As soon as Brady knows, Daddy'll know, and that'll be the end of this. You know how he seeks Daddy's approval."

"He's my friend. I don't want to hide this from him."

She cupped the back of his neck. "You don't

understand. He's been ridiculous lately. He thinks he's my father or something."

"He's hurting."

"Exactly. He needs space to work through Mama's death before we drop this on him. Just a little time to come to grips with the loss."

"I don't know . . ."

"You know I'm right. This has hit him hard. Hit all of us hard."

He brushed a thumb over her cheek, reveling in the notion that he had a right to touch her now. Her skin was impossibly soft. Impossibly fragile. The freckles on her nose stood out in contrast to her pale skin, her cheeks were flushed with color now. Her eyes bright and lively. Beautiful. She was so beautiful.

"Just for a little while. Please?"

When had he ever been able to deny Zoe anything? He sighed. "I guess a few weeks won't matter much."

chapter fourteen

Somehow a few weeks turned into a few months and more. Cruz never took her to his apartment, afraid someone would see them together. At first they hung out at his mom's place. She and Zoe hit it right off, sometimes ganging up on him until they were laughing so hard he couldn't help but laugh too.

When it grew warm they met at the swimming hole near her grandma's orchard whenever they could. Mostly late at night when there was no chance of running into anyone.

Zoe had only confided in Hope and her grandma about their relationship. Granny Nel understood about Zoe's dad and promised not to tell. Cruz liked the way the older woman stood up for Zoe and encouraged her free spirit.

On those warm summer nights they'd spread a blanket in the back of his pickup and lie on their backs staring up into the night. He taught her the constellations, rewarding her with a kiss each time she answered correctly. She was a quick study.

He fell so deeply in love with her under the starry sky.

During the day he'd promise himself that he'd tell Brady soon, but at night when he held Zoe in his arms, he counted the cost. What if her dad forbade her from seeing him? She might be nineteen but she still lived at home, and her father was more controlling than most.

Hiding their relationship from Brady and Mr. Collins meant hiding it from everyone else too. That was never more apparent than one August night at the Rusty Nail. Zoe had filled in as backup singer. It was her first time singing since her mom died, and he could tell her heart wasn't in it.

He could also tell Kyle was interested in her. Cruz didn't like the way he looked at her—onstage or off.

Cruz was already feeling edgy as the two made their way to Zoe's circle of friends at the back of the room. He gritted his teeth as Kyle pulled a chair out for her at the corral of tables and took a seat next to her. Cruz should be sitting next to her. He should be fetching her a drink.

The band was moving to Nashville in about a month. They'd decided they needed to be there if they were going to make it big, and Kyle had made it clear he'd like nothing better than to take Zoe along.

She'd been so excited as she told Cruz about the offer that for a moment he thought she was going to go with them. Then she said she was just flattered at the offer, that she didn't want to leave.

That her dad would have a conniption. That she didn't want to leave Cruz. That the orchard was her future. She'd spent more time there lately, and her dreams seemed to be shifting. Cruz wasn't sure what to think about that. But he wondered if she'd regret saying no to such a big opportunity.

He was still lost in thought when Kyle returned to the table with Zoe's drink. Cruz always felt a little out of his element with Brady's group of friends. They all came from money and seemed to float through life on a cloud of privilege, no thought of college loans or medical bills or financial setbacks.

Their clothes had fancy labels and intentional holes, and though they were nice enough, they talked about things he had no interest in.

"See something you like, Huntley?" Kyle barked, a smirk curling his mouth.

The whole group fell silent, all eyes on him, and Cruz realized he'd been staring at Zoe, probably looking as possessive as a pauper with his last dollar. He was glad Brady had stepped away from the table.

"Cut it out." Zoe laughed, shoving Kyle's shoulder. "He's just doing his job—he's my brother-appointed guardian. Right, Cruz?"

A vise tightened around his heart, and he gritted his teeth against the pain. "Right."

As the conversation turned to local politics

he looked between Zoe and Kyle. Was there something going on? Was it possible Zoe had other reasons for wanting to keep their relationship secret?

He couldn't get the bad taste out of his mouth all night, not even later as he and Zoe lay on the creek's bank, holding hands and stealing kisses under the thick canopy of trees. Physically, things had progressed quickly between them. Last week they'd slept together for the first time, and he was still fighting his guilt over that.

Everything that had seemed so right now seemed secret and wrong. She meant so much more to him than a roll in the hay. But it was hard to restrain himself when being with her meant being alone, way out here where there wasn't a soul for miles.

She pulled back from his embrace, scrutinizing him under the moonlit sky. She'd worked the buttons of his shirt, baring his chest to her touch.

He'd undone a couple of hers too, and her shirt gaped open. He was no saint. What was he doing? It wasn't supposed to happen like this.

"What's wrong?" she asked. "You seem tense tonight."

He opened his mouth to say *nothing,* but he couldn't make the words come out. He sat up and clasped his arms around his knees. A country ballad floated from the radio of his truck, joining the night sounds of crickets and katydids.

Zoe followed suit. "What is it?"

He thought of all the times he'd talked to her about telling Brady—and all the times she'd talked him out of it. He had to know if there was something else behind Zoe's need to keep their relationship a secret.

He turned to her, wishing he could see her features better. "Is there something between you and Kyle?"

Her jaw slackened. "What?"

"He looks at you like he wants you."

"It's just part of the show."

If she believed that, she was more naïve than he thought. "It's not just when you're onstage, Zoe." He hated the insecurity in his voice. It was something he struggled with. A boy didn't have his dad walk away without absorbing some damage.

She shook her head, staring at him, her eyes bewildered. "How can you ask that after last week? There's nobody but you, Cruz. You're all I think about. If you could get in my head for two seconds you'd see there's no room for anyone else." She smoothed her thumb over his jaw.

When she looked at him like that, touched him like she was doing now, how could he help but believe her?

But if it wasn't Kyle, then why all the secrecy?

He wanted to date her openly. He was working so hard to prove himself at the store. He'd even been promoted to assistant manager a few weeks ago. Surely that would impress her father. He was going to make something of himself, prove himself worthy of her.

This relationship couldn't go anywhere until they went public. Until they had the support of her family. But maybe she didn't want it to go anywhere. The feeling that had been niggling at the back of his mind all these months twitched and burned. Maybe he was nothing but a romantic fling to pass the time until she went off to college and started her real life. Maybe she was ashamed of him.

He met her gaze, resolution lengthening his spine. "It's time to tell Brady."

"Not yet. He's leaving for college next weekend. Maybe when he comes home on break."

"Zoe, I need to do this. I need to come clean. I need to be honest." It would've been easier to tell him before they'd slept together. Now his motives would look anything but innocent.

"What does it matter?"

"It matters, Zoe." She flinched at his tone, and he made an effort to soften it. "I want to date you properly. I want to pick you up at your house and hold your hand in public. I want to shake your dad's hand and be invited over for supper. Don't you want that too?"

"Of course I do. It's just—my dad can be so opinionated. And now that Mama's not here to help soften him up . . . He's already fired up about my putting off college another semester. We fought about it just last night."

Excuses. That's what it sounded like to him. She was going off to UGA in January, and she was just biding her time with him till then. Then she'd find a proper boyfriend who came from a similar background. Someone her dad could proudly introduce around town.

His chest tightened. "I'm tired of being your dirty little secret, Zoe."

She reared back. "How can you say that?"

"Well, what do you call it? We're sneaking around like thieves. You won't acknowledge me in public." He finally gave voice to the feelings that had been building all summer. "Are you ashamed of me?"

"*No.* Cruz, I swear I'm not."

"I know I don't come from the same background as you and your friends—"

"Stop it. That doesn't matter to me. I told Granny and Hope, didn't I?"

He looked at her for a long moment. There was nothing but sincerity shining in her eyes.

A breath tumbled from his chest. "Then we'll tell Brady tomorrow. And then I'll go to your dad and—"

"No!" She popped to her feet. "You're going to spoil everything!"

"I'm trying to do the right thing!" He followed

her back to the truck, his open shirttails flapping in the breeze. "Zoe, listen to me."

The grass was high, and she reached the truck before he caught up with her. He planted his hands on either side of her, framing her in.

Her eyes sparkled with anger and tears. He hated getting her all riled up. Seeing her hurt. It was why he hadn't pressed her before now.

"We need to talk about this," he said. "We can't keep putting this off."

"You don't know my dad, Cruz."

"I can't do this anymore." He tried to brush her tears away, but she shoved his shoulder.

"Get away. Just get away from me!"

He started to ease back, but before he could get far pain exploded in his jaw. His body twisted with the impact, and he hit the ground with a thud.

Zoe screamed, and Cruz pushed up to find Brady standing over him, chest heaving with breath.

Anger rolled off him in waves. "Get up."

Cruz held up a hand. "Brady, it's not what you think."

Zoe was suddenly between them, palms flat against her brother's chest. "Stop it, Brady!"

He easily put her to the side. "Get up!"

Cruz came to his feet, and when Brady's fist flew through the air he did nothing to stop it. Pain exploded across his cheekbone. He staggered backwards, Zoe's scream ringing in his ears.

"Stop it! *Stop it!*"

"This is who you've been sneaking around with, Zoe? Seriously?" Brady paced away. "Button your shirt! We're going home."

"I'm not going anywhere with you!" She moved over to Cruz. Her face was streaked with tears. "Are you okay? You're bleeding. Oh, my gosh." She swept her thumb across Cruz's lip.

"Come on, Zoe!"

She nailed her brother with a look. "Shut up, Brady!"

Cruz took her hand. "It's okay. I'm okay. Go on home."

Her lips trembled. "I'm not going anywhere."

His eye was swelling shut, but he could still see Brady in his peripheral vision, wired like a 240 VAC. He wasn't in a mood to listen. This was exactly what he'd been afraid of.

"We'll talk tomorrow," Cruz told Zoe. "After things calm down. It'll be okay."

"I don't want to leave you."

"We'll sort this out. I'll be fine. Go on now." He wanted to kiss her forehead, but touching her seemed like a bad idea.

She wavered, indecision shadowing her eyes. Finally she brushed her thumb over the corner of his eye. "Get some ice on that."

"I will. I'll be fine."

She turned to go, looking back over her shoulder at him before she joined Brady, who reached for her elbow.

Zoe shook him off. "Don't touch me. Don't even talk to me!"

A minute later they were gone. Cruz got into his truck and headed toward his apartment. His head felt like it was going to explode. His one eye had swollen shut, and his lip felt fat too. But he had a feeling his physical injuries would pale in the face of what tomorrow would bring.

chapter fifteen

As the night before came rushing back Zoe closed her eyes, wanting to sink back into the oblivion of sleep. She'd had it out with Brady, and their quarrel had awakened their dad.

Now he knew about Cruz too, and just as she'd feared, he did not approve.

He'd immediately started pressing her to start college the fall semester—a mere two weeks away. He threatened to not pay at all if she didn't cooperate. Without her mother to run interference, the argument had escalated into a shouting match.

She needed to talk to Cruz, but he wasn't answering his phone. She hoped he'd be at church, but she had a sinking feeling he wouldn't be. Unfortunately she'd volunteered to sing.

A few hours later her fears were confirmed. He was nowhere in the small crowd that gathered at Copper Creek Community Church. Of course he wouldn't come. His face was probably black and blue thanks to her ignoramus brother. She shot Brady a sideways glare in the pew, which he missed entirely.

Somehow she made it through her solo of "Lead Me to the Cross" without breaking down. After church she found the opportunity she'd been waiting for. Her dad was chatting with the assistant pastor about a legal matter, and Noah Mitchell had pulled Brady aside.

She slipped out the back door and made her way down Main Street to Cruz's apartment. The heat dampened the back of her neck and by the time she climbed the outside stairs her hair clung there. At the top of the stairwell she knocked on his door, impatience evident in the loud, hard raps.

A long moment later the door swung open.

She sucked in a breath at the sight of his swollen eye and bruised jaw.

"It looks worse than it feels," he said.

"Liar." She touched his jaw tenderly, but he flinched anyway. "I'm going to kill him. Why on earth didn't you hit him back? Or at least defend yourself?"

"I deserved it." He looked over her shoulder as if she might've brought company. "You shouldn't be here. Where's Brady?"

"Who cares? After last night I don't care if I ever see him again. He was so loud he woke Daddy, and now he knows everything."

Cruz ran his hand over his mouth. "Great. I was hoping to at least handle that one right."

She grabbed his other hand, needing to feel connected to him. He seemed distant somehow, would hardly look at her. Even when he did, the warmth was gone from his eyes.

A heavy weight settled in her chest. "It doesn't matter. I don't care what they say. I'm an adult. I can date anyone I want. Why didn't you answer your phone? Aren't you going to let me in?"

He shifted in the doorway. "I don't think that's a good idea."

"Why not?"

The look he gave her made a shiver of dread pass through her. "Zoe . . ."

"What? This doesn't have to change anything between us. They know now. That means we can go out in public like you wanted."

"It changes everything." He paused to give his words thought. "I think we need to take a little break."

"No."

"We need to give Brady some time to cool off."

"I told him it wasn't your fault. That it wasn't what it looked like. That we . . . we have feelings for each other."

Something flickered in his eyes. "They need time to adjust to the idea."

"I'm not going to let them dictate who I see!"

"It's not about that. I need to earn their respect—and their trust. We kept this from them for four months. And we shouldn't have moved so fast—that's my fault. Now they think the worst of me, and I deserve it. We went behind their backs, and that only made things worse. It's going to take some time for me to prove myself."

Tears stung her eyes. "Fine, but you can do that while we're together. Come over to the house for supper tonight." Her dad would have a conniption, but anything was better than taking a break.

"I'm the last person your dad wants to see right now. Not to mention Brady. We need to take a step back and reassess."

"Reassess?" That sounded so permanent. "No, I don't want that."

"I don't either, Zoe, but it's the risk we took when we started sneaking around. Now we have to live with the consequences."

Her muscles quivered as heat flushed through her. "So it's *my* fault?"

"Not at all. I should've done the right thing."

His calm, even tone scared her more than anything else.

"But I talked you out of it, right? You do think it's my fault."

His jaw twitched. "I'm not going to fight with you, Zoe. Brady'll come around in time when he calms down. When he realizes I have feelings for you. But your dad . . . That's going to take longer."

"I don't care what my dad thinks."

"Well, I do."

"You're never going to earn his approval, don't you get that?"

He blinked, hurt flashing in his eyes.

But she couldn't bring herself to take it back. It was true. Cruz came from a different background, and her dad could be such a snob. He'd never support her dating a guy who didn't even go to college, a guy who worked at the local hardware store. And though he'd never said as much, she guessed the color of Cruz's skin didn't help matters much.

"I hope you're wrong," he said.

"Why do you think I didn't want to tell him in the first place? I knew this would happen."

"All we can do now is play it out. And that means stepping back and doing it right this time."

"Aren't you even listening? Time won't change anything. Not with my dad."

He crossed his arms, and the resolute set of his jaw filled her with fear. "I have to have his blessing, Zoe. I'm not dating you without it."

She threw her hands up. "Argh! You're so frustrating!"

"You have to trust me."

She blinked against the sting of tears. She was too angry to cry. How could he do this? He didn't care as much about her as she did about him. Her heart gave a heavy thump.

"I did trust you. I trusted you with my heart, and now you're pushing me away."

His eyes squeezed in a wince. "It's not like that."

"Sure sounds like it to me! You want a break?

Well, that just suits me fine. Let's make it a nice, long, permanent one!" She whirled away, shaking.

"Zoe, come on . . . You don't mean that."

"Yes I do!"

"Zoe!" he called after her as she fled down the stairs.

She didn't want to hear any more excuses. If he cared as much as she did he wouldn't want some stupid break. He wouldn't be able to stand the thought of being apart. He wouldn't let her go.

But when she reached the church and finally looked back toward his apartment he was nowhere to be seen. And the next day there was no phone call. Or the day after, or the one after that.

Three weeks came and went. Zoe was so distracted she barely realized she'd missed her period. After work one day she drove to the next town over and purchased a pregnancy test. Her hands shook as she took it first thing the next morning.

And three minutes later her heart quaked as the pink line appeared in the window.

chapter sixteen

Zoe fretted for the next two weeks. She told only Hope about the pregnancy, and Hope encouraged her to tell Cruz. Zoe knew she had to tell him, but she dreaded it. She'd had nothing but doubts since he'd pushed her away. If he had plans to make her dad like him, she had yet to see them in action. It seemed as if he'd dropped off the face of the earth. As if he'd only been patronizing her with all his talk about winning her dad over.

And all hell was going to break loose when her dad found out she was pregnant.

But she had to tell Cruz. Late at night she lay in bed, mapping out their conversation. He'd do the right thing by her; she didn't doubt that. But she didn't want him to marry her because of the baby. She wanted him to love her as much as she loved him. She wanted him to believe in her. In *them.*

Meanwhile, Kyle was pressuring her to go on tour with the band. They were leaving soon, and he made it sound like so much fun. But she held her ground. She had to deal with this new turn of events.

When she finally got up the nerve she texted Cruz, asking him to meet with her. The text went unanswered, so she sent another, and another. Then she called him. But that went straight to voicemail.

She disconnected the call. She was about ready to tell him the news in a text. She punched his number again and, as expected, voicemail kicked on.

"This is Zoe. I need to talk to you, as I've mentioned to you three times already. It's important, Cruz. Meet me at the creek tonight at eight. If you're not there I'm showing up at the hardware store tomorrow morning, and we'll have this conversation right there."

By the time she disconnected her heart was pounding in her chest. It was humiliating. She felt as if she were chasing someone who only wanted to be left alone. And now she was going to make him feel trapped.

Kyle's words came rushing back. *This is a huge career opportunity. Don't let some guy stand in the way of your future. You're not even together anymore. When's the last time he's checked up on you, huh?* He'd shrugged, an I-rest-my-case look on his face.

But Kyle didn't know about the pregnancy. She'd tell him tonight after she told Cruz. He'd surely give up on her then. The band was leaving in two days, and having some pregnant girl along for his whirlwind tour would surely cramp his style.

Zoe arrived at the creek early, her heart in her throat, her legs shaking so much she stayed in her car. She put her window down and turned off the ignition. A glance in the visor mirror told her she looked as tired as she felt. She hadn't been sleeping well, and she'd been dogged by fatigue. She slapped the mirror closed.

A few minutes later Cruz's truck came rumbling down the lane, kicking up a cloud of dust behind him.

"You can do this," she whispered, placing her hand over her flat belly.

Cruz pulled up beside her and got out. She met him at the front of her car. He looked so handsome in the evening light. There were no dark circles under *his* eyes.

"Nice of you to show up." Okay, so she was still mad. "Obviously nothing's wrong with your phone."

He stopped several feet away, his hands tucked into his front pockets. "I got your texts, but I didn't see any point in meeting. I already know what you're going to tell me."

Her lips parted as nausea twisted her empty stomach. How could he know? She'd only told Hope. She realized belatedly his guarded stance. The strained expression on his face.

"You don't owe me anything, Zoe." His tone

was clipped. "If you want to run off with Kyle and pursue your music together, that's your decision."

Wait. She blinked. "What?"

"You really didn't have to tell me in person. You made your choice. I got the message loud and clear."

Was he really implying she'd moved on with Kyle? After she'd reassured him there was nothing there? She stared at him. She couldn't believe he thought so little of her. May as well just add him to the list, right behind her dad. Her shoulders stiffened.

"Well, glad we had this talk." He was already backing away. "Good luck, I guess."

She was still shaking her head as he walked around the front of his truck. As he got inside and turned it over. This wasn't the way this was supposed to go.

She opened her mouth to stop him. But how could she tell him about the baby now? How could she be with a man who believed as little of her as her father? But he'd know soon enough if she stayed.

Kyle called later that night, and Zoe found herself telling him everything. About the baby. About her conversation with Cruz—as short as it had been. Hearing the compassion in his voice she broke, weeping until she could hardly talk. Until she could hardly swallow against the lump in her throat or breathe for the ache in her chest.

When he pressed her again about going on the tour she hesitated. She couldn't believe he'd still have her. But he was so understanding. He even said she could bring Brownley along. And he made some good points. This would solve most of her problems. If she stayed she didn't know what she was going to do once the baby started showing. Cruz would end up trapped in a relationship he didn't want. And her dad sure wasn't going to be any kind of support.

She would leave. It's what Cruz expected of her anyway.

Two days later, after her dad left for work, she wrote a note for her family and packed up her things. She'd made decisions that had changed the course of her life. All she could do now was take the next step forward.

part three

chapter seventeen

So many emotions washed over Zoe as Hope drove them down the orchard's long gravel drive. How life had changed in the five years since she'd last been here.

Memories rushed back. All the times she and Cruz had spent hiding out in the orchard. At the swimming hole on the north side of the property, stretched out in the bed of his truck or cuddling on the bank of the creek under the moonlit sky.

Memories, good and bad, tangled together like a knotted ball of yarn. There was no going back. Only forward.

She'd hardly slept last night, worried that Kyle would return and make more trouble. But the night had passed uneventfully.

Her jaw still throbbed, and an ugly red bruise marked the spot where his hand had connected. Her efforts at covering it with makeup had been futile.

Behind her in her new booster seat, Gracie slurped her orange juice as she watched the passing landscape. Their trip to Walmart the night before had set Hope back seventy-eight dollars. Zoe was keeping a running tab.

She surveyed the seventeen acres of the orchard and the rolling hills beyond it. It was thinning season now, and harvest would soon be upon them. The trees would require over a dozen laborers.

Zoe was meeting the accountant and orchard manager at the house to go over basic operations. She was completely out of step with any changes they might have made in recent years. She hoped she'd feel more at ease once they brought her up to speed.

Hope rolled the car to a stop in front of the white clapboard farmhouse. Granny's house. Their new home. There would be house bills and orchard bills and financial statements, and she knew diddly about any of it. Kyle had always done the bills. And she was terrible at math.

Hope grabbed her hand. "Breathe. I can see the panic in your eyes. Let's just take one day at a time."

"I don't know if I can do this."

"Why, of course you can. We'll all be right here. Me, Brady, and . . ." Hope bit her lip, something flickering in her eyes. "Honey . . . there's something I need to tell you before you go in there."

A truck pulled up alongside their car, and Zoe's eyes swung to the driver. Cruz sat behind the wheel of the black Silverado, Brady in the passenger seat.

"Mama, it's Uncle Bwady!"

What was Cruz doing here? He was the last

person—well, second to last—she wanted to see this morning. Maybe he was just giving her brother a ride. Obviously the two had overcome the rift in their relationship while she was gone.

But no, he was getting out of the truck. Did he think he could just pop back into her life so easily? Maybe he'd come to her rescue at the Rusty Nail, but that wasn't an invitation back into her life.

Zoe slid from her seat.

"Zoe . . . ," Hope said.

But the door had already shut behind her, and she was busy fighting the rise of irritation. She felt a sharp stab of guilt at the thought of Gracie and the fact that she'd kept Cruz from her.

But he was the one who'd assumed the worst of her. He was the reason she'd gone on the road to begin with. The reason he had no relationship with his daughter. Even now she wanted to gather Gracie up and run far, far away. It was unsettling having them in the same space together.

Too bad she had nowhere else to go.

Cruz adjusted the ball cap on his head, wincing as he caught sight of her jaw. He didn't look so swell either, with that black eye.

"How you feeling this morning?" he asked.

"I'm fine. What are you doing here, Cruz? I don't aim to be rude, but this is a family matter."

Surprise flickered in his eyes. They toggled toward Hope, who was coming around the front of her car, then to Brady. Finally they came back to her.

"I'm obliged for what you did last night," she said. "But I can handle things from here, all right?"

"Um, Zoe . . . ," Hope started.

"Mama! Get me out!"

"I'll get her." Hope skirted Zoe.

"I'll be in the house," Brady said, taking off as if his clothes were on fire.

Cruz was looking at her, that enigmatic look in his dark eyes. "Nobody told you."

A shiver of foreboding passed over her. She looked at Hope, who was pulling Gracie from her booster, deftly avoiding eye contact.

"Told me what?"

He adjusted the brim of his hat. A nervous habit that drew attention to his expressive eyes and held her captive for a beat too long.

"I work here, Zoe," he said. "I manage the place. I thought you knew. Your grandma hired me when Glen moved away four years ago."

She blinked, hearing but not yet digesting the information. "How would I know?"

"I don't know . . . Your grandma, Hope, Brady . . . I figured someone would've told you."

"Well, no one did!"

He seemed to absorb her anger, his jaw twitching once, his eyes steady on her.

Sure, maybe she hadn't kept in touch the way

she should've. Maybe she'd even cut Granny off a time or two when Cruz's name came up.

But this.

Her grandma had left the orchard to Zoe, which was going to put her in very close proximity to the man who'd stolen her heart and forgotten to give it back.

What had Granny been thinking? She'd been meddling, that's what. Meddling from beyond the grave.

She watched a dark shadow move over Cruz's face. Maybe he thought he should've inherited the place. He'd been here, after all, holding down the fort for her grandma while Zoe had been traveling the country. Barely keeping in touch.

"You think she should've left it to you."

He looked away for a long moment before meeting her gaze again. "I never said that."

"You didn't have to."

"I have no claim on the land. I'm glad you're staying."

Her gaze swung to his in time to watch a flush crawl up his neck.

"It'd be a shame to see the orchard pass from the family. A lot of people depend on this place to put food on their tables."

"Of course." Guilt pricked hard. She hadn't even given the laborers a second thought until now. Until it was convenient for her to keep the place. When had she become so selfish?

A flock of geese passed overhead, honking as they flew in their V-shaped formation. Zoe looked at the leader, the one who was strong enough to take the brunt of the wind. She felt like a sickly goose near the back that no one could depend on. And Granny had put her at the apex of the flock.

She wasn't going to be that weak person anymore. She was going to figure this out, and do her grandma proud.

"Let's just make the best of it, huh?" Cruz said.

She thought of Gracie, and a breath left her body on a wry laugh. The child's brown eyes, so like Cruz's. The shape of her ears. The little crescents at the corners of her lips when she smiled. Surely it would only be a matter of time before he saw it.

She should tell him before he did.

But what if he took Gracie from her? What did she have to her name but an orchard she didn't even know how to run? He had a history of stability, and she'd been dragging her baby girl all over the country with a rock band. All the old fears crept in, swallowing her courage.

She couldn't even fire Cruz. Even if she were that cruel, she needed him. She was trapped. Backed into a corner as she'd been so many other times in her life.

She needed a competent manager if she wanted to make it through harvest. If she hoped to make some money and keep this orchard going. She probably wouldn't have to see him much. Hadn't Hope said the place practically ran itself?

"All right," she said, lifting her chin. "I guess we'll have to make the best of it then." She turned to go.

He took her elbow as she passed, releasing her when she stiffened.

"I just wanted to apologize for last night. I-I think I might've provoked Kyle with something I said earlier. That wasn't too smart of me."

She gave him a long, thoughtful look. The flush, rising on his neck, only made her more curious.

She had to ask. "What'd you say?"

"It's not important."

She narrowed her eyes on him, her imagination running wild. "Tell me."

He held her gaze a long moment, and she saw the moment he decided to own up to whatever it was.

His chin edged up, and the cords of his neck muscles stood out. "I asked him how my girl was."

A strangled laugh escaped her throat, a moment of glee at the thought of Cruz putting Kyle in his place. How many times had she wanted to smart off to him, but held back out of fear?

Cruz's words must've made him furious. She was surprised Kyle hadn't decked him on the spot. "Well, you've never lacked nerve, Huntley."

"I'm not afraid of Kyle."

That made one of them. She resisted the urge to touch her aching jaw.

"Anyway," he continued, "it was a stupid thing to say. I was trying to get his goat, and he took it out on you. I'm sorry for that."

"You can't be faulted for someone else's actions."

Her own words pierced her like an arrow into a bull's-eye. Why was it so easy to believe that when she was talking about someone else?

Cruz stuffed his hands into his worn jeans pockets. "Will he come back? I mean, I can't imagine that he won't, what with your little girl."

Zoe's eyes dropped to the ground. "I guess we'll have to wait and see."

"You're not going to stay here alone, are you?"

"I can take care of myself." Maybe she hadn't done such a good job of that lately, but she was turning over a new leaf.

"Still, you should take precautions. You can't be stupid about it."

Heat flushed through her at the familiar words. "I'm not stupid."

Cruz gave her a long, speculative look.

Her skin prickled with heat as a memory paraded through her mind. Sitting at the table on the tour bus while Kyle tried to explain the financial side of the band's business. The look on his face when she still didn't get it the second time he explained. The slap of the financial records book closing. *I give up; you're hopeless. Guess I'll just have to hire this out too.*

The self-doubt came creeping up on her like a lion stalking its prey.

"It was a figure of speech, Zoe," Cruz said. "I know you're not stupid."

The screen door creaked open, and Hope stuck her head through, looking sheepish. "You two about ready to get started?"

"Coming," Zoe called and set her feet in motion. She had a lot to prove. To Cruz, to her family, to the employees depending on her for their livelihood. But most of all, to herself.

⇒•⇐

A long hour later, Zoe looked up from the spreadsheets. They were sitting around her grandmother's table: Phil Blackburn, the accountant; Cruz, Brady, and Zoe. Hope was in the living room entertaining Gracie.

Zoe fixed her gaze on Phil. "So you're saying we're in the red right now."

"That's the long and short of it."

"By that much?" She pointed to a number that took her breath away.

"It's not unusual for farms to take out loans to see them through until harvest."

"But my grandma had all that money . . . Why'd she have to take out a loan?"

"The bulk of her money was tied up in mutual funds. There was a heavy penalty for early withdrawal. A loan made more sense."

"Okay . . . So how much does harvest usually net?"

Phil's eyes bounced off Cruz's. "Well, that varies of course, depending on how good a year it is for the crops."

"And this year?"

Phil's thin lips pressed together. He pushed his glasses up his beaklike nose. He had kind blue eyes, and the sort of patience an accountant needed when going over numbers with her.

Cruz was studying his hands, which were clasped on the table.

"What?" Her gaze toggled between the two. Gracie giggled in the living room, then squealed at whatever Hope was doing.

"I'm afraid it was a mild winter," Phil said.

Maybe she was ignorant about the financial side of things, but she knew her stuff when it came to peaches. She'd learned from the best. The trees needed between seven hundred and a thousand chill hours. Anything short of that meant a late or diminished crop.

"How bad?"

Cruz cleared his throat. "Crop'll probably be about half of last year's."

"Half?" Her stomach clenched as a heaviness weighted her from the inside out.

Phil gave her a sympathetic smile.

Her eyes swung to Cruz, narrowing. "You couldn't have told me this sooner?"

"Would it have made a difference?"

"Yes. No. I don't know." She pressed her lips together, her thoughts bouncing around like a pinball in a machine. "But I should've had all the pertinent information."

"That's what today's for," Brady said.

"Well, it's a little late."

She'd already kissed Kyle good-bye, including her steady paying job as backup singer. Maybe the nomadic lifestyle wasn't all she'd dreamed it would be, but it wasn't an albatross around her neck either—and she was beginning to think that's exactly what the orchard was.

"You can't seriously mean you'd have"— Brady's gaze flickered off Phil before returning to her—"done anything different if you'd known."

"I don't know what I would've done. I just don't appreciate being kept in the dark."

"Nobody intended to keep you in the dark, Zoe," Phil said. "The orchard has had good and bad years, and everything in between. Your grandma always made it work. I'm sure you will too."

"Well, I'm glad someone's sure."

Zoe's mind was spinning by the time the meeting was over. Phil had gone to his office, Cruz to join his pruning crew, and Brady back to his garage. Her brother had offered to fork over the money Granny had left him, but she wasn't taking that. Granny had wanted him to have that money for his business, and he had plans for it.

After the bad news about the diminished crop, they had discussed ideas to make up for the loss. Her grandma had been thinking about opening up a market on the property to sell peaches, produce, and baked goods. There would be a better profit margin this way, and Granny's recipes were the best. The small barn out by the road would be suitable—with a lot of elbow grease.

This was not what she'd signed up for at all. She planted her elbows on the scarred kitchen table and palmed her eyes. What had she gotten herself into?

At a nearby shuffling sound she looked up to see Hope in the kitchen doorway cupping a mug of coffee. "Want some?"

"Better not. My thoughts are already spinning out of control."

From her spot at the table she could see Gracie hunched over the coffee table in the living room, coloring in her Nemo coloring book.

Zoe nailed Hope with a look. "Why on earth didn't you tell me Cruz was the general manager?"

Hope winced. "I tried to . . ."

"Well, you didn't try very hard. Did you also know it was a bad crop year?"

Hope settled into the chair catty-corner to her. "All the farms are struggling. I should've told you, but I was afraid you'd sell the place if you knew, and I couldn't bear the thought. Besides, you belong here, Zoe. I see it, and Granny saw it. I hope you can see it too. You sure don't belong with that loser."

Zoe gestured at the stacks of files in front of her. "Right now this just feels like too much to handle. We're in the red, and the crop isn't likely to get us out. I don't have a paying job. I have a daughter to support. And the thought of getting a market open in time for Peach Fest is just overwhelming. It's barely over two months away."

"You have people handling the day-to-day. The retailers are mostly in place, I'm sure. And Granny trusted Phil implicitly with the finances. Just jump in and get your feet wet. Maybe the crop is down this year, but the orchard has survived other bad years. And it's still the same place you've always loved."

"You're right. I'm sure I'll be fine." Eventually. When she didn't feel like she was drowning. When she had two dimes to rub together again and didn't have to worry about how she was going to work and take care of her daughter.

But she was a farmer now and at the mercy of the elements. It wasn't only chill hours she had to worry about but late frosts. And even a good crop could be ruined by a hailstorm or pests or disease. Nothing was ever sure until the peaches were off the trees.

And on a more personal note, there was Cruz. How was she going to deal with seeing him all the time? It had been hard enough to sit across the table and not be sucked right into those heartbreaker eyes. Not to remember how gentle his touch was. Or how his lips had stirred a fire in her like no one else before or since.

She couldn't let herself go there again. She was done with men. They were nothing but a disappointment.

"Not to bring up another bad subject, but . . . when are you going to tell him, Zoe?"

Her eyes flew to Hope's, her mouth going dry. She squeezed out the words through a constricted throat. "Tell him what?"

Hope gave her a knowing look. "He's going to figure it out. Men are a little slower with the details, but he's not oblivious."

She knew Hope was right, but she couldn't deal with it right now.

"I'll tell him soon. I'm a little overwhelmed with all this stuff right now. If I can just get to harvest I'll be able—"

"Harvest? That's two months away."

"For heaven's sake, Hope, my life just took a drastic turn, and I'm reeling. To make matters worse, I'm meeting Daddy for dinner tonight, and goodness knows that'll be as fun as pulling teeth." When Hope refused to back down, Zoe huffed. "All right. Fine. I'll tell him . . . soon. Just let me get my legs under me, for crying out loud."

Hope's eyes searched hers even as she took a long sip of her coffee.

"I will," Zoe reiterated. "I promise."

Hope's mug clunked quietly as she set it on the table. "Fair enough. But don't be waiting too long. Secrets this big have a way of spinning out of control."

chapter eighteen

The Blue Moon Grill wouldn't have been Zoe's first pick of places to take a four-year-old child. It was the fanciest place in town and a popular special occasion spot. But she supposed it wasn't every day a man met his grandchild.

The restaurant was situated on the outskirts of town, adjacent to Copper Creek. Inside, the dim lighting made the white tablecloths glow and cast intriguing shadows on the brick walls.

She spotted her dad at a corner booth and, holding Gracie's hand, she wove through the tables toward him.

He turned from the window at their approach. She hoped he could see past Gracie's cheap Walmart dress to the wonderful little girl beneath.

"Hi, Daddy. This is Gracie." She squeezed Gracie's hand. She'd prepped her daughter on the drive over. "Honey, this is my daddy. Your papaw."

"Hi," Gracie whispered as her dad fixed his eyes on the girl, perusing her face for a long minute.

"Hello, young lady." He held out his hand and Gracie took it.

His gaze flickered up to Zoe, and she knew the moment he noticed her bruised jaw. She'd done her best to cover it, but makeup only went so far.

The muscle in his jaw twitched. He'd no doubt heard all about Saturday night, but he resisted the urge to bring it up. "She looks like you," he said instead.

Zoe couldn't tell whether he considered that a good or a bad thing. She ushered Gracie into the booth and followed behind her.

A server came by with a children's menu and crayons, and they spent the next several minutes perusing the menu and ordering.

Afterward they made small talk about the town and its residents, steering clear of sticky topics as if by mutual agreement. Gracie, thankfully, loved to color and was busy drawing figures on the back of her menu.

The restaurant wasn't busy on Mondays, so their food came quickly. As they ate the conversation was stilted, her daughter unwittingly smoothing things over with her charming commentary and observations.

Her dad's green eyes fell on Gracie often, and he seemed to be taking her in. But he was not an emotional man and didn't seem to know what to say to a child.

Zoe was on tenterhooks waiting for him to bring up the subject of her leaving five years ago or her single-mother status or Saturday night's events or a myriad of other ways she'd disappointed him.

When she'd scraped the last of her food from

her plate, the server swooped in to clear the table. Her dad folded his hands on the table and leaned forward, his eyes falling to her jaw again.

"Please tell me you pressed charges."

Zoe's gaze dropped to the bread crumbs on the tablecloth before meeting his gaze again. "I just wanted him far away. And he's gone now."

"He should be in jail. I could make sure of it."

Her gaze flickered to Gracie and back to her father, and she saw the knowing look that indicated he understood that discretion was called for.

"I did what I thought best."

"You always do." He tipped his head back. "I heard your grandmother left you the orchard. You probably won't get much for it. I'm afraid Brady got the better end of that deal."

She notched up her chin. "I'm not selling the orchard. I'm going to run the place just like Granny did." She took satisfaction in watching his lips part in surprise. He'd never had much respect for Granny and her spirited ways.

"That's a poor decision."

"Well, it's mine to make." She smiled to take the sting from her words.

He leaned forward, lowering his voice—his version of yelling. "It's a bad year for crops. You must know that by now. By the time you finish harvest you'll be in even deeper. Best to cut your losses now."

"I've got it under control, Daddy." That was a

joke, but confidence was the best way to combat her dad's controlling ways.

"Look, Mama! Sunshine."

"That's beautiful, honey."

"I'm going to dwaw a wainbow next."

"Good idea. Use all your colors."

Gracie went to work on the picture, and Zoe met her dad's eyes. He'd aged in her absence. His hair had receded a bit. The furrow between his brows was deeper. The lines at the corners of his mouth more defined.

He signed for the bill, and the server took it away. Then her dad straightened as if pulled upward by some invisible string. "I have a proposal for you, Zoe—don't look at me like that. Is it so hard to believe I want the best for you?"

"We've always disagreed on what, exactly, that is."

"Well, you've tried things your way."

And been a miserable failure. He didn't have to say it. Heat rose in her neck. "My life isn't up for negotiation, Daddy."

"Just hear me out, will you? Why do you have to get your back up every time I open my mouth?"

She pressed her lips down on a retort. She counted to three. Then ten. "All right. Go ahead and have your say. I'm listening."

"The way I see it, you've got a child to support,

an orchard that's more of a burden than a gift, and nothing more than a high school education."

"Gee, Daddy, must you put such a positive spin on things?"

"There's no sense whitewashing the truth. You need a means of support. A career, not some two-bit dream. You don't survive on hope and a whim. You must've figured that out by now."

She bit the inside of her lip and waited for him to finish.

"It's not too late to think about college. You're a bright girl, and you'd do well if you only applied yourself. In the meantime you can work in my office. Not as an intern. I'd offer you a full salary and benefits. I'll even pay for your college classes."

The full salary and benefits were more tempting than she wanted to admit, even to herself. But no. This wasn't who she was or what she wanted. Besides, she'd only just escaped one controlling relationship. She wasn't falling headlong into another.

"Daddy, I appreciate the offer. I do. But I have no more interest in law now than I did five years ago."

"Don't be so shortsighted, Zoe. It's time to be practical. You need a regular income and higher education."

"There's nothing practical about doing something you don't enjoy for the rest of your life! I love the orchard. I know farming is a gamble, but I'll work hard just like Granny did, and I'll make it work."

"Like you did your singing career?"

"I was doing quite well actually."

"That was no kind of life for you or your daughter. You don't have the luxury of following a pipe dream now. And you don't have your grandmother's business sense. You'll never turn a profit."

She winced as the shot hit its mark. "Well . . . Granny believed in me or she wouldn't have left me the orchard."

"Do you know how many people would jump at the offer I just laid on the table? Must you always be so ungrateful?"

"I don't mean to be ungrateful. I just wish you could support me for once."

"How can I support you when you can't make a sound decision to save your life?"

She ground her teeth together. Drew a deep, calming breath. Her hand squeezed on the purse at her side. "I think it's time for us to go."

"This is a one-time offer, Zoe. I'm not going to continue to offer you bailouts."

"Nobody asked you to, Daddy." She looked at Gracie. "You ready, honey?"

"Uh-huh." Gracie made a final sweep with her red crayon.

Zoe could feel her dad seething across the

table. She grabbed her purse and scooted from the booth.

Gracie followed, extending the picture to her grandpa. "This is for you, Papaw."

Zoe held her breath until he took it.

He gave a formal nod, the corners of his eyes still tight. "Thank you, young lady."

"Thank you for supper, Daddy. It was good to see you. Say good-bye to your papaw, Gracie."

" ' Bye, Papaw."

Zoe took her daughter's hand and led her through the restaurant on shaking legs. Some things never changed. When was she going to stop hoping they would?

chapter nineteen

The next morning at eight o'clock Zoe opened the door to find Ruby Brown on her stoop, purse dangling from her sturdy frame. Her grandmother's friend was a welcome sight. Zoe had nothing but good memories of the cocoa-skinned woman who always had a warm, ready smile.

"Well, you're looking right pert this morning," the woman said.

"Miss Ruby." Zoe pushed open the screen door and was folded into Ruby's soft embrace.

"Come in," Zoe said when Miss Ruby released her. "I aimed to call you. We hardly got a chance to say two words at the funeral."

Miss Ruby had been on Granny's payroll as housekeeper for the past couple of years. Zoe really couldn't afford to keep her on, even if she did work for diddly squat. But she couldn't bring herself to fire her either.

"I have no idea what hours you were working for Granny or if you wanted to continue. Or go to part-time?" *Please, please, please.*

"I was hoping you'd keep me on full-time. I don't know what I'd do if I didn't have this farmhouse to come to every day. I'll miss your grandma like the dickens, though. She was like a sister to me." Miss Ruby dabbed at the corner of her eye.

A knot built in Zoe's throat as she sat on the sofa next to the woman. "She loved you too, Miss Ruby."

"Where's your little one? Nellie showed me every picture she had."

"She's still sleeping. She's having a little trouble adjusting to the new room."

"Well, sure. That's to be expected." Ruby squeezed her hand. "I don't know what your plans were, but you're welcome to leave her with me while you take care of business on the farm if you'd like."

Zoe started. "Oh. I couldn't. It's too much trouble."

Miss Ruby waved her off. "Oh, pshaw. I raised four of my own. I imagine I can handle one just fine." Miss Ruby had to be in her midsixties by now, though she'd always had the energy of a thirty-year-old.

"Of course you can but . . . it's a lot to ask. I can't afford to pay you more." She couldn't afford to pay her at all.

"What am I going to do around here for forty hours a week? A person can only dust so often. Mostly I kept Nellie company—I think she just kept me around because she needed someone to shoot the breeze with. Heaven knows she wasn't afraid of hard work. I'd really love to have a little one around again."

Zoe couldn't believe an answer to her biggest

worry had landed right in her lap. "Ruby Brown, you're an answer to my prayers."

A wide smile stretched across her face. "I do believe I'm going to like working for you just fine, little miss."

⋙•⋘

Josephine Mitchell whipped the black cape off Cruz. "There you go, kind sir. What do you think?"

Cruz ran a hand through his trimmed hair. He had to admit that whatever she'd put on it made his hair soft as a rabbit pelt. "It's great, Josephine. Thank you much."

She accompanied him to the register. Josephine was married to Noah, a friend of his from church. The couple had all but divorced a while back, but last year they'd gotten back together. Whenever Cruz saw the two of them together, so in love, it made him ache for what he and Zoe'd had.

Stop it, Huntley.

"You're back to work already, huh?" Cruz asked. Josephine had recently had a baby.

"It's been a whole month, believe it or not. And the little bugger's still getting up twice a night. About wearing us out. I wouldn't trade it for all the world though."

"Noah's of the same mind, I think. Seems like he's over the moon. I'm happy for y'all."

Her eyes warmed at the mere mention of her husband. "Thanks. We're blessed for sure."

Josephine handed him the credit card slip. "Big plans tonight?"

"Not so much."

She hitched a brow. "I got a girlfriend I could fix you up with. She's sweet as pie and real pretty too. We could double date—my mother-in-law's been itching to babysit for Nicolas."

"Thanks all the same, but I have a policy against blind dates."

She cocked a look at him. "Didn't you just have a blind date with an old friend of Noah's a few weeks ago?"

"And that's exactly why I put that policy in place."

Josephine laughed, her eyes going into half-moons. "Well, let me know if you change your mind, you hear? You're too good a catch to be walking around all footloose and fancy-free."

"Yeah, I look like a real winner, sporting a shiner and all."

"Oh, now. You've just got the rugged, bad-boy look going for you this week."

He chuckled. "Sure I do."

The black eye looked even worse than he'd expected. And he'd had the misfortune of running into Zoe's dad on the way here. If there was any doubt he had the look of a loser, one glance from Mr. Collins had cleared that right up. Yep. Cruz had always known how to make a good impression on Zoe's dad.

A moment later Cruz stepped out in the sultry Saturday morning, walking toward his truck. Already the temperature had to be near ninety. He was relieved to have a day free of the orchard. Since Zoe had returned she'd been like a burr on his brain.

During the day he was constantly alert to her comings and goings, and at night he fretted about her safety, worrying Kyle would come back. Tonight, though, according to the band's website, her *idiota* ex had an event in Nashville. Maybe Cruz could finally get a good night's rest.

He turned the corner and nearly collided with someone. He came up short and found himself face-to-face with Brady, a baby carrier in his grip.

"Hey, bud," Cruz said. "Sorry 'bout that."

"No worries." Brady adjusted the diaper bag slung over his shoulder.

Cruz couldn't get used to seeing his friend like this, hauling all that baby paraphernalia, wearing a cloth diaper over his shoulder and such.

"What are you smirking at?" Brady asked.

"Oh, nothing. Just get a kick out of seeing the stud of Copper Creek High smitten by a ten-pound bundle of joy. How the mighty have fallen."

Brady gave him a look. "He's twelve pounds now, for your information. You'll see how it is one day, just you wait."

Cruz didn't see that happening anytime soon,

with no prospects on the horizon. For some reason Zoe's face flashed in his mind.

"So what's up with you?" Brady asked. "What are you doing in town?"

"Just got a haircut. It's real soft. Wanna feel?"

"I'll pass."

"What are you doing today? Taking the munch-kin for ice cream?"

"He's two months old, Huntley. It's a little early for that. I have an appointment at Mitchell Construction. They're drawing up plans for my new garage. I'm going to get cracking on it right away."

"You're finally going to do it, huh?" Brady was becoming known for his work on high-end sports cars. Wealthy people all the way from Atlanta sent their cars to him, never mind that he worked out of an old barn.

"Thanks to my grandma I can finally afford it. I still have to take out a loan though. These things don't come cheap. I just hope it pays off in the long run."

Cruz slapped his shoulder. "I'm sure it will. You deserve this, man."

A shadow crept into Brady's eyes. The divorce had hit him hard. It was the opinion of his friends that Audrey had only gotten pregnant in order to trap him. Brady was the only one who didn't quite buy it, but he'd been blinded by love. Or something.

"How's it going at the orchard?"

"It's all right. Got the thinning crew out this week." It was a laborious and tedious job. Up to 90 percent of the potential fruit was removed so the remaining peaches could reach market size.

Brady gave him a pointed look. "I wasn't asking about the crop."

Cruz shifted. It had always felt a little weird loving his best friend's sister. Especially since it had caused so much trouble between them. After the long road back to a healthy friendship with Brady, he wasn't eager to return to that particular subject.

"We stay out of each other's way."

Brady pierced him with a look. He had a way of peeling away all the layers with those laser-focused eyes. "Is that the way you want it?"

"There's a lot of water under that bridge."

"Doesn't mean it can't be swum through."

"I suppose."

The baby started fussing, and Brady grabbed a pacifier and slipped it between the kid's little rosebud lips. He quieted instantly, his eyes fluttering shut.

"You're getting pretty good at that," Cruz said.

"What can I say? Parenthood agrees with me." He gazed on the infant like the kid had hung the moon and stars.

Cruz knew without a doubt Brady'd throw himself in front of a bus for the little tyke. He wondered if he'd ever have a chance to feel that way. Wondered if he even wanted to. Seemed to him it would make a man awful vulnerable. And since his own old man had split, Cruz wondered if he even had it in him to be a good dad.

"Kyle hasn't been coming around, has he?" Brady asked. "I'm not sure Zoe would tell me if he had."

"Not that I know of. I've been keeping an eye out best I can."

"I almost wish I'd gotten there first last Saturday. Might feel good to drive my fist right into that punk's face."

"Yeah, well, I would've gotten in a lot more damage if you hadn't stopped me."

"And then I'd have been bailing your rear end out of jail."

"Would've been worth it."

"Part of me agrees. Well, just keep watching for him. Makes me feel better knowing you're on the property. I tried to get her to come stay with me, but you know Zoe."

He used to. "She should get a restraining order and some legal advice."

"I've mentioned it to her. She'll do whatever she's of a mind to do." Brady glanced at his watch. "Hey, I gotta run. Audrey was late, and now I'm running behind."

"See you around."

A few minutes later Cruz found himself taking

the long way home just so he could drive by the orchard. He couldn't even lie to himself and use Kyle as an excuse today.

You're still hung up on her, like a big ol' idiot.

Cruz scowled out the window at the rolling hills. He kept remembering the look on Zoe's face when he'd sat across the table from her earlier this week. The despair in those beautiful green eyes. The tightness at the corners of her lips. The way she'd swallowed hard, blinking at tears she'd probably rather die than let fall.

She'd once been game for any and every challenge she'd come across. But it seemed life—and Kyle—had beaten her down.

The obstacles must seem insurmountable from where she sat, the responsibility heavy. He wished he could help somehow, but a farmer couldn't control the weather, and he was already operating as efficiently as he could. He watched the orchard's dimes and nickels as if they were his own.

Nellie should've opened that market years ago. He'd tried to talk her into it, but she hadn't seen the need or had the energy to put into it.

The blue-and-white sign reading *Blue Ridge Farms* came up on his left. He eased off the gas, though he didn't know why. Habit, he guessed. His eyes caught on the red barn beside the gravel drive. The big front doors were open though there was no car in the lot.

Frowning, he braked and turned into the drive. There wasn't much theft around Copper Creek, and he didn't reckon there was much of value in the barn, but he wouldn't abide someone stealing from the Collinses.

He parked a ways off and hoofed it the rest of the way, creeping up to the entrance. The musty smell of the barn assaulted his nose as he peeked around the corner. All was quiet inside.

It took a moment for his eyes to adjust to the darkness. His gaze swept the rustic interior, the old farm equipment and primitive shelving. Slivers of light peeked through the boards on the eastern side of the building, dust motes dancing around the beams.

A figure shifted a short distance away. Zoe, he realized. Her hands were braced on her hips, and she was staring up at the loft, which was packed with a bunch of junk. Her shoulders sagged, her head was tipped to the side.

He stepped into the dank space. "What do you think?"

She whirled around, a hand flying to her chest. "You scared me."

"Sorry. I was driving by and saw the open doors. Wanted to make sure you weren't getting ripped off."

She gave a wry laugh. "You kidding? I'd pay someone to come steal this junk—if only I had two dimes to rub together."

He stepped closer, taking in her makeup-free face and loose ponytail. He still wasn't used to seeing her as a blond. "Are you thinking about opening the market?"

"Do you really think it would make a dent?"

"It's always a better deal to sell directly to consumers. We get our fair share of tourists these days, especially during Peach Fest. You could recoup a lot of our loss that week. And Miss Ruby's already offered to handle the baked goods. She's eager to get a hold of your grandma's recipes, I think."

"I can't believe Granny never shared them with her."

"She was a little proprietary. You could hire high schoolers and college students to work the register for minimum wage."

"Maybe I should just get a job instead. You're handling the orchard just fine, and I need a paycheck."

"There's money in the account. You need to start drawing an income."

"*Borrowed* money."

"It'll sort itself out, Zoe. You'll be able to pay back the loan after harvest."

"And then what? We have another year before the next harvest. How did Granny do it during the bad years?"

He lifted a shoulder. "Bear in mind she had money none of us knew about. But a market would turn a profit year round. At least you have a vehicle now." Her grandpa's '66 Mercury truck might be ancient but at least it was transportation.

"I'm grateful for that, but look at this place. It's a disaster. I don't have the money to put into it, and frankly, just the thought of all this is overwhelming."

There was panic on her face, and more than anything he wanted to see the confident young woman she used to be.

"You can do it, Zoe. I know you can."

She turned her green eyes up at him, and hope flickered there for a quick, vulnerable moment. He wondered how long it had been since anyone had said that to her.

⧭•⧩

Zoe let Cruz's words sink down deep inside. It was such a simple little statement. Why did it feel like a balm to her soul? And how pathetic was it that she needed someone else to bolster her ego?

"I'll help you get it cleared out. Build some shelving. Noah could help get the place lit up for a reasonable price. You can keep things rustic— it'll be cheaper."

"Why on earth would you help?"

They hadn't exactly parted as friends. Did she even want him around that much? Her eyes fell over his familiar form. Those sturdy shoulders, those sculpted arms, those calloused hands that had touched her with the utmost gentleness.

His ball cap shadowed the top half of his face, but she well remembered the way he used to look at her. Like she was heaven sent, just for him, and he was never going to let her go.

Only he had.

Cruz tugged at his cap. "Your grandma was like family to me. She gave me a chance. She believed in me. I owe it to her to do whatever it takes to keep this place running."

His voice scraped across the wide-open space, making her insides hum. He still affected her. When she'd first felt that pull she'd thought it was because he was forbidden fruit. Her brother's best friend, from the wrong side of the tracks, and definitely not daddy-approved. It was almost a game to her.

It wasn't until later that she realized it was much more than that.

A shiver of fear pebbled the skin on her arms. She clasped her throat. "I-I don't think this is a good idea."

His eyes pierced hers. "The market or . . . us."

She bristled. "There is no *us*."

"You made that abundantly clear when you left, Zoe."

She lowered her hand as they stared each other down. Her breathing had sped, her lungs pulling in the musty air in big gulps. This was a bad idea.

Such a bad idea. There was too much between them—both good and bad.

"Are we ever going to talk about what happened between us?" he asked.

She crossed her arms, looking away. "It was a long time ago."

"Maybe I have some questions. Maybe we should clear the air. Get everything out on the table."

That's what she was afraid of. They couldn't talk about what happened without mentioning her pregnancy, and she wasn't ready to go there.

Her heart beat up into her throat. "I don't want to talk about it. It's in the past."

He exhaled hard, looking away for a long moment before his eyes returned to hers. "Look, Zoe. Let's just call a truce, okay? You're right. It was a long time ago. We've both grown up, moved on. But we're going to have to find a way to work together one way or another."

She wondered if "moving on" meant a current girlfriend for him. Then she chastised herself for the thought. It was none of her business.

He was right. They would have to work together whether she did this market thing or not. And she was going to have to find a way to make some money. Might as well be self-employed, she supposed. She could work the shop herself if need be, and bring Gracie with her.

She gave the space one last sweeping glance,

seeing it all cleared out with rustic shelving and half barrels filled with peaches and apples. She saw her grandma's cobbler and muffins and granola in a lit display, and her heart leaped at the thought of continuing Granny's legacy.

If she was going to make a new life for herself and Gracie, she might as well do it up right. And in time for Peach Fest.

She blew out a breath. "Okay . . . okay, Cruz." She held out her hand and found it enclosed in the warmth of his. "Truce."

A wide smile stretched across his face. "Truce."

chapter twenty

"I don't have time for this," Zoe said. Hope had her by the elbow as if Zoe might run for the hills—and she just might.

Downtown Copper Creek was all but deserted on the Sunday afternoon, the diagonal parking spaces empty. Colorful canopies jutted from brick storefronts and young maple trees lined both sides of the two-lane street.

Hope had snatched her after church. Miss Ruby had swept up Gracie's hand and shooed them out the door, and that's when Zoe realized she'd been conspired against. She told Hope she was supposed to clean out the barn with Cruz, but Hope whipped out her phone and dashed off a quick text to him.

"Done," she'd said.

Zoe was already perspiring under the afternoon sun. There wasn't a cloud in the sky, and the humidity made the air as thick as mud.

"I cannot look at that blond hair another second." Hope pulled out her phone and checked the screen. "Cruz says he'll be at the barn whenever you get there."

Great. She could hardly wait. They came to a stop, and Zoe frowned. "This is a barbershop. You brought me to a barbershop?"

"Don't be fooled. The stylist is a genius."

"They're closed on Sundays."

"I made a special appointment."

The bell tinkled as Hope opened the door.

"Of course you did. I can't afford this, Hope."

"Which is why I said it's my treat. Are we going to stand here arguing all the livelong day, or are we going to go in there and fix that hair?"

She'd worn it blond for years. Kyle was attracted to blonds, and he said the red looked orange under the stage lights. Her stomach quivered at the thought of going back. When had she grown so comfortable in his shadow?

"Well . . . ?" Hope said.

What did it matter? Zoe heaved a sigh. "Fine."

They were met inside by the stunning blue-eyed blond she'd met earlier at the Rusty Nail. Hope all but pushed Zoe into the stylist's chair.

Josephine whisked a black cape around her and Velcroed it snugly at her neck, pulling Zoe's long blond hair out around her shoulders.

The stylist met her eyes in the mirror. "So Hope said you used to be a redhead."

"A gorgeous redhead."

Zoe gave Hope a look before meeting Josephine's eyes again. "It was sort of auburn."

"And curly. She has gorgeous natural curls. I don't know why she's been flat-ironing the day-lights out of it."

"Is that what you want, Zoe? Auburn color and a cut that brings out your natural curl?"

Zoe's eyes cut to her friend. "You mean I have a choice?"

Josephine studied Zoe in the mirror. "Hope's right, the auburn will compliment your skin tone. And the curls will soften your features. A few bangs will call attention to your eyes—they're gorgeous." She ran her hands through the long strands. "It's in good shape. Fresh color, a little trim, and a few layers. What do you think?"

It was only hair. This would be cheaper and easier in the long run. No more touching up her roots or battling her natural curl. It was futile in this humidity anyway.

"Sure. Whatever you think."

Hope gave a little golf clap. "Now we're talking."

Two and a half hours later Zoe stared in the mirror, hardly able to believe her eyes. It was the old Zoe, but updated a bit with side-swept bangs and layers. The stylist had tamed her hair with some miracle product, making her curls tumble over her shoulders in soft waves.

Mi leona. The pet name rushed up from the past, making her chest squeeze tight.

"You are a genius, Josephine," Hope said. "I love it when I'm right."

❧•❦

Cruz pushed the rusty old tiller into the bed of his Silverado and strode back to the barn. He'd made good headway the last few hours. The main floor was almost cleaned out, except for the bulkier items that required more manpower. He'd already made two trips to the dump. He kept thinking of Zoe, wanting her to be pleased with his progress. How pathetic was that?

The radio he'd brought cranked out a country tune, and he whistled along as he pushed an old wagon out of the way. There was wooden shelving piled along the back wall. That should save Zoe a little money.

He wiped the sweat from his forehead with the back of his hand. It was hot, dirty work. The temperatures were in the nineties, and the air in the barn was stale.

He stooped, hefting a rickety wooden ladder. Then he turned and headed toward his truck just as Zoe entered the barn.

She stopped on the threshold.

The whistle died on his lips.

Her face was in the shadows, but the sunshine flooding through the open door glinted off her red hair like sparks off a fire.

Mi leona.

She was a vision from his past. Stealing his breath. Making his heart flip around like it hadn't done since she'd left. His fingers ached to push into those curls. His arms ached to pull her close. His lips ached to taste those rosebud lips again and convince her she was still his leona.

He tightened his grip on the ladder. Cleared his throat and forced himself to speak.

"Hi."

Brilliant, Huntley.

"Hi." She ducked her head, touching her hair as she skirted him. "Sorry I'm late. You sure got a lot done."

"Yeah, just the loft to go now. Except for the bigger stuff."

"Thanks for your help."

"No problem." He turned to watch as she gathered her hair, twisted it up on her head, and clipped it there. A crime, restraining it that way.

She'd thought her hair was ugly back in the day, but he'd eventually convinced her otherwise. He had a feeling Kyle had undone all his work.

"It looks nice." *Nice, Huntley? Try sexy as all get out.*

Her gaze glanced off him. "It was Hope's idea."

"Suits you better."

"Yeah, well . . . It'll be easier this way. And cheaper besides." She began climbing the ladder to the loft.

She'd changed from her church clothes into a pale-green T-shirt and cutoffs. His eyes fell over her feminine form, from her graceful neck to her trim waistline to her long shapely legs.

He dragged his gaze away and headed toward his truck, hitching the ladder on his shoulder.

Seeing her this way, so much like she used to

look, put a bounce in his step. Maybe the upkeep would be easier for her this way, but maybe it was something else too. Maybe she was trying to find her old self. And he couldn't help but hope she would find the part that had once loved him.

❯❯•❮❮

A trickle of sweat dripped down Zoe's back as they scooted an old table from the cobwebbed corner of the loft. Cruz seemed to like her hair color. Not that his opinion mattered. Seemed everyone liked her better as a redhead except Kyle.

She thought of Gracie's reaction when she'd gone home to change. Her little brown eyes had widened an instant before she smiled. "Mama! We match!"

"You can use this, don't you think?" Cruz ran his hand over the table's dusty surface.

"Sure. How are we going to get it down the ladder?"

"Very carefully."

❯❯•❮❮

A couple hours later they'd cleared out the last of the junk except for an old piece of farm equipment. Once that was in Cruz's truck he'd be ready for his last trip to the junkyard.

Zoe dusted off her hands and shelved them on

her hips, surveying the space. She hadn't noticed the beamed ceiling before, but it added character.

Cruz had removed the shutters from the windows, and that let in a lot of light. They'd still need help with the electricity, additional lighting, and plumbing. But Cruz had found a whole bunch of shelving she could use. The floor would do; the wood planks just needed a good cleaning.

"What do you think?" He shuffled to a stop beside her.

"I'm starting to see it. I think the counter and register should be set up over there. And the tables should run in rows going this way. Baskets of fruit. I want the shelving over there. A few rows of it for jams and jellies. I'll have to buy a display case for the baked goods."

"That shouldn't be too costly."

Everything seemed costly when you were buying with borrowed money. She was going to take out an income starting tomorrow. Pay Hope back and buy a few necessities. And just hope harvest brought in enough to pay off the loan and see them through winter.

"Stop worrying. It's going to be fine."

"You don't know that."

"God'll work it all out. You'll see."

Easy for him to say. His life wasn't completely off the rails. Or maybe her life had been off the rails with Kyle, and she was only now getting back on track? She wasn't sure yet. At least she was taking control of her destiny. Surely that was one step in the right direction.

"Ready to move this thing?" Cruz grabbed one end, and she took the other. They walked it sideways out the wide door.

A call buzzed in on her phone, but she ignored it. Kyle had been texting her for a few days. Trying to sweet-talk her like he always did after he messed up. It wasn't going to work this time.

"Have you heard from Kyle?"

Could he read her mind or what? "A little bit."

She hadn't responded to the texts at first, hoping he'd give up. But she'd finally texted back yesterday, asking him to stop. He'd responded by calling, but she hadn't yet answered.

The buzzing stopped, only to start up again as they hefted the equipment onto the truck bed.

"I'd be happy to answer that for you."

Yeah, because another man answering her phone would settle Kyle right down. She gave Cruz a look.

Her nerves tightened with each quiet buzz until it felt as though they might just snap.

By the time they had the machinery in the truck the phone had gone silent again.

"You should file a restraining order."

"I can handle my own life, thank you very much. I don't need you and Brady running it for me."

He angled a look at her. "You're not thinking of going back to him, are you?"

"I fail to see how that's any of your business."

"Darn it, Zoe . . ."

She was in no mood for this. "Drop it, Cruz."

"If you don't do it for yourself, do it for your daughter."

The daughter she'd managed to raise all alone? That daughter? "I can take care of Gracie just fine."

"So last Saturday when he hurt her, that was the first time?"

"That was an accident!"

"Are you seriously defending him?"

She mashed her teeth together until her jaw ached. Then she grabbed the tailgate and slammed it into place. "We're done here."

"Zoe . . . ," he called as she shut and locked the barn doors into place.

But she didn't answer. And he didn't try to stop her as she slipped into her grandpa's truck and drove off.

chapter twenty-one

"What'd Cruz think of your hair?" Hope licked her strawberry ice cream cone, giving Zoe a coy look.

Zoe dabbed at Gracie's mouth with a napkin. "It doesn't matter what he thinks. It's my hair."

"Then why are the tips of your ears red?"

"Because it's ninety degrees out here." Her cone was melting faster than she could lick it, and she was grateful Gracie had a cup instead of a cone.

She'd come into town in the middle of the day to get cash from the bank and pay Hope back. It had been Hope's idea to meet at the Dairy Barn.

"Look, Mama!" Gracie said as she stirred her ice cream. The picnic table shook as she shifted. "I made swirls."

"Very pretty. I like your rainbow sprinkles."

"Are you two, you know, getting closer as you're working together?"

"We're getting the barn ready—that's *all*."

"So he doesn't still make your blood hum? Make you all melty inside?"

Zoe narrowed her eyes at Hope. "I told you way too much back then."

"There've been sparks shooting off between you two as long as you've known each other. I didn't reckon a few years apart was going to change that any."

"Well, we're adults now. Humming and melting only go so far when you've got—" She darted a look at Grace. "Responsibilities. And water under the bridge. Murky, swirling cesspools of treacherous danger."

"Speaking of swirling cesspools . . . Any thoughts on when you're going to tell him?"

Zoe's stomach clenched as it always did when she thought of telling Cruz. "Stop pressuring me. I'll find the right time." Like tomorrow. Or the day after. Or the day after that.

"The longer you wait the angrier he's going to be."

"I'll tell him when we've finished refurbishing the barn. Now can we talk about something else? My dire financial situation? The current state of national politics? The latest natural disaster?"

"Okay, let's talk about He Who Must Not Be Named. Have you heard from him?"

Zoe shot her a look.

"What? It's a change of topic."

"He's out of the picture. I'm ignoring his texts and calls, and eventually he'll give up."

"You know why you were with him, right?"

"Are you fixing to psychoanalyze me?"

"He was like your dad, Zoe. Always trying to control you. You didn't let your dad get away with it, but Kyle—"

"Rolled right on over me. Yeah, yeah, I'm aware."

It hadn't been that way at first. He'd been all about buttering her up and supporting her. But the more success Kyle had experienced, the bigger his ego had gotten and the more controlling he'd become. Once Gracie had been born Zoe'd felt trapped, and somewhere along the line she'd stopped fighting it. He'd critiqued her constantly, and part of her had felt as if she'd deserved it.

"What's wrong with me?" Zoe sighed. "I feel so lost. I don't even know who I am anymore."

Hope placed a hand over hers. "You're the same Zoe you've always been. Find your identity in God, not in any man, ever."

"God . . ." She'd all but forgotten about Him the past few years. "I can't believe how far I've fallen. I've completely lost my way, Hope."

"Well, lucky for you, God specializes in recovery of the lost."

"I just have to get back on track. Start making my own decisions. Take control of my life again."

"Mama." Gracie licked her spoon. "When's Kyle coming back?"

Zoe traded a look with Hope. Her daughter was way too smart. "Remember what I told you? He's living back in Tennessee, and you and I are going to live here now in the big farmhouse."

"With Miss Ruby?"

"Yes, with Miss Ruby."

"She plays Candy Land with me." Gracie caught the eye of a baby at the next picnic table and waved. "Look, Mama, a baby."

"She's a cutie pie."

Gracie went back to her ice cream, making faces at the baby between bites until the little boy giggled.

Hope leaned closer to Zoe. "Kyle doesn't really seem like the type to give up."

"He's got too much pride to keep on for long. But let's talk about something else." Zoe gave her a saucy look. "You, for instance. How's *your* love life going?"

Hope's lips went flat. "I have no love life, as you well know."

"What about that guy you were going to go out with last week? The friend of Josephine's?"

"The one who talked about his ex-wife all night? The one who drank five beers during supper and had to be driven home? The one who ended the night crying on my shoulder?"

Zoe winced. "Yikes."

"Welcome to my world. I haven't had a second date in almost a year. If I had a guy who looked at me the way Cruz looks at you I'd hog-tie him to my bedpost."

Zoe chuckled. "You've never been subtle."

"I'm almost twenty-five, Zoe. That's thirty-five in Southern years. I thought I'd be a radio sensation and married with a whole passel of kids by now."

"Your career is going great. Your show's so popular. And I'm single too, but frankly, better single than in a bad relationship."

Hope tilted her head, looking Zoe in the eye for a long beat. "I'm glad you see that. And I'm glad—" She darted a look at Gracie. "I'm glad he's out of your life. I feel like you're coming back in bits and pieces. I missed you, Zoe. You have no idea how much."

Zoe's eyes burned. "I missed you too. And I'm sorry I pushed you away. I just knew things weren't right with—him—and it got harder and harder to pretend everything was okay. It was easier to just put up walls."

"Well you don't have to pretend anymore."

"Thanks. I wish it wasn't too late for Granny though." A lump welled up in her throat. "I waited too long. She never even got to meet Gracie. I have so many regrets."

Hope squeezed her hand. "Granny loved you. That never changed. And she knew you loved her too. She'd be so happy that you've come home. So proud to see you making a go of the orchard."

A breath left her lungs. "I just hope I can do it."

"You will. Granny believed in you, and so do I."

"Look, Mama!"

Zoe turned to see Gracie's mouth rimmed

with a vanilla coating. "I have a mustache and a beard!"

How she loved her silly daughter. Zoe laughed, the burst of emotion a welcome release. "Well, look at you, Mister."

"I'm not a mister, Mama! I'm a little girl."

"Well let's get you cleaned up then. Little girls don't have beards, not even vanilla ones."

"I'll go get a wet wipe." Hope was still smiling as she entered the Dairy Barn.

Zoe gave a contented sigh as she finished wiping the mess from Gracie's face. She had her girl. She had her best friend, her brother, and her grandmother's vote of confidence. It was a good start.

chapter twenty-two

Zoe set the screw on the tip of the screwdriver and pulled the trigger. The drill whirred to life, driving the screw into the wood wall. The barn's air was filled with the smells of sawdust and pine cleaner. A warm breeze wafted through the open windows, fluttering her bangs, and a country singer crooned from the battery-operated radio Cruz had left behind.

When the screw was in place she tested the sturdiness of the shelf and felt a sense of pride when it remained snugly attached to the wall.

I guess I'm not completely useless after all.

"It's coming along." Hope set her hands on her slim hips and looked around the barn. "Is that the last of the shelving?"

"Yeah. If you're looking for something to do there are more tables in the truck."

"I'll run and grab them. Wanna help, Gracie?"

Gracie grabbed Hope's hand and they headed outside.

Zoe wandered over to the other side of the barn where Brady sprawled on the plank flooring under her new, partially assembled bakery case.

"How's it going?"

"Give me a car engine any day. The directions that came with this thing boggle the mind."

"You read the directions?"

"For all the good it did me. I think I'm doing it right, though."

"That's comforting. Need any help?"

"No offense, but I think I'm better off on my own."

"Probably right."

Zoe brushed back a few strands that had escaped her ponytail. Her shirt clung to her, and a trickle of perspiration ran down her back. She should've had the electricity done and the second-hand air conditioners installed first thing. Now probably wasn't the best time to ask Brady what he was doing tomorrow.

"Doing a great job, darlin'." Hope was carrying a small table into the barn, Gracie at the other end "helping." "Where do you want this one, Zoe?"

"Over here by the register, I think. I was going to fill it with impulse items."

"Good idea."

Noah was coming later today to wire for electricity. She had to find some light fixtures on eBay. They still needed a bunch of baskets to display the varieties of peaches and apples. She was hoping to introduce some locally grown vegetables too.

She needed to find a used cash register and figure out how to handle credit cards. Then there was all the accounting that would need to be done. Phil could handle the paperwork, but she'd still need to figure out how to keep track of stock and how much of what was sold. She had no idea how one went about such a thing. She rubbed her temple. What had she gotten herself into?

"Hey, look at this place." Cruz entered the dim space, surveying their progress. He looked like temptation personified in his snug white T-shirt and faded blue jeans. His dark hair was wind-tossed, making Zoe want to run her fingers through it.

"It's really coming along," he said.

"Cwooz!" Gracie ran up to him and hugged his leg.

Zoe's heart gave a squeeze at her little girl's easy affection. She'd taken a shine to Cruz as they'd worked on the barn together the past week.

"Hello there, *Bella*," Cruz said.

"You just called me beautiful!"

Cruz widened his eyes playfully. "You know Spanish already? And you're only four years old."

"No, silly. You call me Bella all the time."

So many emotions swamped Zoe as Cruz smiled down at Gracie, ruffling her hair. Guilt. Regret. Longing. They all closed in, smothering her with their weight.

She had to tell him. Hope was right. The longer she waited the angrier he'd be. She had to get past the dread and just do it.

She'd do it tonight. She'd ask Miss Ruby to watch Gracie, and she'd go over to his place. It would be wrong to wait any longer. Who was she kidding? It had been wrong to wait this long. Even if her heart did stutter in fear at the thought of sharing her girl, he deserved to know the truth.

⋙•⋘

Cruz watched as Zoe walked toward the window, palming the back of her neck. Something was wrong. He'd known it almost from the moment he'd entered the barn. She was probably over-whelmed. In need of a pep talk. He was just the man for the job.

Hope was busy arranging tables. Gracie had joined Brady on the floor and was handing him tools. She was adorable in a little pink jumper, her red curls framing her face. Zoe's mini-me.

"Hey." He came to a stop beside Zoe. "You all right?"

Her hand dropped to her side. "I'm fine."

"You seem a little frazzled. It's all coming together. You should be set to open by the time we get some peaches in. Just in time for Peach Fest."

"I know, it's just . . ." She placed her hand at her throat, avoiding his eyes. "Listen, Cruz . . . Do you think I could come over tonight? For a few minutes?"

He stared steadily at her until she looked at him. He tried to read something in those green depths, but whatever was there remained a mystery. But she wanted to come over—that had to be good, right? Maybe she finally wanted to talk about their past. Maybe she wanted to talk about their future. His heart tugged at the thought.

"Sure. That'd be great."

"Mama!"

Zoe's eyes jerked to her daughter's. "Yeah, honey."

"Bwady has a necklace just like Kyle's. Look, Mama. It's got a black stwing too."

"Uh-huh. Do you want to help me carry in a table?"

Cruz couldn't hear any more. His ears had caught on something Gracie had said. *Kyle*. Why would she call her dad by his first name? Zoe would never allow that.

Cruz's eyes darted to Gracie, laser-focusing on the girl's face. On her pretty red hair and elfin chin—all Zoe. But he looked a little closer this time. He studied her as she handed a tool to Brady. Noticed her big brown eyes, the same shade as his.

He tried to remember how long Zoe had been gone when he got word that she was pregnant. No more than several months, surely.

Gracie smiled just then, and that too looked

familiar. Because he saw those little brackets at the corner of his lips every time he saw a photo of himself.

Blood rushed in his ears, blocking out all other sound. As realization rushed in, a wave of wonder about knocked him flat on his backside.

She was his.

The girl's eyes sparkled as she laughed at something Brady said. His own flesh and blood. Gracie was his daughter.

His four-year-old daughter. Who didn't even know he was her dad. His eyes fastened on Zoe, who'd gone still, her green eyes wide.

"I-I think I'll go grab a table," she said.

He caught her elbow, holding her fast. "You're not going anywhere."

She looked up at him. If he'd still had any doubt, the fear in her eyes would've told him everything he needed to know.

She looked at him, wary. "Cruz—"

"She's mine." There was as much wonder as anger in the words.

"I-I tried to tell you," she whispered. "Back when I found out I was pregnant. I tried to tell you at the creek that day."

"Is that so?"

"Hey." Brady was there in a flash. "What's going on? Let go of her, man."

Cruz loosened his grip but didn't let go. And he didn't look away from Zoe as he addressed

Brady. "Did you know, amigo?" Betrayed by both of them—he didn't think he could take it.

"Know what?"

"Does he know, Zoe? Does Hope know too? Am I the last flipping person to know?"

"Know *what?*" Brady asked again.

"All right, guys, let's just simmer down." Hope was there too, getting between them. "Bear in mind there are little ears in the room."

It was the sight of Gracie looking at them, wide-eyed, that broke through the swirling fog. Cruz blinked. Pried his fingers from Zoe's arm and let his hand drop to his side. His breaths felt stuffed in his lungs. His body was tense, his muscles quivering with a need for release.

"What's going on?" Brady asked. "Zoe?"

"We need to give them a minute," Hope said. "Gracie, let's go to the house to uh . . . check on Miss Ruby. We'll have pie! Brady, you should come too."

"I'm not going anywhere."

"It's okay, Brady." Zoe looked everywhere but at Cruz. "Cruz and I need to talk."

Cruz felt the weight of Brady's gaze for a long moment before the other three left the barn. A few minutes later a truck roared to life, and then there was nothing but silence.

chapter twenty-three

Zoe's heart beat like a bass drum in her chest, and her breath came shallow and ragged. Brady's engine grew quiet as he and Hope stole away, leaving her to face this alone. Face her past alone.

Face Cruz alone.

The song on the radio ended, ushering in a beat of awkward silence before the next one began. Cruz was across the barn, had put as much space between them as possible. He faced the other way, his hands laced behind his neck, his shoulders rising and falling on deep breaths.

She swallowed hard and told herself to suck it up. It was time to face this. Past time. "I'm so sorry, Cruz. I-I don't know what else to say. I did try to tell you but—"

He whirled around, a flinty look in his eyes. "That last time we talked? Was that you trying to tell me? Because I don't remember the words *pregnant* or *baby* even coming up, Zoe."

"Because you accused me of being with Kyle! You assumed I was leaving to go off with him and his band, which I was never going to do."

"Oh, really? Well, that's not what Kyle said."

"Kyle?"

"And you didn't exactly correct that notion, best I recall."

"You didn't give me a chance!" She wiped at the sweat on the back of her neck. Blinked against the tears of frustration. "I thought you didn't care about me. All you did was accuse me of stepping out on you with Kyle. I was angry and hurt."

"I thought you'd chosen him and your big dream over me."

"That was never the case. You're the one who pushed me away."

"So you weren't in a relationship with him at all while we were on a break?"

"Of course I wasn't! I was in love with you, you idiot! So he just tells you this, and you believe him? You didn't have any more faith in me than that?"

His eyes widened. "You're mad at *me?* What about Kyle? He went behind your back and lied to me!"

"Well, I'd expect that from Kyle—at least I would now. You, though . . . I cared about you, and it hurt that you believed so little of me." *Just like my dad.*

He gave his head a shake. "Don't you try to change this around. This is about you keeping the truth from me. For *four years,* Zoe! I'm a father, and I didn't even know it! How can you excuse that? Do you know how I felt when I got word that you were pregnant? I was devastated to think you and Kyle had shacked up on the road and made a baby together." He turned around, muttering something in Spanish.

She swiped at the tear that had escaped. "I know I should've made more of an effort. But when you jumped all over me about leaving with Kyle, I couldn't think straight. I was angry and hurt that you didn't believe in me, and I was afraid you'd pushed me away because you didn't care about me as much as I cared about you. I didn't want you to be with me only for the baby's sake."

"So you just ran off without telling me about it?"

"I was scared. I knew my dad wasn't going to have any of it with my mom gone. I just didn't see any other options at the time, and Kyle had that opportunity with the band. He promised to take care of me."

"Oh, I'll bet he did." He spat the words out.

"We were only friends, Cruz. I know you don't believe that, but we were only friends until well after Gracie was born. And at that point it was more about loneliness than Kyle."

He shoved the palms of his hands into his eye sockets, as if he was trying to scrub away the image her words invoked.

"I never wanted that break," she said. "You know I didn't. I was head over heels in love with you. And I was so afraid if I told you, you'd do the right thing, but only for the baby."

"You kept my baby from me, Zoe." The quiet tone was somehow worse than his raised voice. "There's nothing you can do to bring back the four years I've missed. She doesn't even know I'm her father—do you not understand how hard that hits me?"

Guilt weighted her chest as she thought about Cruz and his absentee father. After what he'd been through he would never willingly desert his own child.

She swallowed against the lump that rose in her throat. "I know. You're right."

"You could've told me as soon as you came home."

"I-I was going to tell you tonight."

He huffed a laugh. "Sure you were."

"I was. That's why I asked to come over."

He drilled her with a look, staring so long and hard it was difficult not to wither under his gaze. "I want to see her tonight. I want to spend time with her. I'll be over at seven to pick her up."

Fear clawed at her throat. He was so angry. What if he wanted custody? Would he try and take her baby away? She could already feel Gracie slipping away, and the helplessness stole her breath.

"She . . . she goes to bed at eight."

His eyes snapped with irritation. "Five, then." He tugged on his ball cap and stormed past her without a second look.

Zoe didn't breathe again till the roar of his engine had faded into the distance.

chapter twenty-four

Cruz's palms sweated against the leather steering wheel. He'd had a few hours to simmer down, and it was a good thing. He didn't want to scare Gracie by scowling all night.

Gracie—his daughter. He was about to see his daughter.

The words sounded foreign in his mind. Strange. Wonderful. Terrifying.

What did he know about kids? About little girls? What would he do with her? What would he say to her? What if she didn't like him?

She already likes you, idiota.

He'd been wondering since he'd left Zoe standing alone in the barn what Gracie had been told about her father. Clearly she knew Kyle wasn't her dad. He could be grateful for that at least.

Cruz had come to a decision in the three hours he'd spent pacing his house like a madman. He wanted Gracie to know he was her dad, and he wanted her to know tonight. Zoe had waited long enough. It was time the little girl knew she had a daddy who loved her.

And he did, he thought, half dazed by the realization. He couldn't wait to be with her. He wanted to spend a few hours just staring at her, memorizing her features. He wanted to make her giggle and watch her eyes light up again when he called her *Bella*.

He might not know anything about being a dad or about little girls, but he knew one thing. He was going to make sure Gracie knew her daddy loved and wanted her. He knew all too well the repercussions when a child didn't have that assurance.

As he turned into the farm's gravel drive his mind whirled with memories of Zoe and the past. The anguish he'd experienced when she'd left with Kyle, when he'd heard of her pregnancy and nearly doubled over. Kyle had not only lied to him about Zoe and him being together back then, he'd been all too happy to let everyone believe Gracie was his. Cruz wished more than ever that he'd gotten in a few more good swings that night at the Rusty Nail. Kyle'd had it coming more than he'd even known.

He took the slight bend in the drive and blew out a deep breath. He had to forget about all that. Put it all aside for now. His anger toward Kyle and Zoe would have to wait. The only thing that mattered tonight was Gracie.

His daughter.

His lips curled upward at the thought, and he pressed the accelerator a little harder, kicking up dust in the rearview mirror.

He was going to take her for a burger. Every

kid liked burgers, right? Then he'd take her to his house.

And do what, genius? Watch the Braves? Play poker? He didn't have so much as a crayon at his place.

He'd take her to Toy Depot first. She needed some things to keep at his house. He'd let her pick out some toys. Anything she wanted. Good grief, it hadn't even been one day, and she already had him wrapped around her little finger.

His legs were shaking a little as he made his way up the porch steps. He couldn't believe a four-year-old girl had such power over him.

Zoe opened the door before he even knocked.

He steeled himself against the fear on her face, the vulnerable look in her eyes. It had been her choice to keep this secret. He wasn't going to feel sorry for her.

She pulled the door wide enough to allow him entry, and he made a wide berth around her, his eyes sweeping the room for Gracie.

"Where is she?"

"I asked Miss Ruby to stay an extra few minutes. I, um, I thought we might talk first."

He faced her. "Have you told her yet?"

"Not . . . not yet. That's what I wanted to talk about."

He crossed his arms. "I'm telling her tonight."

She walked toward the sofa. "Why don't you have a seat?"

"I'm telling her tonight, Zoe. I've already missed four years of her life. She deserves to know she has a daddy."

"I know, I just—I thought it might be better coming from me."

"Fine. We'll do it together."

She shifted. Tucked her hair behind her ear. "That's fair I guess."

"You think?"

A slow flush crawled up her neck. "We have to keep it simple. And we have to be careful. I don't want her to feel your anger about this. That might confuse her."

"I'm not a monster. I'm not going to scare her. I'm angry at you, not her, and I'm mature enough to put that aside for her sake."

"Good." She had the grace to look chagrined. "That's good."

"What have you told her? About her real dad— about me?"

"Um . . ." She ran a hand over her throat. "Not too much really."

Nice. "Glad to see I rank right up there with international terrorism and world hunger."

"She hasn't asked, and I wasn't going to bring it up until she did. Kyle kind of filled that void, so it really hasn't been much of . . ."

He clenched his teeth.

". . . an issue." She bit her lip, her eyes finding the floor. "Sorry. I know this is difficult. I know

I've made mistakes, but I'm trying to do what's right here. Will you sit down?"

He paused a long minute before perching on the edge of an armchair, elbows propped on his knees.

She shifted on her feet. She must've showered since she'd returned home. Her curls were loose around her face. The sunlight streamed in, glinting off her hair like copper sparks. He tried not to notice the way the freckles on her nose stood out against her creamy skin.

"She knows you're picking her up . . . She's excited about that."

That was something, he supposed.

"She'll want to eat soon."

"I can manage that."

"So . . . I'll tell her, you know, and then we'll just . . . let her respond and ask questions . . . ?"

"All right."

She palmed her neck. "All right, then. I'll just . . . go get her."

He watched Zoe leave the room, wiping his palms down the legs of his jeans. Why was he so nervous? He'd just seen the girl a few hours ago. But everything was different now. Would this be upsetting to her? Did she even want a daddy? Clearly she hadn't missed having one too bad.

He didn't have much time to fret because a moment later his daughter scurried into the room ahead of Zoe.

Gracie must've had a bath too. Her damp hair was held back on the sides with grass-green barrettes, and she wore a matching sundress that exposed delicate freckles on her shoulders.

"Cwooz!" She dashed right over and flung herself into his arms.

He was unprepared for the rush of love that swept over him as he curled his arms around her slight frame. His skin flushed with heat. His heart stopped beating.

"Hey there, Bella." His voice was raspy with emotion.

He got a whiff of apples and sunshine before she leaned back and started tugging his hand.

"Let's go! Let's go!"

"Wait a minute, honey." Zoe sat on the end of the sofa closest to him. "We want to talk to you a minute."

"But I'm hungwy."

"I know, but this won't take very long. I promise."

Gracie faced her mom, still half in his embrace, leaning back against his leg.

Zoe's eye flitted to his, then back to Gracie. "I have something very important to tell you, honey. It's about . . . daddies."

Gracie fidgeted with the string ties on her dress, and Cruz wondered if she was even listening.

"You know how your friend Sophia has a daddy? And how baby Sam has a daddy . . . ?"

"Uncle Bwady."

"Yes, that's right. Uncle Brady."

He appreciated the smile on Zoe's face. The enthusiasm she injected into her voice. "Well . . . um, you have a daddy too, honey."

Gracie's hands stopped their fidgeting, and her eyes darted to her mom's. "I do?"

"Yes, you do. And he's very excited that you're his daughter."

She bounced on her toes. "Can I meet him?"

"Well, honey, you actually already know him. It's, um . . ." She swallowed. "It's Cruz, honey. Cruz is your daddy."

Gracie's eyes flew to his. Her brown eyes widened.

Nothing had prepared him to be sized up by a four-year-old child. His lungs felt stuffed with oxygen and somehow incapable of emptying. It was the longest moment of his life. Belatedly he remembered to smile. He didn't want to scare the poor kid.

"What do you think about that?" he made himself ask, half afraid to know the answer.

Gracie blinked, her long lashes fluttering. "You're my daddy?"

"That's right. I'm your daddy. And your mama's right. I'm so excited that you're my daughter, and I'd love to spend time with you. Would that be all right?"

A thoughtful frown puckered her brows, and

she looked so much like Zoe in that moment that his heart gave a big squeeze.

"Where've you been?" Gracie asked.

The back of his eyes burned, and his throat tightened. He glanced at Zoe, at a loss.

"He, um, he didn't know you were his daughter, honey. Not until today."

Gracie stared at him long and hard. He noticed the amber flecks in the brown depths. Just like his. How had he not seen it before today?

"Do you know how to play Candy Land?"

He breathed a laugh. "Well . . . no, but I'm willing to learn. Will you teach me, Gracie?"

Her eyes lit. "Not Gracie! *Bella*."

He chuckled, the tension slipping from his body. "All right then. Bella it is."

Her little bow lips stretched into a wide smile. She wrapped her ropy little arms around his neck, holding on tight. And just like that his heart swelled ten sizes.

chapter twenty-five

The phone rang almost the instant Cruz left with Gracie. Zoe had known it was coming. Was surprised Brady had waited this long.

"I'd be on your doorstep right now if I didn't have a car I promised would be ready by Monday," he said by way of greeting.

"Save your breath. I've already been taken to task by Cruz and Hope."

"What'd you expect, Zoe? You think you can lie about this for almost five years and have no consequences?"

She winced. "*Lie* is a strong word."

"And yet, perfectly applicable here."

"I was going to tell Cruz back then, Brady. But Kyle got to him first and filled his head with lies. When Cruz jumped all over me, I just saw red."

"And you never felt the need to set him straight? He's the *father,* Zoe."

"I know. I should've told him. But I was angry. And hurt."

A long, tense silence stretched over the line.

"Almost five years, Zoe. And you didn't even tell me. I'm your brother." A short pause. "Or am I?"

All the air left her body as guilt pricked hard.

She'd unwittingly traipsed on Brady's deepest vulnerability, and she hated herself for it. Though he'd always been everything a big brother should be, he'd never quite felt like one of the family.

"Brady, stop it. Of course you're my brother. I've never treated you any other way."

"You didn't tell me the truth. You told Hope, and yet you kept it from me."

"Cruz was your best friend! I wanted to tell you a hundred times, but I knew what you'd say. You'd insist on telling him, and I was afraid he'd only take me back because of the baby. And I didn't want to be with someone who had no faith in me. It felt too much like the way Daddy treated me."

"You're right, I would've insisted. And Dad cares about you in his own weird way. He wouldn't try so hard to lead your life if he didn't."

"Easy for you to say. He wasn't constantly on your case."

Brady huffed. "Yeah, he didn't give a flying fig what I did because I'm not his real son."

"Brady, that's not true." But even as she gave lip service to the thought she wondered if he was right.

"Yes, it is. And that's fine. I've come to terms with it. I got a sister out of the deal, so I'm good."

Her heart squeezed. "I don't know what I would've done without you all these years."

There was a long pause. "I wish you'd felt you could tell me about Gracie."

"I'd already caused a rift between you and Cruz. I didn't want to put you in the middle. It wouldn't have been fair."

"Well, to be honest, it doesn't seem fair that you kept this from me or Cruz."

She palmed her eye. "I'm sorry, Brady. You're right. I should've told you. I should've stayed, and I should've told Cruz about the baby. But I was young and scared, and I ran. If it makes you feel any better, I suffered for my choices."

"Of course it doesn't make me feel any better, you little brat. I want the best for you."

Her heart twisted. "I know you do. I really am sorry for hurting you. Now can we go back to our regularly scheduled sibling rivalry?"

"Cruz is pretty ticked, you know."

"I know."

"It's going to take him a while to get over this."

"I know that too." She closed her eyes. Brady was right. And she had it coming. She just hadn't known it was going to feel this awful.

"Well, if it makes *you* feel any better, I'm betting there's a little four-year-old charmer who'll bring him around eventually."

She remembered the look in Cruz's eyes when her daughter had wrapped her little arms around him.

"I hope you're right."

Zoe put her book down for the dozenth time. She walked into the kitchen and refilled her glass of tea. Carried it into the living room and sat down again.

Maybe she could watch TV. Find a program she could focus on. She fetched the remote from the other side of the room.

Two minutes into a crime-drama her mind was off and running again. What were they doing? Had he fed Gracie? Was he letting her eat a bunch of sugar? What did he even know about taking care of a child?

She checked her watch. Seven thirty. He'd promised to have her home in half an hour.

Fed up with her nervous jitters, she flipped off the TV and dialed Hope.

"Is she home yet?" Hope said by way of greeting. There was noise in the background.

"No. Sounds like you're out."

"At the Rusty Nail." A moment later the background noise grew quieter. "Okay, I can talk now. How was it?"

"We told Gracie."

"Wow, that was fast. How'd she respond?"

"Really well." The memory of her daughter's face lighting up was like a dart to the center of her chest. She shook the thought away.

"You sound real happy about that."

Zoe scrubbed a hand over her face. "I am. Really, I am. But I'm scared too. What if he wants custody, Hope? What if he takes her away from me?"

"Whoa, slow down there, Sparky. First of all, Cruz would never do that. Second of all, this is only day one. He's just getting to know her. He deserves that. And Gracie deserves a loving father."

"I know, I know." She was a terrible mother. She wanted Gracie to have her daddy. Of course she did. But fear was making her panic. She was used to having her daughter all to herself.

"This will be good for her. You'll see. Before you know it you'll be relieved to have an evening alone. We can have a girls' night out whenever we want, and you can remember you're only twenty-four years old and deserve a little down time now and again."

"You're right. This is all just . . . new. I'm used to making all the decisions where she's concerned."

"Cruz will be a far better role model than you-know-who."

"That's true."

Cruz was a good man. Honest and hard-working. Gracie could do a lot worse for a father. Zoe's motherhood had never felt threatened with Kyle. After all, he had no legal claim on Gracie. And Kyle, while he was pretty good with her daughter, hadn't been head over heels for her. His eyes hadn't filled with love when

Gracie hugged him the way Cruz's had tonight.

"You know, Zoe . . . I wonder if your relationship with your dad is weighing in on your feelings a bit. Cruz isn't going to be the kind of father your dad is. A girl needs her daddy, and Cruz will be great for Gracie."

Was that why she was so afraid of sharing her with him? Hope was right. He was nothing like her dad. Kyle had been a lot more like him, and look how that had turned out.

"Did I speak out of turn?" Hope said. "You know how I run off at the mouth."

"No, I'm just processing. You know, he's permanently tied to me for the rest of my life, Hope."

"That doesn't exactly sound like cruel and unusual punishment." Her friend's voice carried a heavy dose of amusement.

Then why on earth did the thought of it make Zoe's chest so tight? Why did dread sit like a peach pit at the bottom of her stomach? She pressed her palm to her pounding heart.

"Listen," Hope said. "Many people share custody peacefully. The kid gets to have a relationship with both parents, and everybody wins."

But Zoe couldn't make the trapped feeling go away. Whether or not the orchard survived the bad year, she was now stuck in Copper Creek. Cruz would never let her take Gracie away, and she would never leave Gracie behind.

"I can hear your panic attack from here. Need me to come over and sit with you?"

"No. No, they'll be back soon." She fiddled with the remote. "He's really angry with me."

"You can't blame him for that."

She'd tried to justify her decision all these years. Before Gracie was born it just hadn't seemed quite real. And after she was born it seemed like it was too late.

"Brady's mad at me too," Zoe said. "He called earlier. This is such a mess."

"It's going to take time," Hope said. "But Brady'll come around and so will Cruz. You'll see."

"You're right. I'm sure you're right."

Needing a distraction, Zoe steered the conversation to Hope's job, and they chatted away the time until she heard a car pull into the drive.

She got off the phone and met Gracie at the door. Her daughter carried a big bulging bag, and Cruz carried two more. It looked like he'd bought out half of Toy Depot. He eased the door shut behind him and set the bags down by the coat rack.

"Mama, look! Look! I got a Pwincess Bawbie! And a new doll baby! Can I play with them? Please?"

"It's pajama time, honey. Did you have fun?" Her eyes shot to Cruz, narrowing briefly.

"But I wanna play!"

"You can play tomorrow. I'll read two books

216

tonight if you go get in your pajamas without arguing."

Gracie pursed her lips for a long, thoughtful moment. *"Amelia Bedelia?"*

"All right. Go pick out two."

"Yay!" Gracie kicked off her sandals and started toward the stairs.

"Wait, little miss," Zoe said. "Don't you have something to say to Cruz?"

Gracie turned back. A smile lit her eyes as she darted back toward him.

He squatted down just in time to catch her, and Zoe's heart snagged as his strong arms wrapped around their daughter.

"Thank you, Daddy."

Cruz's eyes shot to Zoe's, filling with wonder. He blinked rapidly, his arms tightening around Gracie. "You're welcome, Bella."

Zoe's eyes stung as they fell to Gracie's bare toes, which sported new purple nail polish. Cruz must've painted them. Her heart rolled over in her chest.

"Night," Gracie called as she darted toward the steps.

"See you at church tomorrow," he called.

Zoe watched Cruz watch their daughter until she disappeared at the top of the steps. The corners of his eyes were tightened with emotion. His lips slightly tipped at the corners.

Oh, boy. He was a goner.

Zoe forced her eyes to the bags at his feet and

steeled herself for the conversation she had to have.

"So it went all right?" she asked.

His gaze cut to hers, and just like that all the wonder and joy fell from his face.

What an inconvenient time for her to notice his familiar woodsy smell and the way his black T-shirt hugged his chest.

"It went great," he said finally, then turned to go.

She touched his arm. "Wait."

He gave her hand a pointed look.

She let it drop. "We need to talk, Cruz."

"I'd like to end the night on a good note, if you don't mind."

"I know you're new to this, but you can't just . . . buy her everything she wants. She's only four, and she'll come to expect it. I don't think either of us can afford that, and even if we could, it's not good for her."

"I'm not having this conversation tonight."

"You'll spoil her. I know you don't aim to do that."

He turned, one hand flat on the screen door, his jaw ticking. "Zoe . . . I've missed four birthdays and four Christmases. I think I'm due some catching up. She had nothing to play with at my place, so I let her pick out a few things. She was excited and wanted to bring some of them here. That's it."

"*Some* of them? You mean there's more?"

He narrowed his eyes.

Zoe put her hands up. "All right. I get it. I just want to make sure this doesn't become a regular thing."

"I have her best interests at heart."

"I know you do." She remembered the look on his face as he'd watched her run up the stairs. Remembered the purple toenails. "You painted her toenails." She hadn't aimed to say that last out loud.

His shoulders stiffened. "What, was that wrong too?"

He held her gaze for a long moment. His jaw was hard, his eyes steely. Not an ounce of warmth anywhere in those chocolatey depths.

But she envisioned him as he must've looked earlier, bent over her little girl's feet while he painstakingly dabbed at her tiny nails.

A breath left her body in a long, slow exhale. "No. It's really sweet actually."

Surprise flickered in his eyes, and his lips went soft before he closed up again. "I'll see you tomorrow." The screen door opened with a squawk and slapped shut behind him a moment later.

She was still in the doorway as his truck disappeared into the twilight in a cloud of dust.

chapter twenty-six

"Mama, I'm hungwy!"

Zoe heard her daughter but she couldn't make her eyes open.

Gracie shook her shoulder. "Mama! Wake up."

Zoe rolled over in bed. Every muscle in her body hurt. Even her eyelids ached, and the sheets felt too cool against her heated skin.

"Wake up, Mama. Can we have pancakes this morning?"

Zoe cracked her eyes open, smothering a groan. Good grief, it was almost eight o'clock. And she was sick. She covered her face with her forearm. So sick.

"Honey . . ." She cleared the croak from her voice. "You think you can be a big girl and make yourself a bowl of cereal?"

"But I want pancakes." Gracie bounced on the bed. "You sound funny."

"Stop bouncing, sweetie. Mama's sick. I'm going to need your help today."

Zoe felt a cool hand against her cheek. "You have a high temper, Mama!"

Zoe breathed a laugh. "Go make yourself some cereal. I'll be there in a minute."

"Okay." Gracie scampered from the room.

Of all the days to be sick. A contractor was

coming today to work on the wiring, and a plumber was coming at noon. Miss Ruby had taken a personal day to help her nephew's pregnant wife. That meant Zoe was going to have to take Gracie to the barn with her. She was exhausted just thinking about the day ahead.

One step at a time. First, she'd get a shower. Then she'd coax Gracie to get ready.

She threw back the covers and sat up. She shut her eyes against the throbbing pain in her head. Change of plans. First, some ibuprofen.

By the time they were ready all Zoe wanted to do was fall back into bed. Instead she coerced Gracie into packing a day-bag filled with things to occupy her at the barn.

Zoe was suddenly grateful for the new toys Cruz had bought. She would've hugged him if he'd been there. Never mind that he would've stiffened and pushed her away. He'd been politely distant in the two and a half weeks since he'd learned the truth.

Five long minutes later Zoe couldn't bring herself to feel even a moment's pride at the barn's transformation as she stepped inside. She headed straight for the barstool behind the finished counter/bakery case and fell onto it. Why hadn't she bought a sofa? No barn was complete without one.

She cupped her forehead. *Come on, ibuprofen.*

Gracie trotted over, her new dolly clutched in her arm. "You all wight, Mama?"

"I'm fine. I just need to rest a minute." Or a week.

Oh, man. The week she had lined up—how was she going to get through it? She was overwhelmed by the thought of walking across the barn, much less overseeing the remaining renovations. She had to sort through her grandma's recipes and figure out the accounting. She also had two interviews with potential staff and an entire market to stock with inventory.

"Bella will take care of you, Mama." Gracie handed her the doll.

Zoe took it, warmed by her daughter's compassion. "Thanks, honey."

"Anybody here?" Noah Mitchell entered the barn.

"Over here," Zoe croaked.

His face fell as he looked at her, making Zoe realize she must look as bad as she felt. She couldn't help but feel like a mangy mutt in the presence of the good-looking handyman.

"Oh, hey. Are you all right, Zoe? You look . . ."

"Terrible? Disgusting? Like a corpse?"

He gave a sheepish look as a flush crawled up his neck. "I was going to say a little under the weather."

"Sure you were. I was expecting Seth or one of your contractors." Noah and his brother owned Mitchell Construction, but Noah ran the room addition portion of the business.

"The project I'd planned to start this morning got delayed, so here I am." He put his hands on his hips and surveyed the space. "This is looking good. I hear you're wanting to be open in time for Peach Fest."

"That's the plan. But it's a tight schedule."

"Well, let's see what I can do to move things along."

Cruz got out of his truck and walked up the farmhouse's porch steps. He gave the screen door a few hard raps and waited.

He wanted to let Zoe know he'd found her a potential employee. One of his crew had a wife looking for work, and she sounded ideal for the market.

Cruz hadn't wanted to see Zoe at all. He'd avoided her as much as possible the past couple weeks, seeing her only when he picked up or dropped off Gracie. But she hadn't replied to the text he'd sent two hours ago. So after his supper he'd stopped by the barn to be sure she'd gotten his message, but it was locked up tight.

He knocked again and told himself he wasn't there because, deep down, he really wanted to see Zoe. He was still angry with her. She'd cheated him of four years with his daughter, and it was going to take some time to get over that. To rebuild trust.

On a positive note, his mom had come to town with her husband last week and met Gracie for the first time. She'd been overjoyed to have a granddaughter, and after spending a couple hours with Gracie, she was smitten. They were already talking about Cruz bringing Gracie down to Atlanta for a weekend as soon as harvest was over.

He frowned at the screen door, wondering what was taking so long. Zoe had to be home. Her old red truck was in the drive, and the door was cracked open a bit.

"Zoe?" he called through the screen door. "It's me."

He made a face as he realized identifying himself wasn't going to get him inside more quickly. He hadn't exactly been warm toward her lately.

He knocked louder. "Zoe?"

A niggle of worry squirmed inside. What if something was wrong? What if something had happened to Gracie? Zoe would've called, right?

"Cruz? What are you doing here?"

Her voice was a low scrape across her throat. Her red curls were tousled, and she had a pillow crease on her cheek. Even through the screen he could see the shadows under her eyes.

"What's wrong with you?"

"I'm sick. What do you think's wrong?"

"Where's Gracie?"

Zoe checked her watch. "Oh, shoot. I need to get her up or she'll never sleep tonight." She started for the steps, looking like she was about to collapse.

He reached for the door handle. "I'll get her. Go sit down before you collapse."

It was a testament to her state of being that she turned toward the couch without argument.

Upstairs he found Gracie curled on her bed asleep, her new doll tucked in her arms. Her hair spilled over her pillow, and her long eyelashes fanned the tops of her cheeks.

"Bella?" He touched her shoulder. "Time to wake up."

Her eyes fluttered open. They were sleepy and dazed as they fixed on him. Then her little bow lips curved as she whispered, "Daddy."

Be still my heart.

"Am I going to your house?"

"Not tonight. I just stopped by. Did you have a nice nap?"

"Mm-hmm." She snuggled against his leg, and when her stomach gave a growl she giggled.

"Someone's hungry. Let's go see what we can do about that."

He followed her down the stairs and into the kitchen, where Zoe stood in front of the open refrigerator.

"Daddy's here, Mama!"

Zoe startled, then turned, letting the door fall shut. "I know, honey."

"My tummy's gwowling."

Zoe moved to the pantry, wincing as if it hurt to move.

"Why don't you go lie down?" Cruz said. "I'll make her something."

"You don't have to do that." She moved some cans around. "You should get out of here before you catch this."

"You look like you're about to drop." He tugged her elbow. "Go on. I'm kicking you out."

"Have it your way." She shoved a can at him as he ushered her out. "Just make soup or something."

❧⚬❧

Half an hour later Gracie was at the island, happily humming as she ate her pancakes and eggs. Cruz made Zoe a plate and found her in the living room, slumped over the sofa's arm, asleep. Her hair spilled over her flushed cheeks, and she was folded in on herself as if she were cold.

He set the plate down and pulled a nearby afghan over her. She didn't even stir. He hated to wake her, but she obviously needed some Tylenol or something. He wondered if she'd had anything to eat today. Or drink. She could be dehydrated for all he knew.

He touched her shoulder. "Zoe."

Her eyes opened. They were glassy and confused for a long moment before they fell on him.

"Save yourself," she muttered before her eyes fell shut again.

His lips twitched. "Where's your Tylenol? I think you're running a pretty high fever."

"Kitchen cupboard over the sink."

He returned a minute later with the medicine and a glass of water. Zoe seemed to be asleep again.

"Wake up. I have some Advil."

She sat up, wincing, and took the pills and glass of water. "Thanks."

"You should eat something."

"I'm not hungry."

"Have you eaten anything today?"

She found the energy to give him a look.

He picked up the plate and set it on her lap. "Just a few bites."

"Where's Gracie?"

"In the kitchen eating her supper, like a good girl." He gave her a pointed look.

"Fine." She tore off the edge of a pancake and took a bite. "Happy?"

"Don't forget the eggs. You need the protein."

"Yes, Mom."

A minute later he settled at the other end of the couch with his own plate and flipped on the TV to the evening news. She ate slowly, but by the time she set the plate aside, half of the food was gone.

Gracie had finished also and gone to her room to get the game he'd promised to play with her.

"Thanks for your help," Zoe said. She was slouched into the corner of the couch, her eyes on the TV. "You don't have to stay."

"When did you come down with this?"

"This morning."

"And you worked in the barn all day?"

"I'm a mom. That's what we do."

"You should've called me."

She blinked, and he could tell it hadn't even occurred to her.

"You had to work too," she said.

"You don't have to do it alone anymore. Okay, Zoe? I don't mind helping out with Gracie. I like being with her."

Zoe turned toward him, and their eyes met. He saw the moisture there and wondered if he'd said something wrong or if her fever was just getting the better of her. Women were a mystery sometimes.

"I know you do."

"Then let me help. Will Miss Ruby be back tomorrow?"

"Yeah."

"What do you have on your agenda?"

"Um . . ." Her eyebrows crinkled. "I need to oversee the work going on in the barn, interview a couple people, and do some product research."

"You're going to have to postpone the interviews. You're contagious. And the contractors are competent. I'll check in on them throughout the day, and they have your number if they have questions."

"I should be there. And you're too busy."

"I'm just mowing the middles tomorrow," he said, referring to the grass between the tree rows. "You should stay put. You need to get better."

She wilted even further into the sofa. "I guess I could reschedule the interviews for the weekend. And do the research here."

"Now you're talking."

"Got it, Daddy!" Gracie was coming down the stairs, one at a time, her little legs working fast.

"You don't have to stay."

"I don't mind." He got up off the sofa. "Get some rest." And then he led his daughter into the kitchen to play Candy Land.

chapter twenty-seven

The week passed in a blur, but by the time Friday arrived Zoe felt human again. She'd actually found a lot of inventory for the store in between taking naps and forcing fluids. Though he was still distant, Cruz had been a lifesaver, watching over the renovations and keeping Gracie occupied in the evenings.

After answering some questions from Noah in the barn she got a burst of energy. Maybe it was just the coffee kicking in, or maybe it just felt good to feel normal again.

Since her interviews had been rescheduled for Saturday and the work on the barn was progressing just fine without her, she decided it was time to get out of the house. Time to visit her dad. She'd hardly seen him since their supper together, beyond quick greetings at church, and if she was going to have a relationship with him, she had to do her part.

He still carried a grudge about her abrupt departure, but it was time to put the past behind them. Other than Gracie, Brady, and baby Sam, he was her only relative, and she was an adult now. Surely they could get along. She wanted Gracie to have a grandpa. And though he hadn't shown much interest in baby Sam, she hoped he just needed a little nudge.

The sun was shining brightly, but the humidity was bearable, so Zoe packed a lunch from the groceries Cruz had brought over earlier in the week.

"Where we going, Mama?" Gracie asked from her perch on the island stool. She stuck out her sandaled feet, wiggling her toes and admiring the way her purple nail polish glimmered in the morning light.

"We're going to visit your papaw at work."

"What for?"

"We're taking him lunch."

Once the food was packed up, she said good-bye to Miss Ruby and loaded Gracie into the car. It didn't take long to get to her dad's law firm, which was almost in the dead center of town. The green canopy over the door was new, but the sign was the same as it had been when she'd interned there. When her dad thought she would one day be his partner. The top item in a long list of ways she'd disappointed him.

Enough of that.

She shoved the memories down as she opened the door. The cool brush of air condtioning chilled her skin, and the familiar scent of legal briefs and failed aspirations assaulted her senses.

Luanne Watkins sat behind the desk, her chestnut hair teased to the ceiling, same as always.

Her hazel eyes lit up as they landed on Zoe, the crow's-feet at the corners creasing. "Well, look who it is." She came around the desk and greeted Zoe with a warm hug, rocking a few times for good measure.

" 'Bout time you popped in, young lady. And who's this little angel?"

"My daughter, Gracie. Say hello to Miss Luanne, honey."

Gracie smiled shyly. "Hi."

"Well, aren't you just the spitting image of your mama. Look at those red curls. It's like you, running around years ago."

"She's not nearly the trouble I was."

"Now, now, you were just spirited is all."

"I believe Daddy's of a different persuasion."

"Oh, what does he know? How's your grandma's orchard faring? You've probably got your hands full out there."

"I do. I'm opening up a market in that old barn by the road."

"I heard about that. I can't wait to come pick out some fresh peaches and get to my summer baking."

Zoe looked over her shoulder toward the hall that led to her dad's office. "Is Daddy in?" She held up the bagged lunch. "I came with a peace offering."

"Oh, you." Luanne waved her hand. "Just go on back. Maybe he'll actually take a lunch break today."

"That's the hope." With one last smile, Zoe headed down the hall, Gracie's hand in hers. The plush beige carpet was new, and the white walls looked freshly painted. Daddy wasn't one to let things go to ruin. Probably why she'd frustrated him so much. All that lost potential.

She stopped in the open doorway, her hands suddenly trembling. His readers were perched on the end of his nose as he bent over a stack of papers. The light flooded in through a picture window, highlighting his salt-and-pepper hair. He was a handsome man for his age, despite eyes that were set a tad too close and a perpetual pinch between his brows.

She drew a deep breath and readied herself. There was nothing simple about a conversation with her dad. He was the king of subtext. She used to let it get to her, but she was a grown-up now.

"Trying to work up your nerve?" Daddy asked, not taking his eyes from his task.

Zoe stepped into the room and wondered if the sudden chill was her imagination or if the room really was five degrees cooler.

"Hi, Daddy." She squeezed Gracie's hand. "Say hi to your papaw, Gracie."

"Hi, Papaw."

His eyes flickered to Gracie, and Zoe had the urge to step in front of her daughter.

But he merely nodded. "Hello, young lady."

Zoe resisted the urge to wipe her sweaty hand down the side of her jeans.

Her dad fixed his eyes on the papers. "What

brings you by in the middle of the day? Figured you'd be toiling away in that orchard of yours. Or are you finally ready to give up?"

Too bad you didn't get that law degree and set yourself up in my air-conditioned office.

"Cruz is handling that end of things."

He scowled at the mention of Cruz. "I heard the latest scuttlebutt about—" His gaze flickered off Gracie. "Her paternity. Had to hear it from Brady."

"I'm sorry. I should've been the one to tell you, but I've been busy with the orchard, and then I got sick."

"I'd like to say I was surprised."

Zoe cleared her throat. "I'll admit I made a few mistakes, but things are looking up now." She held up the bag of food, ready for a change of topic. "We brought you lunch. Your favorite . . . pastrami on rye and potato salad. Thought we could take it to the park and have a little picnic. Like we used to. Remember?"

He spared her a glance. "You should've called. I have a brief to prepare for a deposition."

I don't have time for you.

Her chest squeezed tight, but she forced a smile. "Well, you have to eat . . ."

"I usually just snack on an apple nowadays while I work."

Even your food's not good enough.

Her skin suddenly felt so warm she wondered if her fever had returned.

This wasn't about a brief or a deposition or about her dad's diet preferences. This was about him punishing her for leaving without a word. For getting pregnant out of wedlock. For embarrassing him and disappointing him many times over.

But she wasn't the young girl who so easily took the bait. She was a single mother who was strong enough to face the past. "Well . . . I'm singing with Last Chance tomorrow night at the Rusty Nail. You should stop by."

He shuffled his papers. "We'll see."

She knew what that meant. "Daddy, maybe we should talk about what happened. Not now of course . . ." She glanced down at Gracie. "But soon."

He cleared his throat. "There's really nothing to talk about, but you're welcome to check my schedule with Luanne on your way out."

You can leave now.

She swallowed against the growing knot in her throat. Her feet itched to retreat, but she forced them to take a step forward—only close enough to set the bag on the edge of the desk.

"Well . . . in case you get hungry." She backed toward the door. "We'll get out of your hair."

On the way out she was glad to find Luanne gone from her desk. Stepping out into the warm day she drew a deep breath of fresh air and wondered how two minutes with her dad could make her feel as if she were suffocating in shame.

chapter twenty-eight

He was stupid to check on Zoe in the middle of the day. She'd texted him this morning that she was feeling good today, but that didn't stop Cruz from running over to the house at lunch anyway.

He was checking in on Gracie, not Zoe. At least that's what he told himself as he pulled up the drive. Her truck wasn't in its usual spot, however, and neither was Miss Ruby's.

He frowned at the deserted house, excusing the sinking feeling in his stomach as disappointment over missing Gracie. He had to admit it had been fun to spend the evenings with her this week. She was a playful and happy child. She only got cranky when she was tired, but the promise of a bedtime story usually ensured her cooperation.

He was putty in her hands. The little girl could flutter her eyelashes with the best of them—and she was only four! She was so much like her mother.

And at fifteen Zoe had been a real handful, he reminded himself. Sneaky as all get out and able to charm the bees out of a tree.

The thought of Gracie following in her mother's footsteps made him want to put a dead bolt on her bedroom door right now. And her windows. How many times had Zoe sneaked out of those late at night? To see *him*.

If karma was a real thing, he was dead meat. They both were.

He comforted himself with the thought that he had another ten years before he had to worry about any of that.

Well, there was no sense waiting around here. As he reached for the gearshift his eye caught on something colorful by the door. Flowers, sitting on the porch table. The kind in a vase, delivered by a florist. He frowned at the large arrangement, thinking immediately of Kyle.

But they could be from anyone. They could even be late sympathy flowers from a distant friend of her grandma or get-well-soon flowers from Hope or Daisy. Though upon closer inspection they looked like red roses—a veritable declaration of love. Zoe had two family members old enough to send flowers, and he could imagine neither Brady nor her dad sending them.

He dithered only a moment before stepping out of the car, drawn by curiosity. Curiosity, not jealousy, he clarified to himself. A fair distinction.

He took the porch steps and paused in front of the arrangement. An envelope from Oopsy Daisy stuck out from the blooms. The back flap of the envelope, he could see easily enough, was merely tucked inside.

He scratched the back of his neck, his fingers itching to read the card.

He cast a glance around. He was being ridiculous. It was a florist card, not an FBI file. And she was the mother of his child. If she was dating someone who was a potential stepdad to Gracie, he had a right to know, didn't he?

Okay, maybe not. But he was going to look anyway. He grabbed the envelope and slid the card out.

I'm sorry, babe. Hope you're feeling better. I miss you. Love, Kyle

Cruz scowled. *Kyle.* So he was still holding out hope, and apparently Zoe was still talking with him. He wondered what Kyle was sorry for. There were so many possibilities. Had she confronted him about lying to Cruz back when?

He looked at the card again. Oh, he missed her, did he?

Well, where was Kyle while Zoe had been passed out on the couch this week? While she could hardly find the energy to get dressed, much less work or take care of Gracie?

Off making a name for himself, that's what.

Didn't Zoe see that? Probably not, if she was still communicating with him. It suddenly felt ten degrees warmer on the porch.

❖

Zoe turned into the orchard drive. There were two work trucks in front of the barn, Noah's and the plumbing contractor's. She'd take Gracie back

238

to the house so Miss Ruby could watch her, and come back to unpack the merchandise that had arrived this week.

She'd taken Gracie to eat at the park first, since her daughter had had her heart set on it. Zoe'd tried to project some enthusiasm into their outing, but after the encounter with her father it was a struggle.

As she pulled up to the house she saw that Miss Ruby's car was missing, and she remembered that the woman had run to the bank. Cruz's truck was there, however.

"Daddy's here!" Gracie had already spotted him on the porch where he stood in his work clothes. His hair was mussed from the wind, his skin bronzed by the sun.

Zoe lifted Gracie from her booster, and as soon as her daughter hit the ground she went running for Cruz. Zoe's heart tugged at the sight of them together, and she pulled her gaze away from the embrace.

As she took the porch steps her eyes fell on a vase of flowers sitting on the table. Cruz's eyes met hers as he stood from Gracie's hug. Her daughter was rambling on about the slide at the park, but Zoe was too busy speculating about the flowers.

"Where'd those come from?" she asked when Gracie took a breath.

He hitched a brow. "Care to take a guess?"

Fresh from her father's rejection, she didn't want to play this game, but some remote part of her hoped they were from Cruz. She reached for the envelope and slipped out the card.

Kyle.

She pursed her lips as her heart seemed to shrink in size. Of course they weren't from Cruz. Why had she even entertained the thought? He'd been helpful this week, but he'd done it for their daughter. He'd shown no interest in her, and why would he after the way she'd betrayed his trust?

Meanwhile Kyle was carrying out a full court press since she'd confronted him about his lies to Cruz, texting her every hour, calling every day, and now . . . flowers.

She stuck the envelope and card into the bunch of flowers and opened the door. Zoe raced past, heading to the bathroom.

"Why's Kyle sending you flowers?" Cruz asked as the screen door shut behind them.

She gave him a look. "You read my card?"

"You're not considering going back to that idiot, are you?"

Zoe pressed her lips together. Wow, everyone just had so high an opinion of her. Daddy. Cruz. Even Brady with his suggestions on how to handle her life.

"Shouldn't you be working?"

"I won't have him around my daughter. Not after what I saw. After what he did."

"I would never endanger Gracie."

"Good. Then you'll tell Kyle to back off."

She bristled. "It's not your place to tell me what to do, Cruz."

Their gaze clashed until the air between them felt taut with tension. His muscles in his cheek twitched.

She had to have boundaries in place. Cruz had a say when it came to their daughter, but not when it came to her love life. She didn't dare tell him that Kyle had been hinting about visiting her. Had been begging her to come back to the band. He'd apologized profusely for that night at the Rusty Nail and swore he'd never raise a hand to her again.

"I've taken care of Gracie for four years," she said finally. "I reckon you're just going to have to trust me."

The corners of his eyes tightened.

Oh well. She wasn't giving up control of her life again. Not to her dad, not to Kyle, and not to Cruz.

When Gracie entered the room a long moment later, Zoe let out a deep breath, relieved the conversation was over. At least for the moment.

chapter twenty-nine

Cruz had never been so glad to see a Friday night roll around. Part of him had wanted to crawl into bed and pull the covers over his head, but Brady wouldn't leave him alone.

That's how he came to be sitting in the crowded Rusty Nail with his friend. Hope had taken a break and joined them. There was no live music tonight, but a country tune blared through the speakers. The smell of grilled burgers and onion rings made him wish service was a little faster.

Hope looked like she was in heaven, cradling baby Sam in her arms, a bottle propped in her hand. She gazed down at the tyke with a wistful smile.

He thought of Gracie and wondered what she'd been like as a baby. Zoe had shown him photos on the computer, but photos hardly scratched the surface. Did she have colic? What had she sounded like when she babbled? What was her first word? He'd never gotten to see her first steps or hear her baby belly laugh.

He took a sip of his drink and forced the depressing thoughts from his mind. The image of those roses on Zoe's porch immediately replaced them. Had she called Kyle to thank him? Did she still have feelings for him? What if Kyle talked her into leaving Copper Creek? After all, he could give her the music career she'd always dreamed of.

"You should go dance," Brady said over the music, a mischievous glint in his eyes. "There's that girl you went out with a while back, the friend of Noah's."

Cruz had given Brady a rundown of the disastrous date. He'd caught the woman in three lies over the course of two hours. And they hadn't even been over anything important.

"Why don't you ask her to dance?" Cruz said. "She seems more like your type."

Brady's grin fell, and Cruz felt a stab of guilt.

Hope eyed Cruz over the bottle. "Low blow, dude."

"What's wrong with you tonight?" Brady said.

Cruz shouldn't have made the reference to Audrey. Brady'd learned his lesson the hard way. "Sorry. I'm just in a mood. Your sister's driving me batty."

"What's she done now?" Brady asked.

Cruz pinned Hope with a look. "Did you know Kyle's still after her? He's sending her flowers and stuff."

"Give her some credit," Brady said. "She's done with him."

"Then why on earth doesn't she tell him to leave her alone?"

"Kyle's not really the type to take no for an answer." Hope gave him a pointed look. "Anyway, since when do you care so much?"

"I don't want him around Gracie. You saw what kind of guy he is."

Hope smirked. "This is all about Gracie, huh?"

Heat pooled in his cheeks, and he was glad for the dim lighting. He wasn't fooling anyone, least of all himself.

He was glad when the server appeared with their food.

"Thanks, Lauren," Hope said after the server unloaded her tray. "You can take your break now if you want."

"Okay."

Seconds later Cruz was tucking into his Bubba Burger, marveling in the flavors of grilled beef, tangy barbecue sauce, and fresh tomato.

"Oh, my gosh, Brady," Hope said, wrinkling her nose. "Your son stinks to high heaven. What did you feed him today?"

Brady pushed his plate back, grabbing the diaper bag. "Give him here. I told Audrey not to give him apple juice, but she won't listen. He's had diarrhea all day. Never seen so many colors in a diaper."

"Thanks for that," Cruz mumbled around a mouthful of juicy burger.

Hope stood with the baby. "Sit tight. I've got this one."

Brady handed over the bag. "You're the woman of my dreams, Daniels."

"Yeah, yeah. That's what they all say."

"Watch out for the up-the-back stuff," Brady called after her.

"Seriously?" Cruz swallowed the bite, his appetite diminished.

"You have no idea."

No, he didn't, since he'd missed out on Gracie's baby years. But he didn't want to think about that anymore tonight. Instead he grabbed a fry and watched Brady's eyes follow Hope as she walked toward the restroom in the back corner.

They'd known Hope forever. Though she was two years behind Brady in high school she'd been around a lot because she was Zoe's friend and, more recently, because she managed the Rusty Nail on the weekends.

She and Brady got along well and often teased each other, but somehow Cruz had never wondered about the two of them.

"So why is it you've never gone out with Hope?"

Brady spared him a glance in between wolfing down his burger. "She's just a friend."

"What? She's not cute enough for you?"

"She's a *friend*. Besides, I think Audrey's scared me off women for good. I haven't dated since the divorce. Haven't even wanted to."

"Audrey's a bad seed. They're not all wily and

manipulative. Look at your sister. She's practically an open book."

"My sister . . . ? You mean the one giving you fits right now?"

Cruz grimaced. "All right, so she's complicated in other ways. But she's all right. Most of the time."

"My attitude toward women right now would make Eeyore seem like an optimist. Wouldn't be fair to subject myself on some nice girl."

Cruz smirked. "You're right. Hope deserves so much better than you."

Brady smacked the back of his head.

Cruz had enjoyed the last of his burger by the time Hope returned.

She held baby Sam out to Brady. "Oh. My. Gosh."

"Told you." Brady took the happy baby and held him over his shoulder, patting his back.

"I'm just . . . speechless."

"Can I enjoy my meal please?" Cruz said.

Hope plopped down and started on her salad as if she hadn't just changed the world's messiest diaper. "Sorry, but yowza. That added a couple years to my ticking maternal clock."

"He shouldn't even be having juice yet," Brady said.

"Well, it's a good thing he's so cute. And he's always so happy."

"You haven't caught him teething yet. But

yeah, he's my little dude. Aren't you, fella?" Brady kissed the back of Sammy's head.

"So what's Audrey up to these days?" Hope asked. "Other than causing conflict, chaos, and confusion everywhere she goes, I mean."

"She's working part-time at a boutique in Dalton."

"I thought for sure she'd move to a big city. She's not really a small town kind of girl."

"She'd like nothing more, but she can't afford it. She's staying at her parents' rental."

"I thought they didn't get along," Cruz said.

"They don't, really. They're the most critical people I've ever met in my life. But she needed a place to stay, and they're not using the villa."

"Do they see Sam much?"

"I don't know. Part of me hopes not. They did a terrible job raising Audrey, and from what I've seen they haven't changed."

"Is she still trying to get more child support?" Cruz asked.

"The court turned it down. I don't mind paying my fair share, but she has to do her part too. I've thought about trying to get full custody."

Hope raised a brow. "Do you think Audrey's a good mom?"

"Believe it or not, as nasty as she can be, she's good to Sammy—apple juice notwithstanding. That's the only thing that stops me from going after custody."

"You've got to be busy with the new building you're putting up," Hope said.

Brady stuck the last French fry in his mouth. "Getting a business off the ground is time consuming."

"Please," Hope said. "It's way more than off the ground. You've got more work than you can handle."

"That's true. I had to turn away a project just last week. It was a Porsche 911 too. 'Bout broke my heart."

"Bummer," Cruz said.

Brady shook his head sadly. "Turbo S. All-wheel drive."

"Poor baby." Hope fished through her salad. "How about you, Cruz? How are you adjusting to fatherhood?"

He couldn't help the smile that formed at the thought of Gracie. "It's funny. If you'd have asked me a month ago if I was ready to be a father, I would've said heck no. But now I can't even imagine not being Gracie's dad."

Hope's eyes sparkled under the lantern lighting. "Look at you. You're totally smitten."

"What'd I tell you?" Brady said to Cruz. "Wasn't long ago you were giving me grief about all this."

"I'm eating my words now." And happy to have it so. "My mom's pretty smitten too. You should've seen her with Gracie. All the rules that applied when I was a kid are out the window now."

"That's how it's supposed to be," Hope said.

Gracie was like a ray of sunshine in his life. He looked forward to seeing her and thought about her in the middle of the workday. If only he could figure out his more complex feelings about her mother.

chapter thirty

Zoe expected the phone call that came later that night. She hadn't thanked Kyle for the roses; why should she when she hadn't even wanted them? Her daughter was asleep, and she wanted nothing more than to drop into bed. She'd pushed herself too hard after being sick all week.

But if she didn't answer the phone, Kyle wouldn't leave her be, and she worried he might show up out of the blue. She sank onto the edge of her bed and answered.

"Did you get the flowers?" he asked as soon as she greeted him.

"They're beautiful. But you shouldn't have sent them, Kyle. I'm still angry about the lies you told Cruz, and I've been clear about how I feel."

"Well, I wanted to be clear about how *I* feel. I still love you, Zoe. I miss you."

"You poked your nose in where it didn't belong, Kyle."

"I gave you your dream, Zoe. I took you on the road, and I took care of you, didn't I? Both of you. And now you're just letting that tool shuttle her all over town?"

She blinked. "How do you know that?"

"It's a small town, Zoe. I have friends."

Zoe sighed. "Well, that really doesn't concern you."

"Is that a fact? Maybe she's not mine, but I treated her as my own for four years. I took care of you both."

He had been good to Gracie, that much was true. "I appreciate the role you had in her life. I really do. But I need some space right now. I've got a lot on the line with the orchard."

"Don't you mean with Cruz?"

She frowned at the phone. "What do you mean?"

"Like I said, I got friends, Zoe."

"Cruz has nothing to do with this. I don't want to argue, Kyle. I haven't changed my mind. I'm staying put. I'm making a go of the orchard."

"I wasn't going to tell you this, but there's been a big development for the band . . . Colonial wants to sign us. Can you believe it? Finally. But the backup singer we've been using isn't nearly as good as you. This is a once-in-a-lifetime shot, Zoe. Come back to me, and we'll take Brevity all the way to the top. We'll do it together."

Maybe she was jaded, but she wondered if this was the real reason he'd been pursuing her so ardently. Even so, for a moment her dream of making it big tugged at her. She did love performing. She loved losing herself in the music, loved the rush of a live audience. But she didn't love the nomadic lifestyle the way she'd thought she would. And she didn't love Kyle.

"I'm really happy for you and the band. You've worked hard for this. But I'm staying put. This is my home now. I have an orchard to run, and I'm going to make it work."

"Get real, Zoe. You're not a farmer. You're a musician. A vocalist."

His words were wired with a familiar kind of tension. The kind that used to make her eye twitch. Funny, that hadn't happened once since he'd left. She was stronger now. Braver. And he was hundreds of miles away. He no longer had control over her.

"You're wrong. I am a farmer. My grandma left me this land, and I'm going to carry on her legacy if it's the last thing I do."

"You're making a big mistake."

"Well, it's mine to make, Kyle."

"This is about Cruz, isn't it? You think now he knows about Gracie you'll be a nice little family. But he's a loser, Zoe. Why can't you see that? He failed you before, and he'll fail you again."

"I'm not talking to you about Cruz."

"Because you know I'm right. Come back to me, Zoe, and I'll make sure you're a household name."

She thought of her old life, going from town to town, dragging Gracie along, stuck on a tour bus with guys whose lifestyle set a bad example for an impressionable young girl. Kyle, making her feel like a little bit of nothing.

Somehow the old dream no longer had the same appeal. "I'm staying here, Kyle, and it's over between us. I'm done answering your calls and texts. We don't have anything else to talk about."

"I was there for you when you needed someone." His voice had grown louder. "When your dad rejected you. When Cruz turned on you. I took care of you for five years."

"Cruz turned on me on account of your lies." She sighed hard. "I wish you the best, Kyle. I really do. But it's time we went our separate ways. Please leave me alone."

"You're nothing without me. You'll change your mind."

"No, I won't."

She wasn't surprised to hear a click in her ear a second later.

chapter thirty-one

The barn had been transformed in the past three weeks. The electrical was finished, and as of this afternoon the plumbing was complete too. With Peach Fest two weeks away, Zoe had already received a lot of merchandise and was beginning to stock the shelves.

In the field Cruz and his crew had started harvesting. The peaches had sized up better than expected. Maybe she'd be able to pay back the loan after all.

If only she could get the rest of this stuff figured out. She headed into the kitchen and started a small pot of decaf. She'd just spent over an hour peppering Daisy Pendleton of the Oopsy Daisy Flower Shoppe with business questions. She'd been a huge help, but now Zoe's head spun with all the advice.

She rubbed her temples as she waited for the coffee to brew. Self-doubt crowded in as her heart sped. Keeping track of money and merchandise was going to be an ongoing battle, and she couldn't afford to hire someone who knew what they were doing. She wasn't smart enough for this. Even a phone conversation about it had overwhelmed her.

You can do this, Zoe. You'll figure it out. Focus on the part of the business you enjoy.

Tending the trees. Customer service. Making people smile. The smell of fresh peaches she'd grown on her own land.

You've got this.

She'd come so far. And she'd kept the renovation on schedule, hadn't she? She'd be open on time, and she was determined to open with a big splash. She already had some marketing in place—not only in Copper Creek but in outlying areas.

She pulled the carafe from the burner and poured a steaming mugful. The house was so quiet tonight. It was going on midnight. Hope had taken Gracie for her first sleepover, and Zoe kept expecting a call asking her to come pick up her daughter. But Gracie was well adjusted, and she loved Hope. Plus she'd slept in a variety of places, so she wasn't attached to her own bed.

Zoe carried her mug into the darkened living room, the wood floor squeaking under her bare feet, the scent of hazelnut rising to her nose.

She wondered what Cruz was doing tonight. He'd probably gone to the Rusty Nail with Brady. There was a new band playing. Her brother had tried to talk her into going, but she'd needed to use her childfree hours to get some work done. Plus she figured Cruz would be there.

She avoided him as much as possible. It was too hard to be around him when he treated her with such polite indifference. She knew he wasn't trying to punish her—that really wasn't his style. But somehow it felt that way.

Kyle seemed to have given up—finally. She hadn't heard from him since he'd hung up on her a few weeks ago. She wondered how things were going with that record label, if what he'd said was even true. Maybe it had only been a ploy to get her back.

The orchard was silhouetted beyond the picture window, the moonlight falling over it like a downy blanket. Her land. Passed down to her, entrusted to her. She drew in a deep breath, letting it fill her lungs until they stretched. Times like this she could almost feel Granny's presence. Hear her words of encouragement. The hymns she hummed while she worked.

"I'm going to keep your legacy alive, Granny," she whispered.

The mountains rose in the distance, an imposing presence against the starry sky. Her eyes climbed to the heavens, to the pinpricks of light, millions of them it seemed, scattered across the night sky.

He's got me this far. I reckon He can carry me the rest of the way.

Granny's words brought a smile to her lips. She wished she'd inherited her grandmother's strong faith as easily as she'd inherited the land. Somehow believing was scary. Zoe's hopes had been raised too many times only to be dashed, and then the sting of disappointment lingered far too long.

She took a sip of the brew and was just turning away from the window when a flare of light caught her eye. She looked back, thinking at first it was only a glare from the stove light behind her.

She moved closer to the window, cupping her hand around her eyes. It was no glare. It was a light. And it was coming from the direction of the barn. She'd turned everything off when she'd left this evening. Hadn't she? But it had still been daylight, and it was possible she'd missed a light.

She'd just resolved to throw on her sandals, pajamas and all, and go shut off the lights, when she noticed that the glow in the distance was flickering. Had it also grown brighter in the last few moments, or were her tired eyes playing tricks on her?

But as she watched, the light flared. Then an orange flame shot up above the treetops.

Fire!

She gasped, her heart suddenly thudding against her ribs. She shoved her feet into her muck boots and grabbed her phone and keys, then darted out to the porch, punching 911 for help. She was halfway to her truck when she remembered the fire extinguisher in the kitchen. She dashed back inside while spewing out the information to the operator.

"Hurry, please!"

She jumped into her truck, gravel churning behind her tires as she sped down the lane.

Please, God. This can't be happening.

But as she neared the barn she saw flames shooting out the window. She rushed into the lot and jumped out. Her fingers trembled as she unlocked the door. The metal of the doorknob wasn't yet hot. Hope flooded through her.

She threw open the barn door and choked on her first lungful of acrid smoke. Her eyes stung. Heat licked at her skin as she entered the building, aiming the extinguisher at the base of the nearest fire.

⇶•⇷

He must be a glutton for punishment. Why else would he be thinking about taking the long way home, driving by Zoe's at midnight on a Friday night?

Don't be an idiot, he thought as he approached the intersection where he'd have to make the choice. *It's a waste of time.*

The band at the Rusty Nail had been entertaining enough. But as much as he'd tried to distract himself with games of pool and small talk, he couldn't get his mind off Zoe. He'd been convicted of his attitude toward her in church Sunday while she'd been onstage singing her heart out. He was harboring resentment, and he knew he had to forgive her.

Yeah, she'd messed up. But he wasn't perfect either. He'd too easily believed the worst of her back then—his own insecurities driving his doubts. Her dad hadn't believed him good enough for Zoe. And deep down Cruz hadn't either.

He'd always thought of her as being in a different league. He'd told himself she was too young, but in truth he hadn't believed he measured up. He hadn't been enough for his dad to stick around, after all.

He pushed the thought away. Amazing how something he could barely remember could impact his thinking all these years later. He'd worked hard to overcome those doubts. A loving mother had helped. Proving himself helped. Remembering God had created him with worth and value helped most of all.

He pulled to a stop at the intersection. Straight toward home, or left toward Zoe?

There was no reason to go left. It was after midnight. She was in bed by now.

But he wasn't tired yet, and he remembered the one time her barn door had been left open all night by one of the contractors. There hadn't been much to steal at the time, but now the barn contained boxes of merchandise.

He turned the wheel. He'd just drive by and give it a quick glance. Make sure the barn was shut up tight.

He chided himself for his weakness even as he drove toward her place. Excuses. Zoe didn't need him taking care of her. She'd done just fine on her own—as a single mom no less.

She'd always been strong, which was why it'd been so infuriating to see that Kyle had snuffed out her spirit. At least she had her spunk back now. He'd rather see her eyes shooting sparks than dull and lifeless, avoiding eye contact, as they'd been when she first returned to town.

He let off the gas as he approached the orchard. There was enough moonlight to see by, and the barn sat close to the road. He'd just give it a quick glance and be on his way.

But a glow over the low treetops made him frown. And as he neared the barn, the sight of flames licking the building was like a sucker punch.

He swerved into the drive, his stomach sinking even further at the sight of Zoe's truck in the lot, the door hanging open.

Querido Dios.

What was happening? He braked hard, shifting into park before his truck even came to a full stop. He threw open his door and leaped to the ground. The fire was a live creature, crackling and roaring. The flames seemed confined to the inside at the moment. But where was Zoe?

He ran for the open door. "Zoe!" He threw his

arm up against the heat that engulfed him on the threshold. Black smoke clouded his vision and burned his eyes.

"Zoe!" He coughed.

Raising his T-shirt to cover his mouth, he crouched lower, darting through the barn. The flames hissed. Something clattered nearby. He couldn't see a thing through the smoke.

"Zoe!"

"Cruz!"

He barely heard her voice. Coming from the corner, he thought. He inched toward her, heat licking at his skin. The glow of fire shone through the wall of smoke.

He found her near the shelving, coughing violently. Her arms sagged as she aimed an extinguisher at the base of a ten-foot wall of flames. The retardant had turned the smoke white.

He grabbed her arm. "Come on!"

She jerked away from him, continuing to spray through another coughing fit.

"Zoe, it's too late!" He tore the extinguisher from her hands and dropped it on the ground.

The heat was almost unbearable. The flames surrounded them, the acrid smoke burning his lungs. Somewhere above them a lightbulb popped.

"We have to get out of here!" He took her hand and weaved through the thick smoke.

Seconds later he stopped to reassess. Where was the exit? He'd turned himself around. He found a wall and slid along it, hoping it led out-side. Which way?

¡*Ayúdanos, Dios*!

They continued along the wall through the endless smoke. The fire crackled and popped all around them, a distant orange glow to the right. Not that way. He bumped something waist high and felt for it. Smooth as glass. The bakery case. He was close. He moved them forward, his lungs begging for cool, fresh air.

Finally the smoke began clearing. He made out the outline of the barn door and burst for-ward through the doorway, still holding tight to Zoe's hand. Cool air washed over his heated skin, and he sucked in a lungful only to cough it back out.

"Where's Gracie?" he gasped.

Zoe was coughing too, hands braced on her knees. She was shaking, ready to collapse. Staring at the burning barn, seemingly in shock.

He caught her around the waist and eased her to the ground.

"Zoe, where's Gracie?"

Mention of their daughter seemed to get through. "At Hope's. She's fine."

A coughing fit seized her. She hacked and hacked as the rush of blood thrashed in his ears. As the coughing spell receded her rigid body slackened, her weight sinking into him.

Cruz sagged with relief, his arms loosening. He

blinked against the sting in his eyes, catching his breath. His heart rate slowing.

"It's gone," she said. "It's gone."

"It's going to be okay."

Moments later a siren sounded in the distance, barely audible over the roar of the fire. Thank God. Zoe needed oxygen. She probably had burns too. Now that the adrenaline was easing up, he noticed his own skin burning.

The flames licked at the building, now moving to the exterior walls. She was right. It was too late for the barn. Anything left after the fire was put out would be ruined by water. But Zoe was all right. Gracie was safe. And that was all that really mattered.

He set his cheek against her temple, brushing the hair from her face. "It's all right," he said softly into her ear. Then he tightened his arms around her, suddenly more grateful than he'd ever been in his life.

chapter thirty-two

"It's over," Zoe said to her brother, the words falling out of her as lifeless as the heap of smoking rubble.

Sunlight shimmered on the horizon, a golden glow fading into the pink morning sky. But the hopeful dawn of a new day was lost in the sight of the ruins. The deputy had just left, promising an investigation. But what did it matter at this point? Her barn was gone. All the merchandise she'd already paid for was gone. All her hard work, gone down in a fiery inferno.

Brady curled an arm around her. "I'm sorry, sis."

"I can't believe this is happening."

Her lungs still burned even after receiving oxygen. She'd been taken to the clinic for an x-ray and observation. She was running now on only a couple hours of sleep, the adrenaline long gone.

"You going to be all right?" He checked his watch. "I have to meet a client at the house."

"I'll be fine." She projected a convincing tone. "I'll head over to Hope's to pick up Gracie in a minute."

"Let me know if I can lend a hand with anything. Insurance or whatever." He gave her a consoling hug and pulled from the parking lot a moment later.

Zoe sagged against her truck's hood, hardly able to take her eyes from what, only yesterday, had been the orchard's last hope.

Why, God? I'm trying to do a good thing here. Keep Granny's orchard running the way she would've wanted. And since I've come home it's been nothing but one trial after another.

The sound of an approaching engine drew her attention, and she turned to see Cruz's black truck. Gravel crunched under his tires as he pulled into the lot.

Zoe's eyes clung to him. She'd been in shock over her loss last night. But now, in the light of day, gratitude swept over her. She would've stayed in that building until she'd collapsed. And where would that have left Gracie? The fear of what could've been tightened her chest.

All right. All right, there's something to be grateful for.

He got out of the truck, his eyes fixed on her. He looked too good to have been caught in a blazing fire last night. Though his eyes were a bit bloodshot, she saw as he got closer. He'd stayed with her through it all. Had driven her home.

Somewhere nearby a bird sang from high in a tree, and a warm breeze tugged at her hair.

"How are you feeling?" he asked.

"I'm all right." Her voice was hoarse. She could still taste the smoke in her mouth, and wondered if it would ever go away. She looked at the ruins. "I can't believe it's gone."

"I know this is a big setback. But insurance will cover it, Zoe. We'll get through this."

"Will we? 'Cause it's looking kind of hopeless right now."

"We'll figure something out. The orchard's been through bad years before."

But her grandma had money she didn't have. All she had at this point was debt and hope. Scratch that last part.

He glanced toward the remainder of the barn. "Any word on what caused it?"

"Deputy Mosley said they'd look into it."

"There was no lightning last night. Who was the last one in the building?"

"I was. I came by to pay the plumber; he finished up yesterday. I shut off all the lights. Locked the doors. I didn't leave anything plugged in, I'm sure of it."

"The plumber, huh? Darren—the guy from Ellijay?"

"Yeah." She thought of that big check she'd written him. Money down the drain. She couldn't even bring herself to smile at the pun.

"I caught him smoking in the barn when you were sick," he said. "I asked him to smoke outside. You don't think . . . ?"

"I didn't smell anything when I was here to pay him, but I guess it's possible."

"Or maybe it was something with the electrical wiring."

"Noah's a competent contractor," she said. "I can't imagine he'd botch something that badly."

"Nobody's perfect. It could even be faulty materials."

"I reckon so. What does it matter, though? Peach Fest is two weeks away, and my market is gone. Next season will be too late. I owe a lot of money, Cruz, and even if the harvest nets enough to pay it back, I don't have any means of getting through till next season."

His eyes clung to hers and held. Something flickered there that made her forget about her financial troubles. Something that reached into the deepest part of her. Made her heart squeeze tight.

He still cared about her. It was apparent in the intensity of his gaze, dancing over her features like a desperate touch.

"I keep thinking about last night," he said.

"Me too."

The way he'd pulled her from the building. The way he'd held her tight, protecting her from the fire. She'd needed him last night, and he'd been there for her. Might not be standing here without him.

"Thank you," she said.

He stepped closer, captured her face, his eyes still burning into hers. "Nothing else mattered to me last night, Zoe. Nothing but you and Gracie. The whole world could've gone up in flames as long as my girls were safe."

She swallowed against the lump in her throat, grabbing his wrists and holding tight.

This. This was what she needed.

Early this morning Cruz had lain in bed, body exhausted, mind spinning. Yet he couldn't sleep. All he could do was lie there thinking, *Gracias. ¡Gracias, Dios!*

What if he hadn't taken that turn in the road? Taken the long way home? Would Zoe even be standing in front of him right now?

A crushing weight fell over him. "If I'd lost you . . ." He shook his head, unable to go on.

"You didn't."

She was so beautiful with the day's new light streaming through her hair, making it glow. Her cheeks were pink, no longer scary pale the way they had been under the clinic's fluorescent lights last night.

He'd wasted enough time being angry. What were four years in light of the rest of their lives? He couldn't change what had happened. Neither of them could.

His eyes sharpened on her, and he reached for her hands. "I don't want to lose you, Zoe."

"You haven't."

Breath he didn't know he'd been holding escaped in a long, slow exhale. He leaned closer, brushing her lips with his. His heart leaped to life, instantly refreshed. His lips tingled, and his body hummed. She awakened him from the inside out. Always had.

Her hands slid up his chest, around his shoulders. Her touch was like coming home. He pulled her closer, her slight weight sinking into his chest. His hands fit just right in the curve of her waist. Her scent wrapped around him, weaving a spell, the sweetness of her shampoo with undertones of smoke. She tasted of morning and coffee and hope.

He released her only so he could hold her closer. So he could tuck her head under his chin. Breathe her in. Remind himself that second chances were one of life's sweetest offerings.

She slid her arms around his waist, clutching at the back of his shirt. "You . . . you just kissed me."

He pressed his lips to her temple, letting them linger. "In my defense, you kissed me back."

She breathed a laugh, snuggling closer. "It was . . . nice."

"Nice?"

He felt her lips curl against his neck. "Maybe better than nice. I don't want it to go to your head."

"Keeping my ego in check, huh?"

"Somebody has to. On the other hand, you could probably do better than a down-on-her-luck girl with nothing to her name but a failing orchard and a burnt-down barn."

"That's all temporary. We'll get through it."

He pulled away, needing to look her in the eye. Needing her to know the seriousness of this moment. Those green eyes, twin pools of heaven, stared back, asking questions he needed to answer.

"I haven't been very nice lately," he said. "I'm sorry."

Her hands clenched at his waist. "You were entitled. I messed up pretty bad."

"We both could've handled things better back then. But I'm done being mad at you, Zoe. I just want to move forward."

He brushed his thumb across her cheek. So incredibly soft. Addictive. His lips tingled with want. But he should probably take things slow. They had a lot to talk about.

He brushed her forehead with a kiss. "We'll talk more later. But let's wait until we're operating on more than an hour's sleep."

Her eyes smiled before her lips did. "Sounds like a plan."

chapter thirty-three

"Uncle Bwady!" Gracie came running as soon as Zoe let Brady in the door. The girl threw her arms around his legs as if it hadn't been only two days since she'd seen him.

Brady swung Gracie into his arms and tweaked her nose. "Hey, squirt."

"I'm not a squirt! I'm Bella!"

He laughed, no doubt at the outrage on her face. "Is that so?"

She squirmed to get down. "Come play Candy Land!"

"Gracie, you know it's bedtime," Zoe said. "Give Uncle Brady a kiss good night and go get in bed. I'll be up in a minute."

Her lower lip pooched. "I'm thirsty."

How could she deny that face? "All right. Go get a drink first—milk or water, not juice," Zoe called after her.

Brady had already made himself at home on the sofa and flipped the TV to the Braves' game. His dark hair was short, as if it had just been trimmed, but a fine stubble covered his jaw.

"What brings you by?" Zoe sank into the arm-chair. "Wait, where's Sammy? I thought you were supposed to have him this weekend."

He made a face. "Audrey was supposed to bring

him, but she didn't show. I finally got hold of her a few minutes ago. Something came up."

"She can't keep doing that."

"I wish she'd at least call or text and let me know what's going on. I'm going to go get him in the morning."

"Bring him by after church if you want. You know how Gracie loves to make him smile."

"Thought you might be busy." He gave her a direct look. "With a certain someone."

"You've talked to Cruz."

"You two going to give it another go?"

"We are."

She'd thought about him all day. Her love life was looking up, but her financial picture had never been so dire. It was perplexing, having something wonderful and something awful happening simultaneously. She wasn't going to think about the orchard right now. Otherwise she'd be up all night fretting.

"How do you feel about all that?" Zoe asked. "Last time Cruz and I got together there were punches thrown—all of them yours."

Brady scowled. "That was different. You were young, and I didn't know he was serious about you."

"I was nineteen, and you didn't exactly give us a chance to explain."

"Guilty as charged. But in my defense, it didn't exactly look innocent."

She thought back to that moonlit night, memories of their stolen moments warming her from the inside out. "I'll give you that."

"Cruz and I are square. He was such a sad sack after you left I couldn't help but take pity on him."

Zoe realized it had grown quiet in the kitchen. "Gracie . . . ," she called. "Up to bed now."

Her daughter scampered in and gave Brady one last hug before heading up the stairs.

"I'll be up in a minute," Zoe said.

Brady watched her go, a reflective look on his face. "You know, maybe God brought you back to Copper Creek for a bigger purpose than just the orchard, Zoe." His eyes pierced hers. "You ever think about that?"

She'd thought about it all day. Could she and Cruz and Zoe become a family? It was a little early to be thinking like that. And maybe just a little too scary.

"I sure hope so," she said. "Because the orchard's future is looking pretty darn bleak."

"Any word from the deputy?"

"Not yet. And frankly I've been too busy trying to make a plan that doesn't leave me thousands of dollars in debt with no hope of recovering to fret about what caused the fire."

Had it only been last night her barn had burnt to the ground? The smoky taste in her mouth said yes, but the hours seemed to have passed at warp speed.

Brady leaned forward, hands clasped between his knees. "Listen, Zoe, I've been thinking. I want you to take my new building and use it as your market."

Her body went rigid. "What? No. Absolutely not."

"Just temporarily. Look, it's already up and ready to go. All you'd have to do is—"

"Brady, I will not take your building! You've been working toward this for a long time. Just because I squandered away my portion of the inheritance doesn't mean you have to lose yours too."

"You didn't squander your inheritance. And I'm not losing anything. Calm down and hear me out. It makes sense. The location's perfect—right down the road, on the other side of the orchard. It's all ready to go—"

"For *you* to move into."

"Hush. It's only temporary, just to get you through Peach Fest. Soon as you get the insurance money you can rebuild the barn. I'll move into my new building, and all will be well."

Zoe could only stare at him.

This was his dream. He'd saved for that building for years before inheriting Granny's money. And now when he was finally on the doorstep of realizing it—he was loaning it to her.

She hadn't exactly been the ideal sister. She'd all but abandoned him when she'd run off with

Kyle. Her eyes burned, and she quickly looked down to where her fingers played at the seam of her jeans.

"I want to do this," he said.

Her chest tightened to the point of pain. She looked up at him, tears and all. "I don't deserve it."

One side of his lip curled up. "You're my little sis. I'm supposed to take care of you. And I kind of blew it back about five years ago. If it weren't for me things probably would've worked out between you and Cruz."

"That was not your fault."

"I didn't help matters." He reached for her hand. "Come on. Let me do this. We can get you up and going by Peach Fest. I may not own it, but I want Granny's orchard to make it as much as you do. She loved this land."

A tingling spread through her chest at the thought of his sacrifice. "Are you sure, Brady? It's an awful lot."

He squeezed her hand. "I'm sure. I won't take no for an answer. And you know I can be as stubborn as you."

She gave a few hard blinks. Life sure could turn on a dime. This—family being family—was the kind of thing that made it all worthwhile.

"All right, brother. Let's do it."

chapter thirty-four

Cruz emptied his bag into the bin and made his way back to the tree where Zoe was two rungs up on a ladder. He took a moment to appreciate the fit of her jeans as he adjusted the thick strap of the bag that wrapped around his neck.

It was a good morning for peach picking. The air was still cool, and the sun hadn't quite burned off the morning fog. The smell of dew and earth hung heavily in the air. His men moved through the orchard, filling their bags, gently dumping them in the plastic bins lining the flatbed truck. Some whistled, others wore earbuds, and still others murmured in low voices.

He reached for a low-hanging peach and twisted. It snapped free from the twig, and he placed it carefully in the bag. Keeping handling damage low was always priority one during harvest.

The ground color on the ripe freestone peaches was yellow, but they had a nice red blush and had sized well. They were slightly tender, and he knew for a fact they were sweet to the taste. From the field the fruit would go to the packing house where they'd be hydro-cooled to slow down ripening and maximize shelf life. Some of the harvest would then go to market, some to Zoe's store, either whole or baked into a pie or strudel.

On the other side of the tree, twigs snapped as Zoe freed the higher hanging peaches.

"You sure you don't have better things to do?" he asked. Her grand opening was just one week from today.

She'd been busy the past week reordering merchandise and getting Brady's building set up for temporary sales. They hadn't seen as much of each other as he would've liked.

"I'm sure. Not much I can do until merchandise starts arriving. Miss Ruby's baking up a storm. The house smells like temptation on a stick."

"I'd be happy to offer my services as chief sampler."

"Funny, you're not the first to offer. I'm afraid I've sampled more than my fair share. Good thing I'm burning off a lot of calories these days."

His gaze cut over to her legs, the only part of her he could see through the tree. "Your figure looks fine to me."

She stepped down from the ladder, hitching a brow. "Just 'fine'?"

He winked. "Well, maybe better than fine, but I wouldn't want it to go to your head."

She pursed her lips. "Humph."

He smiled as she tossed her chin and headed to the flatbed.

"Did I tell you I decided to brand Granny's baked goods?" she asked when she returned a few moments later.

"No, you didn't. That's a great idea."

Her auburn hair was pulled back, exposing the tender flesh of her neck. A tempting sight. And since they were hidden from the rest of the crew by the low hanging branches . . .

He pulled off his bag and trapped her, one foot a step up the ladder.

She turned carefully, eye level with him. "I'm calling them Granny Nel's Baked Goods."

He eased closer. She smelled sweet, like the peaches they were picking, and he was suddenly desperate for a taste. "Oh yeah?"

"A couple of the local stores are going to carry them. Goudeman's, Mercer's . . . Daisy's drawing up a logo for me."

He pressed a kiss to the cradle of her neck and shoulder. It was just as soft as he remembered, slightly warm from the sun. Delectable.

Her shoulder rose, and she giggled as he hit a ticklish spot. "Are you even listening to me?"

He placed a series of kisses. "Branding . . . Granny Nel . . . stores and . . . something else."

"I didn't come out here to serve as a distraction," she said, but her arms had curled around his neck.

"Not your fault. You can't help it."

She chuckled. "So generous."

"I'm a generous guy." His lips found hers, teasing and playing until her smile was long gone, her laughter a dull memory.

Zoe wove her fingers into the hair at the nape of Cruz's neck. It was warm from the sun and soft. Nearly as soft as his lips.

He deepened the kiss until Zoe forgot where she was. What she'd been thinking. Everything but the feel of his hands pressing into her back. The smell of his spicy soap weaving around her. The taste of his mouth, hot and hungry on hers.

It was a dream. Like coming home where she belonged. How had she forgotten this? How had she ever settled for Kyle after what she'd had with Cruz? The relationship had been a pale imitation.

His fingers threaded into her hair, making tingles shoot down her limbs. Her body thrummed with delight, every cell alive and pulsing with energy. What he did to her.

Somewhere in the distance—in another world—a throat cleared.

Cruz drew back, and the coolness of the morning pressed in, chilling her. Zoe wobbled, and he steadied her on the ladder's rung.

She followed his gaze to Deputy Mosley, who was standing a car's length away in his tan-and-brown uniform, shifting awkwardly. He pushed his frameless glasses up his nose.

"Howdy, deputy," Cruz said, clearly having more faculties than Zoe at the moment.

"Sorry to interrupt your morning." His white

mustache twitched as he hitched his pants up to his belly.

Zoe stepped down from the ladder. "You're out and about early. Do you have word about what caused the fire?"

"I do." He tugged his hat down. "According to the investigator the fire was definitely caused by an accelerant."

Zoe traded a look with Cruz, her stomach sinking. "Like . . . like maybe a cigarette?"

"More like gasoline."

"What?" Her legs wobbled beneath her, her breath suddenly trapped in her throat. "You mean someone set it on purpose?"

"Are you sure?" Cruz asked.

" 'Fraid so. The fire originated at a point near the rear window. There was a large rock in the ashes, likely tossed through the window with a gasoline-soaked rag. Burn patterns and other factors corroborate the point of origin. It's an open-and-shut case."

"But . . . but who would do something like that?"

"That's what we'll be trying to figure out. Arson cases pretty much revolve around opportunity and motive since the evidence tends to get burned up." Deputy Mosley drilled her with a look. "Is there anyone you've had words with, Zoe? Someone who'd be wishing you ill?"

"I—" She glanced at Cruz. A shadow flickered in his jaw. "No. Not that I can think of."

"Is the building insured?" Deputy Mosley asked.

"Why, of course. They knew of the renovations. I had to get a building permit."

"I have to ask . . . Are you the beneficiary?"

"I—" Her gaze sharpened on Deputy Mosley. "Wait a minute. You're not thinking—"

"Come on, Deputy." Cruz shelved his hands on his hips. "That's ridiculous. Zoe's been working her butt off trying to get this market ready in time for Peach Fest. She was depending on it."

Deputy Mosley lifted his shoulders, looking somewhat sheepish. "I've been a friend of your family for years, Zoe, and I'm trying to help. But the fact is, you stand to come into some money, and it's no secret harvest is down this year. Unless you can think of someone else who'd do this, this is probably the direction the sheriff's going to go. That's why you need to be thinking about who else might've done this."

Cruz nailed Zoe with a look. "What about Kyle?"

"He-he's in Nashville."

"Is he? How do you know that?"

"Kyle Jimmerson?" the deputy asked. "What's he got to do with all this?"

"He wants Zoe back, that's what," Cruz said.

Mosley's eyes sharpened on Zoe. "That true?"

"I reckon so . . . yes." Zoe folded her arms over her chest. "He's been trying to get me to rejoin the band." But he wouldn't do anything like this. Would he?

Cruz gave her a pointed look. "He's been sending her flowers and harassing her with phone calls and texts."

Zoe palmed her throat. "Harassing is a bit strong, maybe."

Cruz gave her a look. *Whose side are you on?*

"I just can't believe he'd go this far."

"He hit you, Zoe—have you forgotten that already?" Cruz's eyes swung to the deputy. "We called in the assault from the Rusty Nail."

"I remember the report. Well. That's certainly a place to start. We'll definitely look into it."

"How long will that take?" Zoe asked. She needed that check.

"Shouldn't take long. In the meantime, if you think of anything else that might be helpful, let me know." He left his card, tipped his hat, and said good-bye.

When the hum of his engine started in the distance, Cruz pinned Zoe with a look. "I knew that guy was bad news."

She didn't want to believe it of Kyle. Even now, when it would absolve her. But what would happen if there was no evidence against him? Would they find her guilty of a crime she hadn't committed?

"Hey . . . come here." Cruz framed her face with his work-roughened hands. "It's going to be all right. If Kyle did it, they'll figure it out."

"I hope you're right."

chapter thirty-five

"Everybody's staring at me." Zoe lowered her fork and washed her pancakes down with a glass of ice water.

"Let them look," Cruz said. "You've got nothing to hide."

Saturday at the diner was crowded with neighbors and a sprinkling of tourists. The savory smells of bacon and omelets that had welcomed her through the doors now made her stomach turn.

Dorothy Winslow tossed a look over her bony shoulder. She sat with two other ladies from the auxiliary. In a nearby booth Allison Blevins, one of Cruz's old flames, sat with her folks, stealing glances every few minutes.

She didn't know why the speed of the town grapevine surprised her. She'd sure provided her share of gossip lately, what with the ruckus at the Rusty Nail and the revelation of Gracie's paternity. Then again, it seemed she'd always given the residents of Copper Creek something to talk about.

"More pancakes, Mama." Gracie eyed Zoe's plate.

Zoe forked a silver dollar pancake onto her daughter's plate and wiped a dot of syrup from her chin.

She lowered her voice for Cruz's ears only. "Everybody's staring. What if they think I really did it?"

"Nobody believes that. You're well loved here." He covered her hand with his. "This'll pass soon enough."

Her gaze flickered to his hand. "Do you know what the penalty for arson is?"

"Stop looking things up on the Internet. They're going to get Kyle."

"If it even was him. If they can't find who really did this I could get jail time, Cruz, on top of a fine, not to mention a nice criminal record to go along with it."

He squeezed her hand. "Hey. You're getting way ahead of yourself. Give the sheriff's office a chance to get to the bottom of it."

"And in the meantime, what? Just forget all the drama that seems to follow me around like a bad smell?"

"In the meantime, get your store up and running. We've got a bunch to do before the grand opening. Now let's get the check and get out of here. Take Gracie to the park for a few minutes."

Gracie perked up, pushing back her plate. "I'm done!" she said around a mouthful of pancake.

Cruz made quick work of the bill, and minutes later they spilled out into the late morning. The sun glimmered overhead, and the humidity stole her breath and seeped into her clothing. They clasped Gracie's hands between them and started up the sidewalk toward Murphy's Park, named for the man who settled the town back in 1832.

As they walked, they lifted Gracie between them. She squealed with delight as she swung above the sidewalk.

Zoe's arm was tiring by the time they hit the center of town. "All right, all right!" Zoe said, laughing. "Mama's getting too old for this."

As they passed the storefronts a glass door opened, and Zoe's dad stepped out from his law office. He stopped, blocking their path, and his shrewd eyes quickly took in the trio.

"Well. Isn't this a pretty picture." Dressed in a suit and tie, he exuded the kind of confidence and power that made Zoe want to either shrink ten sizes or toss her chin in the air.

She opted for the latter. "Hi, Daddy."

She resisted the urge to tame her frizzy curls or tuck in her shirt as his eyes roved over her.

Cruz gave a nod. "Mr. Collins. What are you up to this morning?"

"Working." He fixed Zoe with a look. "As maybe you should be too. Sounds as though you've had quite the week. It's too bad about your barn."

Cruz stiffened beside her. "Your daughter nearly died in a fire this week, sir."

Her dad looked Cruz up and down, clearly

sizing him up and finding him wanting. "I've heard all about it." He turned that look on Zoe. "If there's anything you excel at, Zoe, it's keeping the tongues wagging around here. You've made an art form of it."

Cruz stepped in front of Zoe. "Now, listen here—"

"No, you listen. My relationship with my daughter is none of your business. Never was, never will be." He drilled Zoe with a look. "You should've taken me up on my offer. Don't come to me for help. You got yourself into this mess. Get yourself out."

He spun toward his Mercedes, the soles of his dress shoes grinding the pebbles into the sidewalk. He tossed his briefcase inside, started the car, and pulled from the diagonal slot.

At his departure all the fight seemed to drain from Zoe in one long exhale. She didn't realize she was shaking until Cruz grabbed her hand.

"Come on." He tugged her forward. "You okay?"

"Sure."

She could feel his gaze on her for a long moment. "Liar."

She tossed him a wobbly smile. Her dad made her feel so incapable. Like she was nothing but one big disappointment. And she had made a wreck of her life, hadn't she? She'd gotten pregnant at nineteen, failed to inform the baby's daddy, run off with a man who was at best a mean person, at worst an abusive narcissist. She shook her head. What was wrong with her? Why on earth couldn't she do anything right?

"Hey . . . ," Cruz said.

She looked at him, the tenderness in his brown eyes instantly soothing her ragged spirits. She allowed herself to soak up the warmth for a long moment.

"I'll never make him happy. I'm nothing but a disappointment to him."

"It's not your job to make him happy."

She thought of Cruz's dad, completely absent from his life. "I'm sorry. I shouldn't complain about my dad when yours—"

He squeezed her hand. "Your hurt is my hurt."

Still, at least her dad had been there. He hadn't abandoned her. He'd provided a roof over her head and more advantages than most children had. "I'll keep trying. Maybe someday he'll come around."

"If he doesn't, it's his loss. You're an amazing woman, Zoe. You're smart and hardworking, and you're a great mom."

Gracie moved to Zoe's other side, taking her hand. A frown flattened her brows. "Mama . . . I don't like Papaw."

Zoe floundered for the right thing to say. Should she scold her daughter for being unkind? But she'd only been stating her feelings. And how many times had Zoe thought the very same thing?

Before she could decide, the park came into view at the end of town. The playground equipment crouched on the shady mound of grass.

"Race you to the swings, Bella . . . ," Cruz called, taking off at a slow jog.

Gracie ran after him. "Wait for me, Daddy! Wait for me!"

The corner of Zoe's lips turned up at her daughter's excitement. At the sight of the two of them running toward the park. Her daughter had a good daddy. One who'd accept her as she was and give her a solid sense of confidence. It gave her hope. And that was the very thing she needed most right now.

⇒••⇐

Cruz gave Gracie a push on the swing. "Pump with your legs. That's it. Look at you go."

"Higher!"

"Say *más alto*."

"Massado!"

He chuckled. "Close enough." He gave her another push.

Gracie leaned back, her little legs extended, then leaned forward at the peak, tucking her legs under her. The chains squeaked rhythmically.

"Massado, Daddy!" she called a moment later.

"That's high enough. You're going to flip right over the swing set."

Gracie giggled. The wind blew her hair back as she sailed forward. Her little legs worked hard. One of her shoelaces flapped in the breeze. He'd already braved the high slide with her and pushed her and Zoe on the merry-go-round until Zoe got sick to her stomach.

He glanced over at Zoe, who'd parked herself on a green bench under a broad oak tree. She'd been quiet since the run-in with her dad, and who could blame her? The man had a way of making a person feel small. Cruz used to resent not having a dad of his own. But after seeing what Zoe's dad was like, he wondered if no dad at all was better than a bad one.

He was going to be a good father for Gracie. He was going to be the kind of father he wished he'd had. The kind Zoe had deserved.

He looked at her, sitting on the bench with her shoulders slumped, her chin tucked.

He gave Gracie one last push. "Keep up the good work, Bella. I'm going to go sit with your mom."

"Okay," Gracie said. "Mama! Look how high I can go!"

Zoe smiled. "You're such a big girl."

Cruz admired the graceful curve of Zoe's neck as he approached the bench. She'd pulled her hair back in a ponytail today, and he loved the creamy perfection of her skin against her red hair.

Good job, God.

"Feeling better?" he asked.

"Yeah. I guess I'm done with the round-and-round thing."

"We all have to grow up sometime." He sank onto the bench beside her, setting an arm around her.

The shade felt good, and the breeze felt even better. Leaves fluttered overhead, and somewhere in the branches a robin tweeted. The smell of lilacs and cut grass permeated the air.

"What are you thinking about over here, all quiet?" He tugged her closer, loving the way she felt, all nestled into his side.

She gave him a sideways look. "All the girls you've dated."

He blinked at her. That wasn't at all what he'd expected. "You say that like there've been a lot."

"Well, I may have been gone awhile, but I hear things, you know." She set her hand on his leg. "So were any of them . . . you know. Serious?"

His lips quirked. "Not really, no."

She bit her lip, and he watched the plump pink flesh go white. Wanted to soothe the spot—but maybe now wasn't the time. She clearly had other things on her mind.

"So . . . this Daphne person," she said. "I don't think I know her."

He sighed. It appeared they were going to do this. He wasn't sure why she needed to know about his past. Heaven knew, he didn't want to know a single detail about her and Kyle.

"She's a bank teller from Dalton. We dated for several months last year."

"I hear she's quite the looker."

"Not as pretty as you."

Zoe smirked at his pat, though very true, answer. He ran his fingers down the back of her neck, to that little spot in the cradle of her shoulder, just begging for a kiss. His lips tingled with want.

"So what went wrong between you?" she asked. "Why'd you part ways?"

"I broke up with her. She—I don't know. We didn't have much in common, I guess."

"I guess . . . ?"

When he failed to fill in the blanks, she moved on. "Okay, what about Sarah McAllister?"

Sarah was a kindergarten teacher at Copper Creek Elementary. She was a kindhearted and warm woman who was now married to Derek from the hardware store.

Cruz toyed with a strand of hair that hadn't quite made it into the ponytail. What he really wanted to do was kiss her silly and make her forget all the women he'd ever dated—just as he had.

But she pressed on. "Sarah . . ."

"We dated a while. I don't know . . . eight months maybe." He gave Zoe a look. "And I broke up with her because she was talking about how many kids we were going to have and where we were going to live, and I just wasn't ready for all that."

"Typical male. Okay . . . and Allison Blevins."

Ah, that's what had started all this. He'd spotted Allison at the diner. "We went out for maybe a year. It was pretty casual for a long while."

"And then what happened? What was wrong with Allison?"

He sighed hard, then turned her in his arms, his gaze sharpening on hers. "You really want to know what was wrong with Allison Blevins? She wasn't *you*. And Sarah McAllister? She wasn't you. And Daphne Stevens?"

"She wasn't me?"

"No . . . She was a Gators fan."

Zoe jabbed an elbow in his gut, and he grunted, chuckling until a smile curled her lips.

But there was nothing funny about the vulnerable longing in her green eyes, the wistful look on her face. Her father had planted so many insecurities in her by knocking down her ideas and making her feel incapable. The insecurities went core-deep, and he wanted nothing more than to assure her of her value.

He cupped her face, looking at her with all the intensity in his heart until her smile was long gone.

"When you left back then I was devastated,

Zoe. I'm not saying that to make you feel bad," he added when she winced. "Maybe that was the journey God needed us to take to fully appreciate *this*." He stroked her cheeks with his thumbs. "But when you left, you took my heart with you. Every woman I've dated since has just been a placeholder for you."

She gasped as her eyes went glossy. "Oh, Cruz. Leaving you was the most painful thing I've ever done. But when you believed the worst of me, I just kind of snapped. All my fears of being a disappointment surfaced. All the times Daddy expected me to fail, all the times he looked at me like I was his life's biggest disappointment—it just made me wither up inside."

"I'm sorry I fell for Kyle's lies. I should've heard you out. Believed in you. I think it's fair to say we both have issues we're working through. Let's do it together."

Her lips curved. "I like the sound of that."

"You're still mi leona. Always have been. Always will be."

She huffed. "More like a mouse."

"Mi leona," he said firmly before pressing a kiss to her cheek where a tear had tumbled down. He pressed another to the corner of her lips, then finally soothed that spot she'd bitten earlier.

Her lips were soft and pliant as she slid her arms around his waist and pressed closer. He could hardly believe she was back in his arms again. His. It had been a rough few years, but so worth the journey. He'd never stopped loving her, he realized, the thought hitting him like an avalanche.

A childish laugh floated through the fog of his thoughts. "Daddy! You're kissing Mama!"

Zoe's lips curved against his. "Yeah, Daddy," she said in a throaty whisper.

He turned and watched their daughter scamper through the high grass toward them, her curls flying behind her, her mama's smile stretching across her face.

"Kiss me too!" Gracie said as she flew into their arms, puckering her rosebud lips.

Zoe kissed her daughter with a loud smack, and Cruz followed suit.

"My two favorite girls." His heart was so full of joy his eyes stung with emotion, and his throat tightened around the words. He was never letting them go.

chapter thirty-six

Brady's new steel building was red with white trim, reminiscent of the barn he'd started his business in. It sat in the back corner of his property, conveniently located a stone's throw from the front door of his farmhouse.

Zoe adored the high-ceilinged front porch, which gave the building a cozy feel. She'd placed barrels along the wall, which she planned to fill with sale items. The interior was wide open with a shiny gray concrete floor and only an office and small restroom partitioned off at the back.

Zoe unpacked the last of the Georgia mugs, lining them up neatly on the shelves near the used cash register. There was no bakery case for the baked goods. That would have to wait until she rebuilt the barn—if the insurance money ever came through.

"Where do the bags of peanuts go?" Hope asked.

"Over by the jams and jellies."

She'd had a lot of help getting the shelves up and the merchandise unpacked. Brady had taken off more time than he could probably afford, as had Hope and Cruz. Miss Ruby had put in extra time watching Gracie. With Peach Fest only two days away, Zoe was grateful for the extra help.

Other neighbors had pitched in too, offering discounted produce and promising to tell all their friends about her grand opening. The Peach Barn was even trending locally on social media sites. It felt good to be a part of a real community again.

They still had a lot left to unpack and arrange, and she was going to lose Brady's help any minute. His ex-wife had been due to drop off baby Sam over an hour ago. Zoe was getting bonus time out of him as it was.

She might have to call in reinforcements. She'd hired a local girl named Ava who lived at the Hope House, a place for girls who were orphaned or had unfit parents. She seemed very responsible, and Zoe felt the girl needed someone to give her a chance. She'd also hired the wife of one of Cruz's laborers.

Zoe put her hands on her hips and surveyed the space. It seemed a little empty after the close confines of her barn, but it would work nicely. The building was well lit with fluorescent lighting and carried the "new" smell.

Out near the road Brady had installed the large sign she'd had made. *The Peach Barn*, it stated in large red letters. The building was a long way down the gravel drive, but she didn't think the little jaunt would deter too many people.

She'd borrowed tables from church, and tomorrow the baskets for the peaches would arrive—fingers crossed. It would take all day to arrange and label all the varieties. The baked goods would go last. The Peach Barn was almost ready. A nervous knot tightened in her stomach. Now if only people would show up.

Cruz hauled in a box from Zoe's car. He looked so appealing in his white T-shirt and soft-worn denim. His biceps bulged under the weight of the box. She was half tempted to grab him and plant one on those supple lips of his.

He set the box near the register and glanced up at her, doing a double take as he honed in on her face. No doubt reading her mind.

A flicker of male appreciation appeared, and his eyes became hooded. "Are you ogling me, Zoe Collins?" he asked softly.

She cocked an eyebrow. "Maybe."

"Like what you see?"

"Oh, definitely."

"I missed you last night."

Hope dumped her empty box into the nearby pile. "Oh, my gosh. I'm drowning in pheromones. Just kiss her already."

"Where do the magnets go?" Brady asked as he entered the building.

"Get out while you can," Hope said.

Zoe couldn't tear her eyes from Cruz's. She forgot about the mugs and the magnets and the peanuts. Was she supposed to be working on something? What was her name again?

"Oh, geez," Brady said. "Can you two please wait till we're done to make cow eyes at each other?"

"Oh, Brady," Hope said with dramatic Southern flair. "I do declare you're the most handsome man I ever met. I'm so sweet on you I'm fairly swooning."

Cruz's lips twitched. "I think they're making fun of us."

"They're just jealous."

"I don't blame them," Cruz said, stepping closer. "I'd be jealous of us too."

"Well, you are the most handsome man ever."

"And I'm definitely swooning." The rough texture of his voice made her heart roll over as he palmed her cheek.

"Ugh," Brady said, turning away.

"There's a bathroom in the corner if you need to barf," Hope said helpfully.

"I guess I should be grateful my stomach's empty."

"Mine too. Wanna grab lunch at the diner?"

"Sure, if Audrey ever shows up."

A shuffle sounded at the door, finally drawing Zoe's eyes from Cruz. Deputy Mosley entered, his gaze sweeping the interior space.

All the pheromones seemed to evaporate on the spot.

"Well, this is certainly coming along nicely," the deputy said.

Zoe stepped toward him, something in his expression making her stomach flutter with nerves. "We've been working hard to get it open by Peach Fest. Do you have news for me?"

Deputy Mosley took in the others. "Maybe we should have a private word."

Zoe shook her head. "This is my family. They'll be the first to hear whatever you tell me anyway."

"All right." He gave a nod, his eyes sliding briefly to Cruz. "Maybe that's for the best. I'm afraid Kyle's alibi checked out. His band was performing that night in Huntsville."

"How late did the show go?" Cruz asked.

"Past midnight. No chance he could've made it here in time to set the fire."

"He has friends here in town who could've done it for him," Brady said.

"Checked into that already. Pete Townsend and Devon Brooks were playing poker with some buddies."

Zoe hated to mention Axel since he was Miss Ruby's nephew, but he was also a good friend of Kyle's. "What about Axel Brown?"

"I checked with him too," the deputy said. "He said he was in bed with his wife, and she corroborates."

"What about Garret Morgan?" Cruz said.

"We've been unable to reach him so far. He's away on a camping trip."

"Sounds pretty convenient to me," Cruz said.

"Garret's sister said he'd been planning the trip for months. We'll reach him soon enough. But his sister said he left the day before the fire."

"You can't just take her word for it," Hope said.

He held up a hand. "We'll check into it."

"If Axel's wife was asleep, how would she know if he slipped out?" Cruz said.

"Well, there's always that possibility. But we have nothing linking him to the crime, and he stood to gain nothing from the fire personally."

Cruz stiffened beside Zoe. "As opposed to Zoe."

Deputy Mosley's eyes shifted to Zoe. "Out of respect for your family I'm probably telling you more than I should." His eyes flittered around the building. "But it's striking the sheriff as awfully convenient you have this building just waiting in the wings."

Zoe's breath left in a rush.

A scowl darkened Brady's face. "It's only temporary. Everyone knows this building is for my business."

Cruz stepped forward. "Why on earth would she have invested all that time and money into the barn if she only planned to burn it down?"

"Besides," Zoe said, "I was on the phone most of the evening with Daisy Pendleton. She was helping me with some business stuff."

Mosley's eyes were apologetic. "It doesn't look good that you were the first one on the scene, Zoe."

"Well, for heaven's sake, the barn's on my property."

"I had to drag her out of there. She suffered from smoke inhalation, for crying out loud."

"Making you the second person on the scene. I need to ask where you were before the fire broke out, Cruz."

"Hey!" Zoe said. "He did not do this."

"I was at the Rusty Nail with this guy." Cruz gestured to Brady.

"He was," Brady said. "A dozen people would corroborate that."

"The direct route from the Rusty Nail to your place is down Old Mill Road. Mind if I ask what were you doing out this way so late?"

A flush climbed Cruz's neck. "I just wanted to check on the barn. Make sure it was locked up tight."

"Because . . . ?"

"One of the contractors left it open once. I just wanted to double-check it on my way home."

"The problem is it wouldn't have taken long to throw a rock through the window."

"This is ridiculous," Zoe said. "All this for a little insurance money? If that's what I was after I could've torched the house."

Deputy Mosley nodded. "I hear you. And I'm sorry to be here under these circumstances, Zoe. I just stopped by to catch you up on things. I have to be running, but if you think of anything that might be helpful in the investigation, let me know." He tipped his hat and then he was gone.

Zoe didn't realize she was shaking until he'd left. Her legs seemed made of jelly. She sank onto a half barrel near the wall. This was going from bad to worse. Now they suspected Cruz too?

She met his stormy eyes as he approached. "I'm so sorry. I can't believe this is happening."

He came behind her and rubbed her shoulders. "It's going to be all right. We both know we didn't do it. The truth will prevail."

"He's right," Hope said. "It'll sort itself out."

"I'll bet it was Garret," Brady said. "Camping trip, my rear end. He's in cahoots with Kyle."

"I think you're right," Zoe said. "Or maybe Axel slipped out of bed without his wife knowing, or Pete and Devon's poker partners are covering for them."

"Any way you slice it, Kyle's at the bottom of this mess," Cruz said. "I guarantee it."

"I think we're all in agreement about that," Hope said.

Zoe leaned back into Cruz's chest, hating the feeling of adrenaline shooting through her system. "But what if the sheriff doesn't look too hard for another culprit?" She turned and met Cruz's gaze. "What if we both end up charged with this?"

He squeezed her shoulders. "That is not going to happen."

But the heaviness in her stomach told a much different story.

The quiet moment was interrupted by someone's phone.

Brady reached into his pocket. "Finally she bothers to call. Better not be canceling."

He checked the screen and frowned. "Hello?" Ridges deepened between his brows. "Yes, this is Brady Collins." He went still as he listened, staring off into the distance. Then his head jerked back. His eyes widened and his lips slackened, disbelief etched on the sharp planes of his face. Fear flickered in his eyes. "What about Sam? Where's my son?"

A shiver of dread chased up Zoe's spine. Cruz's hands tightened on her shoulders.

Brady ran a hand over his face. His shoulders rose and fell with his rapid breaths.

Zoe had never seen him look so shocked, so distraught. She got up and went over to him, needing to be nearby.

He met her gaze, giving nothing away as he listened for what seemed like forever. She wished she could decipher more from his end of the conversation, but he was doing all the listening.

Finally he spoke. "Yeah. Of course. I'll be right there."

"What happened?" Zoe demanded, the second he turned off the phone. Hope and Cruz had come to stand nearby too.

Brady looked around frantically. Felt his pockets. "I have to go. Where are my keys?"

"You laid them on the counter," Hope said.

"Wait." Zoe grabbed his arm. "What happened? Is Sammy all right?"

"He's fine, I think. He's at the hospital in Dalton. That was the Whitfield County Sheriff's office. Audrey had an accident." His eyes pierced Zoe's, giving his head a shake of disbelief. "She's dead."

Hope sucked in her breath.

"Oh, no." Zoe tightened her grip on Brady's arm. She'd been no fan of Audrey after what she'd done to Brady. None of them were. But baby Sam had just lost his mama. Her eyes burned at the thought.

"Audrey's parents and sister are away on a trip. They want me to come and identify her remains."

Zoe's heart sank. "Oh, Brady, I'm so sorry."

"I have to go." Brady dashed toward his keys.

"I'll go with you," Zoe said.

Hope went for her purse. "We all will."

Brady grabbed his keys off the counter. "No, guys. There's nothing you can do. You have too much to do here."

"I don't care," Zoe said.

"Well, I do," Brady said.

"You're shaking," Cruz said. "Let me drive."

"No." Hope looked between Cruz and Zoe. "I got this. You guys stay put and finish. I'll drive Brady to Dalton."

"You don't have to—"

"Hush." Hope shouldered her purse, her chin notching up. "I'm going, and there's nothing you can say to stop me."

Brady paused a moment on the threshold, his eyes still a little dazed. "All right," he said after a moment. "Let's go."

chapter thirty-seven

Zoe was dragging her fingers through her damp curls when a knock sounded at the door.

"Miss Ruby," she called down the steps. "Can you get that please?"

Zoe had overslept this morning and felt frantic from the moment she opened her eyes. She'd been up late talking to Brady on the phone. They'd checked Sammy over at the hospital in Dalton, and he was fine. He'd been safely fastened in his car seat, and the impact had been on the driver's side.

Zoe's mind spun with all that was happening. With Brady and with the arson investigation and with the rapidly approaching grand opening.

A knock sounded again.

"I've got it!" Miss Ruby called up the stairs.

Thank God for that woman. Zoe didn't know how she would've gotten through the past couple months without her. The smell of something sweet and yummy drifted up the stairs. Peach crisp, she guessed by the hint of cinnamon. It was increasingly difficult to stay out of all the baked goodies.

She'd left Gracie downstairs in the kitchen, having a bowl of cereal. Zoe felt a pang of guilt. She hadn't spent as much time with her daughter lately as she wanted to. Things would calm down after Peach Fest. She'd have more time then.

If you don't end up in the county jail.

She shook off the dark feeling that rose inside. Absurd. She couldn't be convicted of a crime she didn't do. That didn't happen, did it?

She thought of all the *20/20* programs she'd watched where just such a conviction—and worse—had happened to innocent people just like her.

Please, God. Let the truth come out. Gracie needs me.

Zoe gave up on her unruly hair. She was sweeping it up into a ponytail when the stairs outside the bathroom squeaked.

Miss Ruby approached, her warm smile nowhere to be seen. Her cloud of white hair was like a halo around her face.

Zoe lowered the brush. "What's wrong?"

"It's Deputy Mosley," Miss Ruby whispered. "He wants a word with you."

Just what she needed. Zoe's stomach rolled, and she swallowed hard. What if he was here to arrest her? What if he handcuffed her, read her her rights, and carted her off right in front of her daughter?

Her heart took off in a sprint, but she forced a smile. Miss Ruby looked nervous enough for the both of them. "Tell him I'll be right down."

⇒•⇐

The deputy was standing by the front door when Zoe came down the stairs a moment later. She'd asked Miss Ruby to keep Gracie in the kitchen just in case this wasn't a friendly visit. Her legs wobbled like stilts as she took the last step.

Her chin automatically thrust upward. "Deputy Mosley." She was glad her tone came out strong.

He pushed his wireless glasses up his nose. "Zoe. Sorry to disturb you so early this morning. And I was sorry to hear about Audrey. How's Brady holding up?"

Didn't sound like a man about to make an arrest. She allowed herself a breath. "He's in a bit of shock, I think."

"Understandable. I'm real sorry for his son."

"Thank you. We all are." Zoe shifted. "Well, I'm sure you didn't come to talk about that. Do you have news? Did you get hold of Garret?"

"Maybe we could have a seat?"

Her cheeks warmed. "Of course. "

Her grandmother would roll over in her grave at her appalling manners. Even if he did seem more foe than friend at the moment, she'd known the deputy all her life. He'd even been invited over for Sunday supper when she was younger.

"Would you like some coffee?"

He sank onto the center of the sofa, removing his hat. "No thanks. I've already reached my caffeine quota for the morning."

Zoe took the armchair, unable to do anything but perch on its edge. She tucked her hands under her thighs.

"I'll get right to it, Zoe. The phone records did corroborate your statement. You spoke with Daisy from 10:47 to 11:57. Since your 911 call was made at 12:02, there wasn't adequate time to set a fire."

She released a breath and took a second to feel the pleasure of vindication. "Why, of course not. I tried to tell you that. You've known me since I was in diapers, Deputy."

A flush rose in his neck. "I'm just trying to do my job, Zoe. The sheriff's office has to do its investigation, and it hasn't gone unnoticed that you've caused a scuffle or two in your day."

"So I set off fireworks on the bridge a couple times and got a couple speeding tickets. I was only a teenager. Hardly a hardened criminal, Deputy." She threw her hands up.

He held his hand up, palm out. "I'm not here to dig up your past, Zoe. I hate that I have to be here at all."

"I had nothing to do with this fire. For heaven's sake, I nearly died trying to put it out. Probably would've if Cruz hadn't dragged me out."

"I believe you. The extinguisher was found in the ashes."

Her shoulders sank a good two inches on her exhale. "Then why on earth are you here questioning me instead of chasing down Garret?"

"We've already spoken with Garret. He checked into a campsite in Tennessee the day before the fire."

"Well, that doesn't mean he couldn't have come back."

"It's over a four-hour drive. Highly unlikely he would've gone to all that effort. And we confirmed his reservation had been made two months ago. Zoe, I need to talk to you about Cruz."

She pressed her lips together. "You're wasting valuable time that could be spent chasing down the real culprit. Cruz did not start that fire."

"The sheriff wanted to bring you down for questioning, Zoe. But out of respect for your family, I'm trying to keep things casual."

Zoe huffed. She sure didn't want to add fuel to the fire—so to speak. "Fine."

"Cruz says he diverted his route to check on the barn. That it had been left unlocked in the past. Tell me about that."

"A framer I hired to help shore up the stairs left the barn unlocked one night. He said he forgot. His name is Allen Carlisle, and he's part of Merck Framing and Construction out of Ellijay. Feel free to contact him. I spoke with him about his negligence."

"That's helpful. I'll do that." The deputy planted his elbows on his knees. "It's no secret you and Cruz have gotten tight lately. Or that your orchard is limping along."

"We're having a hard year, as is every orchard in the area. It's hardly the first low-yield year. Besides which, it's not as bad as we'd feared.

And just because Garret was camping the day before the fire doesn't mean he couldn't have—"

"Zoe, you're grasping at straws here."

She had to make him understand. "Deputy, Kyle has been trying to get me to come back to him for both personal and professional reasons. He's been texting, sending flowers, calling . . . harassing me. The band is ready to sign with a label, and he wants me back, but I've refused. I made it clear I'm staying here and running the orchard. Kyle knows how critical the Peach Barn is in my plan to turn things around. He's the one responsible for the fire. He was sabotaging my efforts in order to get me to come back to him."

Interest flickered in the deputy's eyes. "Suppose that's true. Kyle and all his friends have an alibi. Can you think of anyone else who could've done it?"

"I don't know. Maybe he hired someone."

"We've subpoenaed his bank records. There's nothing suspicious there, Zoe."

"Well, maybe somebody's lying about an alibi."

"I'm afraid the sheriff has followed every other lead."

"Kyle's a very controlling man, and he doesn't like to lose. This is just the kind of thing he'd do. He was very angry about my rejection the last time we spoke."

"And when was that?"

Zoe winced inside. "A few weeks before the fire."

"It sounds like maybe he'd given up, then. Listen, Zoe. I know you don't want to think this way, but we have to look at the facts. Cruz was the first on the scene after you. It seems like an awful big coincidence that he came along so late at night, just as the barn was going up in flames."

"He did not do this. Kyle's the one who—"

"Kyle has an airtight alibi."

"So does Cruz! He was at the Rusty Nail with Brady."

"No one can pin down the exact time of his departure. It was somewhere between eleven thirty and twelve. But if it was closer to eleven thirty that allows enough time." He sighed, his hazel eyes piercing hers. "Zoe . . . just consider. It's not uncommon for an arsonist to stick around after setting a fire. Especially when the woman he's involved with is trying to—"

"All due respect, sir, you are barking up the wrong tree."

He held his hands out, palms out. "Just listen for a minute. Suppose Cruz had nothing but the best intentions. Perhaps he might even feel a bit responsible that the orchard isn't faring well. As the manager, there's quite a bit of weight on his shoulders, and he wants the best for you. Nobody doubts that."

"He's hardly at fault for the mild winter."

Deputy Mosley held out his hand again, and Zoe folded her arms, pressing her lips together. Fine. She'd appease him.

"Suppose he thought he'd help you out with a little insurance money to tide you over until next harvest."

"He knew I needed to get the market open by Peach Fest. We've both been working our rear ends off to get it ready in time."

"And he also knew Brady had a perfectly nice building waiting in the wings."

"And so he threw a rock through the window? With a gasoline-soaked rag? How stupid do you think he is?"

"It wouldn't be the first time an arsonist started—"

"Cruz is not an arsonist!"

He nailed her with a look for a painfully long moment. "Hear me out."

Zoe pressed her lips together. Locked her jaw. Clearly he was going to have to get all this nonsense out before he listened to a word she had to say.

"Imagine that he's just set a fire—in order to help, mind you. But before the fire could get out of control, you show up. You enter the building and don't come out. He starts to fear that you aren't coming out at all so he rushes in after you. He just wants the insurance money, he sure doesn't want you getting hurt.

"Just think for a minute. Would he really have

gone out of his way when he left the Rusty Nail that night? It was going on midnight. He had to be tired after a long day in the orchard. Does that make sense to you?"

"Yes, it does. He wanted to make sure it was locked up tight. He feels a high level of responsibility to this place."

Deputy Mosley tipped his head back, and she realized her mistake. "That's exactly what the sheriff is thinking."

Her mouth snapped shut. Everything he said made sense.

But Cruz wouldn't have done something so heinous, not even for her. That wasn't his style.

It sure was Kyle's though.

"Zoe . . . I don't believe you're at the bottom of this. But I can't prove you weren't in cahoots with Cruz, not even with the fire extinguisher. People do all kinds of crazy things to make themselves look innocent. You need to think long and hard here. Someone's going down for arson. It's a serious crime. We're talking about heavy fines and possible jail time. You're a single mother—think of Gracie."

Heat flushed through her body, and she gave him a flinty look. "You're pitting me against my boyfriend? The father of my child?"

"I didn't set the fire, Zoe. I'm only trying to get to the bottom of it. And I'm afraid you're the one with the most on the line."

chapter thirty-eight

Zoe was shaking by the time Deputy Mosley left the house. She tried to calm Miss Ruby's fears and put on a brave face for Gracie, but by the time she arrived at Brady's barn twenty minutes later the weight of the deputy's accusations had settled in her midsection like a cement block. She pounded her fist against her steering wheel.

God, this isn't fair! I didn't do anything wrong, and neither did Cruz! Kyle did, and he's going to get off scot-free.

Her eyes burned at the injustice of it. Regardless of what Deputy Mosley said, one thing was obvious. The sheriff had already reached a conclusion about the fire.

Cruz was going to get blamed for this, despite all her denials.

She couldn't let that happen. But what could she do? It was obvious to her that one of Kyle's cronies had set the fire. If only she could figure out who and get him to admit it. But none of them considered her a friend.

Distinct lines had been drawn that night at the Rusty Nail when Kyle hit her. They weren't going to throw their friend under the bus no matter what.

The hum of an approaching engine drew her from her thoughts, and she looked over to see

315

Hope swinging her red Civic into the adjoining space. Zoe had completely forgotten that her friend had offered to help her unpack and label all the peaches.

Hope came around to the open window at the driver's side of Zoe's car, the gravel crunching under her feet. As her eyes honed in on Zoe, her smile went flat.

"Are you all right?"

The stinging behind Zoe's eyes increased at the concern in Hope's voice. But first things first.

"How are Brady and Sammy?"

"They're doing okay, all things considered. Brady was pretty shaken up last night after identifying Audrey. He felt better once he had Sam safe and sound though."

"I don't know how he's going to manage his business and full-time parenthood."

"The same way you and every other single parent does, I guess. One day at a time. I told him I'd pitch in until he finds someone permanent. Others will too. Now, how 'bout you tell me what's got you all upset?"

Zoe heaved a sigh. "I got a visit from Deputy Mosley this morning."

"Bad news?"

"It's terrible." Zoe spilled the entire story, ending with how helpless and overwhelmed she felt that all the blame was shifting to Cruz no matter what she said.

"Unbelievable."

"Isn't it? You hear about people getting falsely convicted of crimes. I guess this is how it happens." Zoe pressed her fingers to her forehead. "I'll never forgive myself if Cruz gets blamed. I have to fix this, Hope."

"Well, we don't know who actually set the fire, but we sure know who's behind it. Maybe we can get Kyle to confess somehow."

Zoe scowled. "Why would he do that?"

Hope leaned on the doorframe, a frown puckering her dark brows. "He wants something from you, Zoe. Maybe if he thinks he's going to get it, he'll admit to what he did."

Maybe Hope was right. Maybe Kyle was the weak link. He'd made no bones about wanting Zoe back. Maybe she could leverage that somehow.

"So you're saying I should set up a meeting, wear a wire, go all FBI on him?"

Hope backed off. "Whoa. I was just thinking of taping a phone conversation or something."

Zoe considered that. "I don't think he'd come clean on the phone. It wouldn't be convincing enough. I was pretty adamant last time we talked."

Hope grimaced. "You know, I don't think this is such a good idea after all. He has a volatile temper—I saw it firsthand, remember? Maybe you could bring the sheriff into this. Offer to help them set him up."

Zoe bit her lip, stared out the front windshield, thinking. A moment later she shook her head. "The sheriff seems pretty sure Cruz is responsible. At best he'd refuse to pursue this with me. At worst, he'd warn me to stay out of it. And then where would I be? No, I think this falls under 'easier to ask forgiveness than permission.'"

"What about taking Cruz along then? You can't meet him alone. I don't like to think what he might do to you if he suspects a trap."

"Take Cruz? Are you kidding me? Kyle would never admit to anything in front of him."

"He could stay hidden. He Who Must Not Be—"

"Oh, for heaven's sake, just say his name!"

Hope scowled. "Fine. *Kyle* wouldn't even have to know Cruz was there."

"I don't want Kyle coming to Copper Creek at all. I don't trust him, and I don't want him anywhere near Gracie."

"Now you're thinking smart. Let's leave this in the sheriff's hands."

"I was thinking more of going to Nashville and trapping him into a confession there." She was starting to feel convinced this could work.

"Are you crazy?"

"Probably."

"You'd have to take Cruz. It's way too risky to go alone."

The more Zoe thought on this, the more she

realized what kind of tack she'd have to take with Kyle. She'd have to play up to his ego and let him think he'd won. Tell him he'd been right all along. That she was giving up on the whole idea of the orchard. She'd have to sweet-talk him and make him believe she wanted him back.

She was already shaking her head. "There's no way Cruz would go along with this. Especially when he knows I'm doing it for him. He'd want to strong-arm Kyle himself. And that's no way to get Kyle to talk. Trust me. I know his weaknesses."

Cruz would want to do this his way, and it wouldn't work. She was done letting other people control her life. Her dad had never known what was best for her. Kyle sure hadn't. It was past time she took the reins of her own life.

Hope straightened, pulling her elbows from the window frame. "It's not safe to meet Kyle alone. I can't go along with this."

"I'll meet him someplace public. Someplace he wouldn't dare cause a scene."

"That didn't stop him at the Rusty Nail."

"We were in a dark parking lot. He thought we were alone." Zoe was feeling less helpless with every second that passed. She was going to get this done.

"I don't know about this, Zoe."

"Don't worry." She gave her friend a confident look. "This is going to work. You'll see. I'll put out the bait right now and plan to move on it after Peach Fest." She grabbed her phone from her pocket and opened her texts.

"Wait!"

Zoe looked up, raising her brows.

Hope didn't speak; she just ran her hand over her throat and gave Zoe a pained look.

"What am I supposed to be waiting for?"

"For me to think of something to say that'll stop you from doing this."

"It was your idea!"

"That should've been the tip-off. You know I'm full of bad ideas."

"It's a great idea." Zoe tapped on Kyle's name. "He'll be expecting me to contact him. He's thinking his plan to ruin my business was brilliant, and he's just waiting for me to come crawling back to him." She started texting.

> Hi Kyle. I've been thinking . . . reconsidering some of my recent decisions. I was thinking of coming up to Nashville soon so we could talk. You were right about so many things.

Hope made a gagging sound.

Zoe shot her a look as she sent the text. "There. He'll respond to that. Knowing him, he'll probably make me wait, but that'll give me time to get through the grand opening."

She should be ready for this, though. Making Kyle wait would only anger him. "Do you still have that little hand-held recorder?"

Hope gave her a pained look. "Maybe . . ."

"Perfect. I'll pick it up later today." A small wave of euphoria washed over her. She was actually going to manipulate Kyle. Now there was a switch. Imagine how she'd feel when it was all over. "We are so doing this," she said.

"*You're* doing this. I don't want anything to do with it." Hope stepped away from the truck as Zoe got out.

"Fine. When I nail his rear end to the wall, all the credit will be mine."

"Promise me you'll tell me before you head to Nashville. Someone needs to know what's going on."

"I promise. Maybe we can even rig it up so you can listen in just to be safe. But you cannot tell anyone else."

"I don't like this, Zoe."

"We'll hammer out the details later. I have a grand opening to get through first." Zoe shut the door behind her, her chin nudging north. "This is going to work, you'll see."

"I sure hope you're right."

Zoe headed to the barn. She felt good about this. Okay, maybe her knees were a tad wobbly. Maybe her pulse was a bit jumpy, her muscles a little twitchy.

But she knew Kyle better than anyone. He was eager to believe she was coming back to him. Eager to believe he was so incredibly clever for having found a way to make it happen.

All she had to do was play to his ego. Then she'd have him right where she wanted him.

chapter thirty-nine

Cruz stopped at Brady's place to check on him first thing the next morning. The baby had apparently been up since the break of dawn, and Brady looked pretty spent. Cruz was glad to hear Hope was coming over later in the morning to lend a hand so his friend could have a break.

Cruz looked up at the clear blue sky as he approached the Peach Barn. It was a beautiful day for Zoe's grand opening. The sun shone bright, obscured only by fluffy white clouds. A light breeze, carrying the scents of pine and loamy earth, ruffled the trees that towered over the red building.

He was so proud of Zoe. She'd taken a lot of hits lately, but she'd come up swinging. It was good to have his leona back.

He walked through the entrance, the sweet smell of pastries teasing his senses. Baskets filled with a dozen peach varieties sat atop the skirted tables, along with apples and produce from other area farms. The tables featuring the bakery items were lined up neatly near the register. Miss Ruby had sure outdone herself.

Zoe was behind the cash register with her new hire. His girl looked cute as can be in her red apron bearing the slogan "Sweet as a Georgia Peach."

Zoe rubbed her forehead, scowling at the register, as she punched buttons. She looked a little frazzled, and the day hadn't even started. It would be officially open for business in—he checked his watch—twenty-five minutes.

"Happy Grand Opening Day." He came around the makeshift counter and gave Zoe a peck on the lips that he would've gladly extended—except for the teenaged girl hovering nearby.

He reluctantly drew away from Zoe. "Hi, Ava. How's it going?"

The girl smiled at him, a slight blush blooming on her cheeks. "Hi, Mr. Huntley."

While Ava went outside to sweep the porch, he and Zoe took a moment to catch up on Brady and the investigation. Cruz didn't mention that the deputy had been by to question him again. She didn't need more stress today.

"So . . . ," he said, looking around. "What do you need done right now?"

"Well . . . now that you mention it. How much do you know about stubborn cash registers?"

⇒•⇐

By the end of the day Zoe was feeling cool and confident as she rang up a bag of peaches for a customer. She gave the couple a smile as she finished the sale, then watched Cruz helping a customer.

"These are the clingstones," he was saying.

324

"They have a soft texture, and they're very sweet and juicy. Great for snacking. These are freestones. They're lower in sugar and less juicy, so they're ideal for baking. You'll see here we have a cross hybrid. And these Red Tops over here are great if you like a little tartness."

"My wife wants to make a cobbler."

"In that case I'd definitely advise the free-stones."

Cruz finished helping the man before turning him over to Ava at the register and turning to another customer. Zoe felt her pocket, suddenly realizing she hadn't checked her phone all day. In all the chaos of the opening, she'd forgotten to charge it last night and had plugged it in as soon as she'd arrived this morning.

She slipped into the office, wondering if Kyle had responded to yesterday's text.

"Everything all right?"

She jumped as she looked over her shoulder, placing a hand on her heart. Cruz had followed her. "You scared me." She pocketed her phone without checking it.

"Sorry. You seem distracted today."

She gave him a lame smile. "I'm a little on edge. All this stuff with the fire and Deputy Mosley, I guess. I feel responsible."

"This is not your fault. It was my decision to swing by the barn the night of the fire, and I wouldn't take that back even if I could."

That detour had probably saved her life. "Nothing's working out like I thought it would."

"Hey." He brought her in close, locking his hands around her waist. "Let's think positive. God's got your back, and mine too." He nudged her toe with his. "Let's not talk about that today. It's your grand opening, and it's going pretty darn good, don't you think?"

She settled her arms around his neck. "It's been steady. I think everyone I know has been through here today, and a bunch of new folk besides."

He rubbed her back. "And everyone was buying. It's been a good day."

"I'm glad you were here. I underestimated how many would turn out."

"It's a supportive community. Everyone wants to see you succeed. Me most of all."

Her gaze darted away. "Well, I still have some pretty big obstacles."

He set his finger over her lips. "Not talking about that today, remember?"

His lips replaced his fingers. He'd only been going for a soft brush, but once that was done, he couldn't seem to help himself.

Zoe didn't mind. She tightened her arms around him, and he pulled her closer. He fit against her like he was made for her. He deepened the kiss, and she responded wholeheartedly. His fingers threaded into her hair, making a chill race down her arms.

His hands moved restlessly, seeking her curves and bare skin. His touch felt like home and he tasted like heaven. She was the luckiest woman alive.

They'd been so distracted lately by the fire investigation and the grand opening, they'd hardly had a spare minute alone. She wasn't even sure when he'd kissed her last. Unacceptable. And a mistake he was, apparently, all too happy to correct.

Her phone buzzed in her pocket.

She pulled away, sliding her hands down his chest. She would've pulled away completely if he hadn't kept his hands locked around her waist. Apparently he wasn't done.

"I should get back out there," she said. "And you were going to go check on the orchard."

"I'd rather kiss some more."

Her eyes smiled. "Me too, but I don't want Ava overwhelmed on her first day." She gave him a quick peck. "I have to stay till closing. Ava's up for Miss Georgia Peach, so she has to leave early to get ready for the parade."

"I hope she wins."

"Me too. Want to just meet in town then? At seven, outside the barbershop? We can watch the parade together."

He buried his lips in the curve of her neck. "And eat our way through junk food alley."

"Sounds like a plan."

"Need me to pick up Gracie on the way?"

"No, that's all right," she said. "I'll want to go home, shower, and change anyway."

"I can't wait to ride the rides with her. She's tall enough, right?"

"For some of them." She lifted her shoulder as he hit a ticklish spot. "She loves carousels."

He planted random kisses on her neck. "I might have to buy her cotton candy. And a candy apple. And maybe an elephant ear."

"I can see where this is headed."

"Miss Zoe?" Ava said from the doorway.

Cruz released Zoe, allowing her to step from his arms.

"Sorry," Ava said, her cheeks going pink. "Didn't aim to interrupt. A large group just came in on a bus, and I thought—"

"Thanks, Ava," Zoe said. "I'll be right out."

Cruz took Zoe's hands, pulling her closer again, setting his forehead on hers. Her lips tingled with the need to kiss him again. But if she did, she didn't think she'd be able to stop, and she had a bunch of customers waiting.

"Stupid customers," he said, reading her mind.

"They tend to be good for business."

"Stupid business."

She chuckled, darting away even as she gave him a shove toward the door. "Off to the orchard, Mr. Huntley. Or there will be severe repercussions."

"Do these repercussions involve kissing?" he called over his shoulder.

Zoe could only laugh as he slid out the door. She was still smiling as she pulled her phone from her pocket, but the grin quickly slid from her mouth. There were seven unread texts, six missed calls, and a voicemail. The texts had started at 9:06 that morning.

> I knew you'd come around. Drive up today. I've got a busy schedule tomorrow.

> Zoe?

> Answer your freaking phone!

> YOU texted me

> Done waiting on you. I'm coming there

> Flight lands at 5:30. Be there to pick me up.

> You're really ticking me off! Where are you? Devon picked me up. I'll be at your house at 6

"Oh, no!" She checked her watch. It was 5:40. She had to divert him from the house!

> I'm so sorry I missed your messages! I won't be at the house. Meet me at the Ferris wheel. I'll be there at 6.

She sent the text and paced the office. *Please get the message.* She grabbed her purse and keys. She'd have to leave early and tell Ava to lock up when she left.

She checked her phone. Nothing. She sent another text.

Did you get my message?

Should she head toward home just in case? Take Gracie somewhere safe? Oh, what had she done?

A text dinged in. So you can make me wait hours and you can't wait two seconds for me?

I'm really sorry. My phone was dead. Meet me under the Ferris wheel?

Six o'clock. Don't be late.

I won't be.

Zoe rushed through closing instructions for Ava, apologizing profusely for leaving her with a busload of customers.

She started up her truck. She'd be lucky to make it by six with the festival traffic. At least her daughter was safely tucked away at home. At least she'd been able to divert Kyle. She sent Miss Ruby a quick text to let her know she'd be late and hoped that didn't ruin her plans for the evening.

It was going to be okay. This isn't the way she planned it, but she could work with this.

Thank God she'd gotten the recorder from Hope last night. It was in her purse and ready to go. All she had to do was clip the thing into her waistband. She took a deep calming breath as she pulled from the lot. She had to plan what she was going to say. How she was going to get him to confess. All was not lost. If tonight turned out as she planned, this turn of events could work in her favor.

chapter forty

The atmosphere on Main Street was celebratory, despite the June heat. A heavy bank of clouds rolled in, offering Zoe a welcome reprieve from the sun. A portion of the street was blocked off for the coming parade, so she rushed down the crowded sidewalks, skirting the folks who waited curbside in their lawn chairs.

A large banner reading *41st Annual Peach Fest!* was draped from one side of the street to the other. Colorful flag banners waggled in the breeze, and twinkle lights spiraled up lampposts, awaiting nightfall. A light breeze cooled the perspiration on the back of Zoe's neck. Her stomach twisted at the smell of peach cobbler and elephant ears.

Nerves, not hunger. As much as she wanted to nail Kyle for what he'd done, the thought of being with him again made dread unfurl in her gut like a coil of barbed wire.

The far end of Main Street was blockaded for carnival rides as the parade route took a turn up Maple Street. She followed the crowd around the barricades and began weaving between rides. The squeals of children and the hum of the rides' motors filled the evening air.

She'd quickly clipped on the recorder in the

truck and turned it on. Hope said she had at least an hour's recording time. That should be plenty. She hoped it wasn't too noisy to pick up Kyle's voice. But she couldn't get any farther from the band playing at the other end of the street and still remain in public.

Up ahead the sphere of the Ferris wheel extended high into the sky, the spokes already lit red, white, and blue. It was the slow kind of Ferris wheel, offering more in the way of grand views than high motion thrills.

Her mouth went dry at the thought of what she was about to do. What if this ended in disaster?

No, she couldn't think that way. She was doing this for Cruz.

As she neared the Ferris wheel, she spied Kyle through the crowd. He was frowning at his phone, which gave Zoe a minute to get her game face on. She was right on time.

He wore a ball cap, the brim pulled low, and a black T-shirt hugged his lean upper body. The girls went crazy for him when he was onstage, and Zoe got that. He was muscled and handsome, and he could sure turn on the charm when he was of a mind to.

But he was also demanding and demeaning, and he had a nasty backhand.

She felt the vibration of a call coming in on her phone, but just as she registered the thought, Kyle looked up from his phone, his eyes zoning in on her, a direct hit. His gaze raked her over from head to toe and back.

She forced a smile as she closed the distance between them. "Hey there."

She knew she had her work cut out when he only scowled in return.

She touched his arm, hoping to soften him. "I'm really sorry I didn't get your messages. I missed you."

He looked at her long and hard before pulling her into an embrace that somehow felt more like possession than passion.

Her heart stalled as his hand settled at the small of her back. But she'd anticipated this and had put the recorder at her side. Though every instinct begged her to push away, she softened into him, praying his hand wouldn't edge over.

"You owe me." His breath on her ear made a shiver shimmy down her spine. The familiar smell of him made a fist tighten in her gut.

"You've been very patient. Thanks for coming all this way." She gave him a squeeze before releasing him. Her smile felt carved in stone.

He pinched her chin gently, holding her head still. His eyes roved over her hair before they narrowed on her eyes. "Heard you dyed it back."

Her chin nudged up before she could stop herself. She was never letting a man control her again. Not her hair color or her decisions or her future. She was done being a doormat.

His lip curled as he stared at her, his eyes going dark. He tsked. "My little wild child. Taming you is half the fun."

She bit her tongue. Hard. And worked to keep the disgust off her face.

She thought of Cruz and his patience. Of the tender and reverent way he touched her. She felt such a longing for him right then, it took everything in her to stand her ground.

Kyle was oblivious, though. He was already looking around, scoping out the area. "Where do you want to do this? The diner's closed, and the park's a madhouse."

"There's a bench over there." But just as she said it a little boy with a blue cloud of cotton candy parked himself on it.

She bit her lip.

"Let's just go sit in your car. Or better yet, go somewhere quiet and make up for lost time." He slipped his arm around her waist and pulled her into his side, leering at her. "Been looking forward to that."

"I-I had to park way across town at the post office. And I'd really rather talk first." And last. Because the thought of touching him again turned her stomach.

Kyle scowled at her. "I don't know what we have to talk about. This place is a dead end for you, Zoe. Especially now."

Because of you. She bit back the words. He

was getting antsy, and she needed to calm him down.

She made herself smooth the cotton material at his chest. "You promised we could talk this out. Please, Kyle?" He loved her eyes, and she used them to full advantage. "I want the chance to apologize properly. I was wrong before."

After a moment the tightness at the corners of his eyes relaxed. "Whatever. Let's just ride this thing. We can talk up there. But after that we're leaving."

Zoe's pulse stuttered as she followed him to the ticket line. After that they moved to the short Ferris wheel line. She didn't know how she was going to get rid of him when their talk was over.

She looked up at the slow-turning wheel with its little cages. She didn't like the thought of being trapped in that seat with him, thigh to thigh, but she needed him close. And it would be quieter up there, right? In full sight, more or less, of the viewing public. Safe.

Kyle took her hand in his as they waited. His grip was too tight, and her palm soon began to sweat. They stepped forward as they worked their way up in line.

She needed to ease into this. Get him relaxed. "How was your flight?"

He gave her a sideways look. "Expensive."

She bit the inside of her lip. "How's the band doing? How's Brandon's little boy?"

"The band's good. Eli came through the bone marrow transplant all right. He's still pretty tired, but he's home. They think he's going to be okay."

"I'm so glad to hear that. I can only imagine how scary that was for Brandon and Beth. Are Dave and Joelle still together?" They'd just started dating when she'd returned to Copper Creek.

Kyle grunted. "Hardly. He's been through two more girls since."

"That's too bad. I really liked Joelle." She tried to think of something else to say and came up blank.

Kyle pulled his phone from his pocket and responded to a text, tucking it back when he was finished. "We'll leave after this and drive back tonight. I've got a lot to do tomorrow."

She fiddled with the hem of her shirt. "I really need a week or two to tie up loose ends, Kyle. And besides, this is not all settled between us. I missed you but—"

He pressed a hard kiss to her lips. Then he backed away, still hovering over her. "As far as I'm concerned, there is no *but.*"

She fought the urge to wipe his kiss away.

"You were made for me, Zoe. You're coming with me. We'll make music together, become famous together." He nuzzled his nose in her hair. "Everyone will want to be us."

So full of himself, she thought, as they took another step forward.

The Ferris wheel stopped, and two women emerged from a chair. Their heels clanked as they descended the metal ramp. As they passed by they caught Kyle's eye, giving him flirtatious smiles. His shoulders went back, and his lips curled. The women faded into the crowd, giggling like a couple of schoolgirls.

Kyle was practically preening as he looked down at Zoe, smirking. *See how lucky you are?*

Zoe fought the urge to stick her finger down her throat. Instead she pressed closer to him, as if staking her claim. He liked her best when she was jealous.

They were next in line. She had to focus. She went over her dialogue in her head. She had to soften him up. That would be easier when she got him alone in the chair.

"When we get back you'll have a few songs to learn, but we'll get you up to speed. Colonial loves our stuff. They don't want to change us or remake our image. They're going to make us the hottest band going, Zoe. They're really invested."

"That's . . . that's very exciting."

A moment later the boy stopped the wheel again, and an older couple stepped off. Kyle let Zoe in first, and she was glad he ended up on the side closest to her recorder. As she settled into the metal chair, the recorder dug into her side, reassuring her. When Kyle settled beside her, the operator slammed their door with a clang, and then they were moving forward.

"So go ahead," Kyle said. "Have your say."

She glanced at him. "Well, I guess I just wanted to spend a little time with you mostly. It's been a while. I haven't heard from you, and I just wanted to make sure—"

"You haven't heard from me because you told me to stop calling." Kyle had stiffened beside her.

"I did. That was my fault. I was so focused on the orchard and trying to make a go of it." She shook her head as if she were disappointed in herself.

The wheel took them upward, and the breeze toyed with her hair.

"I told you you weren't cut out for farming."

"You did. You were right. But when Granny left it to me I thought maybe it was a sign—" *From God.* She pinched off the words. Kyle always bristled at the mere mention of her faith. That should've been her first clue.

"Then when I realized the orchard was having financial difficulties, and I came up with the idea of the market, I guess I just dug in."

His hand settled on her thigh, hot and heavy. "You always were too stubborn for your own good."

She clamped her jaw tight and made herself set her hand on his. If nothing else maybe that would keep it from sliding up her leg.

Play to his ego. Soften him up. She looked up at him. The sunlight hit his face as they hit the pinnacle of the ride. Its light reflected off his blue eyes, making them look like ice.

"You're right," she said. "I'm really sorry, Kyle. I was so set on making it work that I tuned out everything else, including you."

Those cold eyes snapped with fire. "Not everything. Seems like you had plenty of time for Huntley."

Her heart thudded so hard she wondered if the mic was picking it up.

She caressed the back of his hand with her thumb the way he liked. "He's not you, Kyle. He's nothing like you." Truer words had never been spoken.

His eyes softened before something malicious flickered there. His gaze fell over her face, over her red hair. "You've got a lot of making up to do."

He cupped her face and kissed her.

She prayed it would just be a quick one. But then he tilted his head, deepening the kiss. A moment later his tongue swept past the barrier of her lips, offering the yeasty taste of beer.

She repressed the shudder that moved through her and forced herself to reciprocate. Kyle pulled his hand from hers and slipped it around her shoulders, pulling her into him. His lips were all over hers.

Her stomach heaved at the feel of him. The motion wasn't helping either. She set a hand on his chest, pressing gently.

"You're getting me all worked up," she said, breathless. "Maybe we should—"

"You had your talk." He swept several kisses up her neck.

She tipped her head to the side, allowing him access. Her head spun with dizziness. She thought of Cruz's lips there just a few short hours ago and wished with everything in her that it was him with her right now. Maybe if she pretended it was she could survive this.

But no. Cruz's kisses were soft and reverent. Kyle's were hard and forceful. And he smelled faintly of cigarette smoke and sweat. Her stomach churned.

She needed to get a confession out of him. She was running out of time.

Think, Zoe. Think.

The Ferris wheel swept them upward yet again, and she swallowed against the bile in her throat.

The wheel slowed to a stop, leaving her stomach a few feet south. Worried she might actually get sick, she pressed against his chest, leaning back. They were near the top.

Her head spun. "I'm feeling dizzy."

He backed off, giving her a little space to collect herself.

"I forgot the effect you had on me." Her smile felt strained as she patted his chest.

"It's been too long."

She had to move this forward. The ride wouldn't last forever.

"I'm really grateful things turned out the way they did. If it hadn't been for you I'd still be holding out hope I could pull that place out of its death spiral."

"What do you mean, 'if it hadn't been for me'?"

She touched his face with her fingertips. Dragged them along his scruffy jaw and gave him a besotted smile. "Come on, Kyle. I know you set the fire. Who else would've cared enough to get me back on the right track?"

He leaned back and narrowed his eyes ever so slightly. "You know I was in Nashville."

Their chair swept low, past the crowd, and back up again, leaving her stomach on the ground.

She swiped her thumb over his lip and hoped she imagined the flicker of suspicion in his eyes. "Why, of course. One of your friends, I mean. If that hadn't happened I wouldn't have taken a second look. Got my head on straight. I didn't realize how much I'd miss you when you stopped calling. You were right to do what you did. It made me reconsider . . ."

Her words tapered off as something shifted in his expression. Her throat constricted. "You-you're pretty amazing to go to all that effort for me."

His eyes hardened, and his lips pressed together as his nose flared. "You must think I'm pretty stupid."

"What do you m—"

Then his hands were all over her. "Where is it, Zoe?"

She pushed at his hands. "What are you doing?"

"Where is it?"

She tried to shimmy away, but it was hopeless in the confines of the cage.

He jerked the recorder from the waistband of her pants.

Her gaze flew to his, widening.

His face screwed up in the ugliest snarl she'd ever seen, and he spat a curse word. Then his eyes narrowed on her. His nostrils flared, and his lips twisted.

"Kyle . . . it's not . . ."

Think, Zoe. Think!

"Kyle . . . please, I just—"

He grabbed a handful of hair at the back of her head and squeezed until her scalp burned. She sucked in a breath.

He was up in her face. So close she could smell the beer on his breath.

"What's this, Zoe? Huh? What's this?"

The ride shimmied as it started up again. They were headed over the top. Soon they'd be back down where the crowd was. He'd have to let her go then.

Her eyes stung at the pain. "I—it's not what you think."

"Oh, it's not, huh? Think you can play me for a fool, Zoe? Is that what you think?"

"No, no, it's not like that."

Something cruel flared in his eyes.

"Let's talk about this. Please, Kyle, I—"

When he jerked her head back she opened her mouth to scream, but he shoved his other hand over her mouth.

"Oh, no you don't. You're not as smart as you think," he hissed, spittle hitting her in the face. "You think I didn't smell a setup? Well, the joke's on you, Zoe. Guess who has your little girl right now?"

The hair on her arms lifted as a cool chill washed over her. She tried to speak, but his hand was still over her mouth.

"Not so smug now, are you." He slowly removed his hand from her mouth.

Zoe drew a deep breath. "What are you talking about? Where's Gracie?"

His cold eyes never left hers as he fished his phone from his pocket.

Zoe's eyes flashed to the screen, and the photo there sucked the air from her lungs. It was Axel Brown, looking rather pleased with himself, and on his lap sat an unsmiling Gracie.

Her breath left her lungs. *O God, help!*

Her prayer was cut short when Kyle pressed

her forehead against his, hard, until white dots speckled her vision.

"You're going to pay for this, Zoe," he whispered harshly.

"Don't hurt her!" Her eyes burned with helplessness. She had to do something. But what?

"Give me your phone."

Think, Zoe!

"Give it to me!"

She reached into her purse and handed it over.

The ride stopped again, just over the crowd's heads. Anyone who might look up wouldn't see a man holding a woman hostage. They'd only see lovers locked in an embrace.

"We're going to get off here," Kyle said into her ear. "And we're going to walk to your truck. You're not going to make a peep. You're not going to draw attention. Understand?"

"Yes," she whispered.

The ride jimmied into motion. Zoe could hardly draw breath as he eased away. He stuffed the phone and recorder into his pockets, keeping his eyes on hers.

"Not one word." His gaze sharpened on hers. "Be a shame for something to happen to Gracie, huh?"

How dare he use her daughter against her. She blinked away the tears.

"Say you understand."

She unlocked her jaw. "I understand."

The wheel swept them lower, slowing until their cage hovered over the platform.

He took her hand, squeezing it painfully tight. "Don't be stupid."

The operator opened their door and Kyle stepped out, pulling her along behind him.

She tried to get the boy's eye, but he was busy flirting with the girls in line. Kyle passed the line, setting a harsh pace. It took all her effort to keep up with him in the crowd. He kept her right at his side.

She had to get to Gracie. But what would he do with them then? He'd clearly come unglued. Her gaze darted around, praying for help. Someone in a uniform. Someone who might see the panic on her face. But they were all too engaged in their own little worlds to see that hers had just turned upside down.

chapter forty-one

Kyle took the keys from Zoe, opened the passenger door of her truck, and pushed her inside. "Slide over! You're driving."

She slid across the seat, maneuvering around Gracie's booster seat. She was breathing fast from their long, fast walk and from the panic his cruel stare induced. What was he going to do?

He slammed the door. Then his hands were all over her.

A scream built in her throat. She pushed frantically at his hands, crowding the driver's door.

"Settle down!"

The fog of panic cleared enough to realize he wasn't groping her. He was patting her down. She forced herself to go still.

He finished patting her pockets, front and rear, all the way down to her ankles, taking his time.

When he was satisfied he leaned back. "Drive."

Shaking, she started the truck, put it in drive, and pulled from the lot. Her clammy hands trembled on the wheel. "Where are we going?"

"We're getting Gracie and we're going back to Nashville where you belong."

"Where is she?"

"Your place."

"Please don't hurt her."

"Maybe you should've thought of that before you set me up!"

The back of her eyes burned. What had she done?

"Turn left at the light."

She did as he said. Her nerves were quaking with fright. Think. She had to think. But her thoughts were scrambled when they most needed to be clear.

O God. I need you. I need you now. Please! Show me what to do.

He grabbed her arm in a bruising grip. "Who else knows about your little game, Zoe? Who knows I'm here?"

"Nobody. Nobody knows."

He squeezed her arm until she gasped. "Who else, Zoe?" he yelled.

"No one! I was afraid they'd try and talk me out of it." She turned onto the road that would lead them to the farm. Every second brought them closer to her little girl. She hung onto that thought.

God, please help me! I don't know what to do.

"You thought you could play me for a fool! You have no idea who you're dealing with. Somebody got a little too big for her britches the last couple of months." His fingers dug into her flesh. "But we'll fix that soon enough."

She winced against the pain. She had to talk some sense into him. "Think . . . think of your career, Kyle. You don't want to do anything to mess that up."

"That's exactly what I'm thinking of. You won't ruin this for me. You're coming back with me, and you're back in the band where you belong. You'll thank me soon enough."

She took a slow blink. He was deluded. Completely mad. There would be no reasoning with him. Taking her had nothing to do with wanting her or helping the band, and everything to do with his need to control her. She was nothing but a possession to him. Her heart felt like it was going to explode in her chest, and she struggled to slow her breathing.

He let go of her arm, and she wilted with relief.

"Where's your brother?" he asked.

"He's taking his son to the parade."

"And that loser you've been seeing?"

She discreetly checked the time. She was supposed to meet him in ten minutes. He'd be on his way to meet her now.

"Where's Huntley?" he yelled.

"He—he's on his way to the parade, I guess."

"What were your plans tonight? Who were you meeting?"

He'd never believe she was going to sit home on Peach Fest's opening night. "I was going to take Gracie to the festival to ride rides."

"Were you meeting Huntley?"

She bit her lip. If he knew she was meeting Cruz he'd know it wouldn't be long before he'd worry and come looking.

"Tell me the truth!"

"Y-yes. We were meeting him before the parade. At seven o'clock."

He let loose a string of curse words, jerking at the brim of his ball cap. His breaths were shallow and harsh in the confines of the cab.

She swallowed hard, trying to gather her thoughts. Fear ignited inside. If only she'd agreed to let Cruz pick up Gracie. Regret nearly engulfed her.

But Kyle wouldn't really hurt Gracie, would he? An image surfaced of his stony face when he found the recorder, of the crazed look in his eyes. She didn't know this man. Didn't know what he was capable of.

She took the turn that put her on Old Mill Road. They would be there soon. She gripped the leather wheel with her damp palms.

"This is what we're going to do, Zoe. You have five minutes to grab your things—all of them. You're going to leave a note on the door for Miss Ruby to find in the morning, explaining how you just can't do this anymore. How you realize this isn't the life for you. Got it?"

"Yes."

"Don't even think of trying anything."

She gritted her teeth. "I understand. Where's Miss Ruby?"

"Seems she was meeting some friends, and you were running late. She was all too happy to let her nephew babysit for a few minutes."

The house was quiet when they pulled up. The sunset glowed pink on the white clapboard siding. Home. She thought of Gracie and Cruz, and everyone else she was letting down.

"Pull up over there."

A minute later they climbed the porch stairs. When she walked into the house, Gracie came running.

"Mama! Let's go wide the cawousel!" Her little girl looked up, her innocent eyes sparkling with anticipation.

Oh, baby. Zoe checked her over. She was okay. Axel hadn't hurt her.

"Hi, sweetie." Zoe took a breath and gathered herself. "Where's Mr. Axel?"

"Right here." The man came around the corner, wearing a smug smile. "She was a very good little girl."

Zoe bit back a remark.

Gracie's eyes swung past Zoe to Kyle. She froze for a second before she went running into his arms. "Kyle!"

It took everything in her not to snap Gracie up as she darted past. Zoe's stomach bottomed out as Kyle scooped her baby into his arms.

"Hey, kiddo. How's my girl?"

"Where you been, Kyle? I missed you."

He gave Zoe a triumphant look. "I missed you too, Gracie-girl."

"Not Gwacie-girl!" She fluttered her lashes. "Bella!"

Something shifted in Kyle's eyes. His jaw twitched as he nailed Zoe with a lethal look. "Yeah, well," he said, not taking his eyes from Zoe. "We'll see about that."

He set Gracie down and went to have a powwow with Axel in the corner.

Zoe's gaze darted toward the door. Even if they could get away he'd taken the truck keys. She didn't even have a way of calling for help. Why, oh, why, had she disconnected the land-line?

Her gaze trailed back to where Kyle and Axel stood. Something black glinted in Axel's hand. Her blood froze. He was holding a gun out to Kyle.

Kyle took a step back, lifting his hands, but Axel leaned in, whispering harshly until Kyle took it and tucked it into the back of his jeans.

Gracie tugged on her hand. "Mama, let's go! Let's go!"

"In a minute, honey."

A gun. How would they ever get away now? She thought of the knives in the kitchen. But she hadn't a prayer of getting past two men.

Axel must've been the one who set the fire. He was up to his neck in this now and wanted to make sure it played out right.

"Kyle, are you gonna wide wides with us? I'm gonna wide the cawousel! A white howsey!"

"Yeah, yeah. First things first, though," he said, joining them by the door. "I need you to grab all your toys and put them in a bag. Can you do that for me?"

Gracie's brows pinched together. "What for?"

"It's a game. I'm going to time you. You and your mama are going to race, and we'll leave as soon as you're done. Are you ready?" He checked his watch.

She bounced on her toes. "I'm weady!"

"Set . . . Go!" He gave her a smack on the tush, and she scrambled up the stairs. "Huwy, Mama! Huwy!"

The ease with which he manipulated her daughter made heat flush through Zoe. Sure, it was only a little game designed to ensure her cooperation. But Zoe's stomach twisted hard as she realized he'd once controlled her so easily.

His methods had been much more subtle—it had been little things at first. How she folded his clothes or wrapped the mic cords during tear-down. But before she knew it, she'd been doing everything to his liking. When the littlest thing went awry she worried that he'd get aggravated with her. His moods had controlled her behavior.

Not anymore, though. Not anymore.

⇒•⇐

Five minutes later the note was written and hanging on the door, and Axel had left. Gracie was in her booster seat between Zoe and Kyle, and all their belongings had been tossed into the bed of the truck.

Zoe put the vehicle into drive and eased down the lane.

Kyle had kept his tone friendly for Gracie's sake, but the cold look in his eyes was enough to remind Zoe that rage boiled just below the surface. He'd stayed right with her every second in the house, giving her no opportunity to leave some kind of clue or pick up something she could use as a weapon.

Gracie squirmed eagerly in her booster seat. Zoe couldn't keep track of her chatter. She was so excited about the festival. Her daughter wouldn't be happy when she realized there was no carousel at the end of this trip. Her eyes would fill with tears, and then the crying would start.

Kyle would lose patience with her quickly, and his temper would flare. Not what they needed when he was already hanging by a thread.

Zoe discreetly checked her watch. She was ten minutes late to meet Cruz. Too soon for him to start worrying. He probably figured she'd gotten caught in the festival traffic or was having trouble finding a parking space. He'd probably text her soon.

"Are we going to the wides now, Mama?"

"Be patient, honey."

Kyle handed her a spinning lollipop he must've swiped from the house.

Gracie's eyes lit up. "Thank you, Kyle." The wrapper crinkled as she took it off. She flipped the switch, making the lollipop buzz quietly, and popped it into her mouth.

"Look, Mama!" she said around the sucker.

"It's spinning, huh?" That would hold her over for a bit.

"Wound and wound and wound," Gracie said.

Zoe pulled the truck from the drive and turned onto the street, heading toward 76. The sun was hanging low in the west, striping the sky with bold colors.

The parade was well underway. Cruz must be wondering where she was. If a text had come in, Kyle hadn't said anything.

Minutes later she took the turn for 76 West. The road straightened as it left town. She wiped her sweaty palms down her jeans and tried to foresee what might be unfolding in town.

Cruz would be getting worried, but he wouldn't be able to reach her. He'd eventually call Brady—who knew nothing—and then Hope. But Hope didn't know Kyle had come into town. Why, oh, why hadn't she told someone?

chapter forty-two

Cruz checked his watch for the dozenth time in the last half hour. The parade was well underway. The high school band passed by, the horn section blaring out "Ramblin' Man," the percussion following in a line behind them delivering a lively cadence. The Bulldog mascot danced to the tune while the crowd cheered him on.

Where was Zoe? He surveyed the crowd lining Main Street, looking for her red hair. She was always a standout. Beside him the barber's pole spun, its red, white, and blue stripes going in an endless circle. She'd said right outside Josephine's, right?

It wasn't like her to be late. The band moved past, and a group of little girls sashayed by in sparkly red outfits. Once it was quieter he stepped around the corner and dialed Zoe, but there was no answer.

He called the market, but there was no answer there either. He dialed Brady. The phone rang through to voicemail. He was probably somewhere along the parade route, unable to hear or feel his phone in the chaos. Hope was next on his list. She finally answered on the fifth ring, distracted by the parade. But she hadn't heard from Zoe all day.

He checked again for a message, then pocketed his phone and went back to the storefront, perching his hands on his waist.

A fire truck paraded by, volunteers waving from the back. Next was a seventies model convertible red Chevelle. Ava sat atop the back seat, smiling and waving. Her Miss Georgia Peach banner crossed her upper body, and her tiara sparkled under the setting sun. Zoe would be disappointed that she'd missed Ava's big moment.

A feeling of foreboding swept over him like a strong summer wind. Something wasn't right. Before he could even finish the thought his feet were already headed toward his truck.

⤜•⤛

Twenty minutes later he arrived at Zoe's. Her truck wasn't there, but he charged up the porch steps anyway. As he did his eyes zeroed in on a note taped to her front door.

He scanned the contents, frowning.

She couldn't do this anymore? This wasn't the life for her? This was bull. He ripped the note from the door and wadded it in his fist.

He barged inside the house. "Zoe!" he called, though he didn't expect an answer. After covering the first floor he took the stairs two at a time. "Gracie!" The house was as silent as a tomb.

Upstairs he turned into Zoe's room first, his

357

eyes scanning the space. The bed was made, but her things were gone. He went to the closet and found it empty, hangers and all. He dashed across the hall. All of Gracie's toys were gone, her closet empty.

He stopped, his hand still on the closet knob. They were gone.

His stomach sank to the floor as he reviewed the last several days. Sure, it hadn't been easy. Between the grand opening, the investigation, and the insurance refusing to pay up, Zoe was stressed. But she'd gone through with the grand opening, and it had been successful.

She had a few months of peach season to look forward to, and the investigation wasn't finished yet. There was still a chance they'd catch the real culprit. That she'd be able to rebuild her barn and pay off her loan.

The old insecurities came flooding in. The ones that made him fear he wasn't enough. Hadn't been enough for his own dad. Flesh and blood. Why would he be enough for Zoe?

He shook the thought from his head. He wasn't that man anymore. What his dad did was on *him*. Not Cruz. He had God-given value, and no one could take that away.

The suddenness of this, on the heels of her grand opening, didn't make sense. None of it was ringing true. His gut was screaming. Because Zoe wouldn't do this. No way. No way would she leave. No way would she take Gracie away. She'd come too far. They'd come too far.

This whole thing reeked of Kyle. Cruz didn't know how or why, he just knew.

He tried Zoe's phone again, but it rang over to voicemail. He left a message begging her to call and tried to get through twice more before he hung up and slammed the closet door shut.

If anyone could shed some light on this it would be Hope. He pulled his phone from his pocket even as he rushed from the room. She picked up on the third ring.

"Have you heard from Zoe?"

"You mean . . . she's still not with you?"

"No, she's not with me. I'm at her house. Her stuff is gone, and she left some note, making it sound like she was leaving for good."

"What? Zoe wouldn't do that." Then Hope mumbled something unintelligible. "Oh, no. Oh, no. Cruz . . . there's something I have to tell you."

"Tell me everything you know, and say it fast."

As the story tumbled out he rushed toward his truck. He started the engine, then pressed on the accelerator, the speedometer inching upward as he hit a straightaway on the drive.

Zoe squeezed the steering wheel. A drizzle had begun, and she turned on the windshield wipers.

Her breathing had gone so shallow she felt as

if she were going to hyperventilate. She forced a few deeper breaths, casting a look at Kyle. The smirk on his face was less than comforting. He'd checked her phone a few minutes ago. She was sure there'd been a text or call from Cruz.

He gave her a long, amused look. "Don't worry, Zoe. I'm sure he'll get over you fast enough. He'll probably buy the orchard, if he can afford it, and be glad to cut you loose. He's probably already forgotten about you."

As if refuting his words, the phone buzzed an incoming call.

Kyle checked the screen, his lips twisting. He set the phone down, not even bothering to turn it off. Tension built in the cab as she waited it out, wanting with everything in her to answer. It had to be Cruz.

Finally the buzzing stopped. A moment later a voicemail buzzed in.

"Well, let's see what he has to say." Kyle placed the phone on his ear. A few seconds later he chuckled. Then he hung up.

"What'd he say?"

He only ignored her, that smug smile making her want to strangle him.

The phone started buzzing again.

Gracie stopped the spinning sucker. "Who's calling you, Kyle?"

"Nobody, Gracie-girl."

The phone rang on, shrinking the air in the cab

until it wrapped around Zoe tight as Saran Wrap.

Cruz wasn't giving up so easily. He'd know she wouldn't go, wouldn't leave him, wouldn't he?

The ringing continued. "Maybe I should just answer it, Kyle."

His eyes narrowed on her as the ringing stopped. Zoe waited for the voicemail, but none came. A breath she didn't know she'd been holding escaped.

The phone began buzzing again.

Kyle shifted in the seat, his muscles tensing. He tugged the brim of his hat down. Emotion tightened the corners of his eyes, and his upper lip was dotted with sweat. He jabbed the button that turned off the phone. The ringing stopped, and the cab was suddenly silent except for the hum of the spinning sucker.

Zoe drove on, but she could sense the tension on the other side of the cab. If she could just talk to Cruz maybe he'd be able to figure out what was going on. Maybe she could slip him a clue or something. She just had to get Kyle on board. And somehow manage that without angering him.

Her fingers tightened on the wheel. "Turning off the phone's not going to fix this, you know. He's not going to let this go with a note on the door. He won't believe it without hearing it straight from me."

He turned wild eyes on her. "If you think I'm going to let you talk to him you're crazy."

"What can I possibly do, Kyle? You're sitting here with my daughter, and you have"—she thought of the gun tucked in his jeans—"plenty of incentive to inspire my cooperation."

He gave her a long hard look until Zoe turned to look out the rain-speckled windshield. "Answer's no."

Zoe stared ahead at the road stretching out in front of her. She'd once thought Kyle would never harm her daughter, but the crazed look in his eyes was making her doubt his sanity. He was livid about losing Zoe to Cruz and felt she'd played him for a fool. She'd bruised his precious ego, the unpardonable sin.

chapter forty-three

Zoe drove on, regretting every mile she was putting between herself and Copper Creek. She'd kept a light foot on the accelerator, going five below the speed limit. Fortunately Kyle hadn't noticed. The truck was so old and rattly it felt as if they were going much faster. The rain had begun in earnest, and she turned the windshield wipers to a higher speed.

"Mama, I want to wide wides now!" Gracie tugged on Zoe's shirt.

She patted her daughter's leg. "Be patient, honey. Where's your sucker?"

If only she could unwind this night and do it over. She would start yesterday when she'd had the bright idea to bait Kyle. Her plan had completely backfired.

And that was the key right there. It had been *her* plan. Since she'd been back home she'd been working so hard to make her own decisions. To fight her way back to the spirited young woman she used to be before she'd fallen prey to Kyle.

It was true that the reins of her life didn't belong in any man's hands. But they didn't belong in hers either. They belonged in God's. She'd forgotten that one critical thing. He was the One who'd placed the planets and stars in the sky and set the moon in orbit around the earth. He'd created the pulls of tide and gravity. He'd created every human being who ever existed.

Maybe, just maybe, He knew what was best for her.

All this time she hadn't asked Him about the orchard's direction or about the Peach Barn. And she sure hadn't stopped for a single second to ask Him about baiting Kyle. She'd just taken control of the situation. It had felt so good to do her own thing. But it didn't feel so good right now.

I'm sorry, God! Oh, what have I done? Help me!

Kyle caught her looking at him and sneered at her. "Poor, poor Huntley," he said over Gracie's whimpering. "I hope he is all broken up over you. Serve him right, trying to take my place."

Heat roiled in her belly at his smug attitude. Her chin thrust up of its own accord. "Maybe he won't buy it at all, Kyle. He's a pretty smart guy."

He reached across the back of the seat and smacked the back of her head with enough force to make her head spin.

"Mama!" Gracie cried, burying herself into Zoe's side.

"I'm all right, honey." Zoe blinked, orienting herself, working to keep the truck between the lines. Just the fact he'd take such a chance when she was driving proved he'd already lost it.

"You're just as stupid as ever. Bear in mind *you* texted *me* yesterday. This is all your fault. Huntley's going to see that note you left, and he's going to believe it."

Doubt pricked her hard. "He—he'll trust me. He knows I wouldn't leave him."

Kyle gave a cruel laugh. "Like he believed you last time, Zoe? Huh?"

Pain flared in her heart as the arrow hit its target, a direct shot. The memories flooded back, making the back of her eyes burn. She remembered the way Cruz had been so quick to believe she was leaving him for Kyle and the band. Remembered the accusation in his eyes.

"Just like last time . . . ," Kyle continued. "I didn't even have to do much convincing. Just laid a little lie out there, and he snapped it right up. Easy pickings."

Her heart hammered in her chest, and heat flushed through her body. She set her jaw, glaring out the speckled windshield, hating him for being right.

"Know what?" Kyle said, his eyes like a heavy weight on her. "I can see I have a little work to do with you. I don't think we'll be heading back to Nashville just yet. Not until I've had a chance to knock some sense into you. I know of a nice little place we can be together to bond again, just the three of us."

His gaze raked over her, long and slow.

Cold fingers of dread wrapped around her throat, squeezing tight. If they didn't go to Nashville their chances of being followed shrank to almost nothing. And as he'd said, those chances were looking pretty slim.

She could only imagine Kyle's plans for her. She'd always suspected he had a dark side, but he'd mostly kept it under control. It seemed to have surfaced with his swelling ego.

"I know of a nice little fishing cabin on the back side of nowhere," he continued. "Once you've learned to behave I'll take you back to Nashville. By the time Huntley comes sniffing around, you'll be begging me to let you stay."

He probably planned to lock her and Gracie up in that cabin until he believed he could trust her. God only knew what he'd do to her in the meantime. But she'd endure anything as long as he left Gracie alone. He would leave Gracie alone, wouldn't he?

Maybe it wasn't too late to change his mind about Nashville.

"What . . . what about the band? Aren't they expecting us?"

He scowled. "Don't worry, you've got plenty of songs to learn. That'll keep you busy for a while. Can't you do something about her?" he said over Gracie's whining.

"It's all right, honey," Zoe said. "Settle down now."

"Mama! When we gonna be there?"

Kyle shifted in his seat as Gracie's complaints rose over the sound of rain beating the roof. His hands fisted.

"I wanna wide the cawousel."

"Be patient, Gracie," Zoe said. "Where's your lollipop? Let's make it spin again."

"I wanna wide wides with Daddy!"

Kyle pulled off his hat and flung it to the floor. "That's enough, Gracie!"

Gracie's cries filled the cab. She turned back into Zoe's side.

Kyle snapped on the radio, turning it up ear-piercingly loud. An old Johnny Cash song blared out. The music merged with the sound of the rain and Gracie's cries, a discordant clamor.

If only Zoe had something for Gracie to play with. But she didn't have anything in her purse. There was nothing in the glove compartment but some old receipts and maintenance records.

"Do you still have Tinkerblocks on your phone?" she yelled over the cacophony. "Maybe that'll settle her down."

"I ain't giving up my phone! You think I'm stupid?"

"Mama . . . ! I want Daddy!"

Kyle pounded his fist on the windowsill, glaring at Zoe. "Shut her up! Now!"

She had to calm Gracie down before Kyle hurt her. Zoe tightened her arm around her daughter.

"Maybe if you drove I could keep her occupied. I'll get one of her toys out of the back."

"Fine! Just shut her up."

Zoe started to pull over, but there was no place to do so. The road was just busy enough to make it dangerous, and there was a deep ditch on their side. As she scanned the highway ahead, an idea materialized like a mirage in the back of her mind.

Her heart accelerated as the idea took shape. It was a huge risk. Was it worth it? Maybe she was a slow learner, but she wasn't foolish. She wasn't doing anything without running it by God first.

Should I do it? I don't know what else to do, but You've got to get us out of this. Please.

The song ended, and the sound of Gracie's wails filled the cab before another began.

Do I do it, God? Do I take the risk?

She wouldn't do it without a sign. She'd already taken things into her own hands, and look how that had turned out. But she needed an answer, and she needed it now.

"Pull over!" Kyle said.

Zoe realized the ground beside the road had leveled out, giving them an area to pull off before the woods began. She put on her signal, her heart a jackhammer in her chest.

Directions, God! I need directions!

This noise—it was enough to drive anyone batty, much less an agitated and unstable man.

368

Even she could hardly think past the crying, and the rain, and the ear-splitting music.

The singer's name registered: *Anne Murray.* The voice was belting out the chorus, and Zoe's eyes flew to the radio as she recognized the song.

Sunday Sunrise.

Her breath left her body in a wry laugh. It was Granny's favorite song. The one she'd hummed so many times in those early mornings in the orchard. Zoe stared ahead, disbelieving. If that wasn't a sign she didn't know what was.

Okay. Okay, I get it, God. If Kyle gives me the opening I'm going to do this.

"What's so funny?" Kyle glowered at her over Gracie's head.

She wiped the smile from her face as she braked harder, slowing the truck to a crawl. "Nothing."

He continued to glare at her.

Her shoulders sagged when he finally turned his attention to his seat belt. She gulped down breaths, trying to calm her racing heart. There was no time to think or plan.

Here we go. Let's do this.

She brought the truck to a full stop and put it in park. She unclicked her seat belt and made like she was reaching for her door handle.

Kyle couldn't get away from the noise fast enough. He was already out of the cab and heading around the front.

Zoe threw the truck into drive and punched the

accelerator. The truck darted forward, spewing dirt and gravel. Kyle scrambled out of the way, sliding on the slick pavement.

She caught sight of his wide eyes and red, rage-filled face as she flew by. Heaven help her get away. If he caught up to her, he was going to kill her.

"Mama!" Gracie sobbed, gripping Zoe's arm as they accelerated.

"Hang on, baby!"

A loud pop rang out. Zoe shrieked, terror flooding through her.

"Gracie, get down!" She pushed Gracie down, then focused on getting control of the swerving truck.

Another gunshot rang out.

"Mama!"

"Stay down, Gracie!" With the truck under control, she pressed the pedal to the floorboard, shrinking down in the seat.

She winced as another shot pierced the evening. A boom reverberated through the truck, and it slowed drastically. Tugged hard to the right. She fought the wheel, trying to gain control, but it spun the other direction, fishtailing. Out of control.

"Oh, God. Oh, God, help us!"

chapter forty-four

Cruz squinted through the rainy windshield as he pressed the truck's accelerator. The ashen clouds made the sky darker than usual, and he was driving faster than he should be, given the conditions.

But all he could think about was his girls. If he lost either of them, he'd never forgive himself for not being there.

Hope's explanation had made his chest constrict. Made terror run like acid through his veins. What had Zoe been thinking, trying to set Kyle up like that? She'd placed herself right into the hands of a crazy man.

Kyle must've come to meet her. Maybe Zoe had tried to trick him into confessing, and he'd caught on. If that's what happened Kyle would be livid, and Cruz didn't even want to think about what he might do to them.

They had to be on their way to Nashville, and Cruz had to get to them before it was too late. Hope had already put in a call to the sheriff's office, but with the traffic in town Cruz wasn't sure how long it would take to get them out here and start looking for Zoe's truck. Hopefully they had put out an APB.

He had to find them before they reached

Chattanooga. There were too many side roads, too many places to hide—assuming they were even headed to Nashville.

He gave his head a shake and pressed harder on the accelerator, whizzing past a semitruck going the opposite direction.

Red taillights glimmered ahead in the distance. He squinted through the rain, his own headlights doing little in the dim evening light. He was coming upon the vehicle quickly. He took a bend in the road and realized it was off on the side.

He started braking, shutting off his headlights. As he grew closer his heart sped. It was a red truck. Zoe's, he realized as he got within a hundred yards. He slowed, assessing. The truck was off the road, tilted down an embankment against a copse of trees.

A movement on the road ahead snagged his eyes. A man in black was jogging toward the truck, favoring one leg.

Cruz recognized Kyle's build. Rage welled, his blood pressure soaring, his muscles quivering. He'd run the monster down. His foot poised above the accelerator.

But he spotted something in Kyle's hand. It glimmered in the light as it swung. A gun?

Kyle hadn't noticed Cruz yet. The sound of his approach must've been drowned out by the torrential rain. But if Cruz accelerated now he would hear it all right. And if he shot Cruz, where would that leave Zoe and Gracie? Assuming they were still okay.

Cruz braked, then threw open the door and hit the ground running. He estimated the time it would take to reach Kyle, who seemed to be limping. It would be close. Rain pelted Cruz's face as he ran full out. His shoes gripped the pavement, the force of his steps reverberating through him. Lights from an oncoming vehicle blinded him, and rain dripped into his eyes.

Kyle was off the road now. Almost to the back of the truck. He disappeared around the corner.

Cruz dug in, pumping his arms. *Get there! Get there!* He was a car length away when Kyle reached for the door handle.

Then Kyle stopped and turned around. His eyes widened, and he raised the gun.

Cruz plowed into him, and a gunshot fired as they went flying. A second later they hit the earth with a thud.

Kyle's breath left in a grunt, and his head *thunked* against the ground. Cruz reached for the gun and found Kyle's wrist instead. He banged his hand against the ground until the weapon slipped from Kyle's grip.

A fist connected with Cruz's jaw, and lights flashed behind his eyes.

Kyle twisted from under him, scrambling for the gun, inches away.

Cruz delivered a jab to his gut. It caught Kyle

off guard, and the moment's hesitation was all he needed.

He flipped Kyle to his stomach, straddled him, and cranked his arm up behind his back until he let out a string of curses.

"Hey! Hey, what's going on down there?" A burly man approached the road's edge cautiously. His truck was parked on the other side of the road.

Cruz struggled to keep Kyle restrained. "Call 911. He kidnapped my girlfriend and our daughter. Got any rope?"

"Yes, sir. Just a second," the trucker said as he punched numbers into his phone. He trotted back to his truck.

Kyle squirmed beneath him. "Get your hands off me!"

"Be still!" Cruz tightened his grip, shoving one arm up until the man cried out in pain and began cussing Cruz out again.

Cruz kicked the gun a safe distance away, his eyes flashing to the cab of Zoe's truck. He desperately wanted to check on them. He couldn't see anything inside from this angle. Why wasn't Zoe getting out? What if they weren't even in there? What if they were—

He couldn't think the word.

God, please. Let them be all right.

He wished the trucker would hurry. The rain had slackened a bit, and he became aware of music blaring from the cab. He listened, his ears homing in on a sound that wasn't part of the song at all. And yet it was the most precious music he'd ever heard: a muffled wail.

Gracie.

The trucker returned with two short bungee cords, handing Cruz one of them.

"Help's on the way."

"We may need an ambulance."

"I told 'em as much."

Cruz tied Kyle's hands while the trucker captured his feet. Tricky work with Kyle struggling against them and the rain making everything slick.

Cruz put a tight knot in the cord at his wrists. "Stay with him, and don't trust him."

Cruz sprang to his feet, barely resisting the urge to plant his boot in Kyle's gut as he passed by. The man had a nasty case of road rash running up one arm, but that hardly seemed like punishment enough.

Cruz picked up the gun and tucked it in his pants, then waded through the tall grass back toward the truck.

"Zoe!" He called over the music. The front of the truck was smashed into a huge tree, the hood curled up, the engine hissing.

As he took the slope, he made out a shadow behind the rain-speckled driver's window. She was hunched forward. Unmoving. His heart kicked into high gear, adrenaline surging through him.

No, God. Please no.

He reached the truck and wrenched open the door. The music split the air, as did Gracie's wails.

Zoe was slumped lifelessly over the steering wheel.

"Zoe! Oh God, please."

He reached for her, carefully easing her back against the seat. She had a bump rising on her forehead and a minor gash at her temple. Her face was pale. So pale. He quickly scanned her body for injuries and found nothing else.

He slid two fingers to the side of her neck. *"Zoe."*

With all the racket he had trouble feeling anything under his shaking fingers. He made himself hold perfectly still, his own thumping heart and shallow breaths making it difficult.

There. There it was. She was alive. She was going to be fine. His breath left in one long exhale.

"Daddy!" Gracie's shriek pulled his focus from Zoe. Her face was flushed red and twisted in anguish, her eyes full of fear. She held her little arms out to him.

Oh, his poor baby. "Bella."

He leaned across Zoe to pick her up only to realize she was still belted in. He released it and lifted her carefully across Zoe's lap, pulling her into his arms.

"It's okay, baby girl. I got you."

She pressed into the curve of his neck, clinging to him like ivy to a fence. He checked her over quickly, finding no injury. His heart gave a deep sigh. He shifted Gracie, then leaned over Zoe and snapped off the radio.

Blessed silence filled the cab. Even Gracie's cries had given way to quiet sniveling, her little stomach quivering against his chest. In the distance he heard the muted sound of a siren.

Thank God.

He returned his attention to Zoe, cupping her cheek with a trembling hand. "Zoe, honey. Wake up."

The knot on her forehead was worse than he'd realized. A stream of blood flowed down the side of her face.

"Come on, honey."

"Everyone all right in there?" the trucker called from somewhere behind him.

"She's unconscious. Bumped her head on the steering wheel, looks like."

Kyle was saying something, but Cruz couldn't make it out. He heard a grunt, then the trucker saying, "Shut it!"

Cruz caressed Zoe's face, wiped the blood away. His girl. She had to be all right. He couldn't stand the thought of anything else. Maybe there was an injury he'd missed. Worry churned in his gut.

The siren slowly grew louder. They couldn't get here soon enough. Time had slowed to a crawl.

"Wake up, Zoe. Open your eyes."

Her eyelids fluttered.

A jolt of hope made his limbs tingle. "That's it, honey. Wake up. Everything's all right now."

Her lashes fluttered slowly, finally opening. She blinked against the pain.

He gingerly wiped it away, avoiding her injury.

Her eyes drifted dazedly, unfocused.

"Thata girl. You're all right."

Her gaze grew focused, finding him, widening in awareness. They shifted to Gracie, and her breaths grew labored.

"She's okay. You're both safe. Just a little bump on your head."

"Where's Kyle?" Her voice was laced with panic.

"All tied up—literally. He can't hurt you. The sheriff's on his way."

She shifted, reaching for Gracie. "Baby."

Cruz stayed her with a hand on her shoulder. "Be still. I got her."

"Mama, you're bleeding," Gracie whined.

Zoe touched Gracie's arm with a trembling hand. "Mama's all right. Everything's okay."

"Does anything else hurt?" Cruz asked.

"No." Zoe's eyes drifted shut. Her Adam's apple dipped as she swallowed. A crease formed between her brows. She probably had the head-ache to end all headaches.

He wiped away the blood with the tail of his shirt. The siren wailed louder, and Cruz looked through the window to see an ambulance approaching, strobes flashing in the waning light.

"Hang in there, honey. The EMS is almost here. They're going to fix you right up."

She opened her eyes, focusing on him for a long moment, more lucid now. Her gaze was steady, her eyes softening as something unfathomable flickered there. A sweet smile curved her lips.

Inside him, the sun shone, rays of light warming him from the inside out. All she had to do was smile at him, and he knew he was the luckiest man alive.

"What's that smile for?" He had to know.

Her eyes filled with tears, glistening over green like the most beautiful gem he'd ever seen. "You believed in me."

"Oh, Zoe." He brushed her cheek with the back of his finger, unable to look away from every-thing he saw there. "Of course I believed in you. I always will."

He palmed her face, his thumb brushing over her cheek, feelings welling up in him like a storm surge, impossible to hold back. "I love you, mi leona. Maybe this isn't the right time or the right place, but for a while there I was afraid I'd never have the chance."

Her breath escaped in a sigh, her smile widening. "I love you too. I will never leave you, Cruz Huntley. You can count on that."

A lump thickened in his throat as his own eyes grew wet. Her words filled up something deep inside him. Some hollow spot he'd only been vaguely aware of before this moment.

As if weighted, her eyelids drifted shut again.

In the distance doors slammed. Finally. Help was on the way.

"Over here!" he heard the trucker call.

Gracie snuggled in closer, her breaths growing deeper even as her world righted. When Cruz looked back at Zoe, her eyes were fixed on him again, her love shining for all the world to see. She was everything to him. They both were. And he was going to spend the rest of his life proving it.

Epilogue

"Where are we going?" Zoe asked when Cruz took a turn off her driveway.

They'd just had a most excellent meal at the Blue Moon Grill. They were celebrating—Zoe had received the insurance check for the barn and its contents. She'd be able to start rebuilding immediately.

"Can't you guess?" He gave her a sideways smile that made her pulse leap.

His truck bumped over the rutted dirt drive. There was only one noteworthy destination down this lane.

"I haven't been back there in ages."

"It's high time we fixed that then."

She gripped his thigh as they bounced along the uneven ground. A few days ago the jarring would've made her head pound.

But she'd fully recovered now, except for a little soreness in her chest and bruising on her forehead. The gash in her temple had only required a few stitches. Gracie had been completely unharmed.

Her papaw's truck hadn't fared so well, though. It was presently sitting in Brady's driveway, awaiting parts. He'd promised to have it back to its original condition soon, but she wasn't holding her breath. He had his hands a little full right now with baby Sam.

She was glad when Cruz had suggested a date tonight. The week had been jam-packed as she'd attempted to manage the busy Peach Barn and answer all the questions from the sheriff's office and insurance company.

Kyle had been denied bail and was being held in the Murray County jail until his hearing. He and Axel would be tried for arson. They'd also added a few more charges to the list last Friday, including kidnapping and assault with a deadly weapon. Kyle was going away for a long time.

Miss Ruby was horrified about her nephew's role in all of it. She felt terrible about trusting Axel with Gracie. She'd tried to call and leave Zoe a message that night, but Zoe had been in too much of a rush to answer.

A few minutes later Cruz stretched his arm over the seat behind her and backed his truck up to their old spot by the creek. He put it in park and turned off the ignition.

"I hope you're not wanting to go swimming," Zoe said. "It took Hope an hour to fix my hair."

He gave her a mysterious smile as he got out of the truck. "I have something else in mind."

She arched a brow at him as she stepped out into the warm evening, shutting the door quietly so as not to disturb the evening. Crickets chirped from the nearby pine grove, and the creek rippled quietly by. A warm breeze rustled the leaves.

Overhead the full moon floated like a glowing balloon, casting a silvery sheen over the landscape. The familiar peace of this place took her back in time, the memories washing over her like warm water.

All the talks . . . the kisses . . . the little girl they'd conceived right about here. They'd come so far since then. Been through so much. But they were finally together again. That thought warmed her from the inside out. A shiver of gratitude swept over her.

"You chilly?" he asked as he met her around the back of the truck. "I have a jacket in the cab."

"No. It's a perfect night. I forgot how peaceful it is out here," she said, looking around at the familiar trees and hills and boulders.

He lowered the tailgate and unfurled a sleeping bag in the bed of the truck.

She met his gaze with a knowing look. "Are we stargazing tonight, Mr. Huntley?"

"That depends. Do you remember all the constellations I taught you? There might be a test later."

She remembered the way he used to quiz her, kissing her for every one she got right. "I may just need a refresher." She gave him a sassy smile as he lifted her up into the truck bed.

"Accommodation is my middle name."

"And here I thought it was Anthony." She lifted

her skirt and scooted back against the cab where he'd tossed a few fluffy pillows. "Look at this. You've thought of everything."

She admired his masculine grace as he hopped into the bed and lowered himself beside her. When he stretched his arm around her and pulled her into his side, she found other things to admire. The hard curve of his bicep, the strength of his hands, the familiar woodsy smell that made her wish she never had to exhale again.

"Comfortable?" he asked.

"I may never leave." She leaned back, tilting her head to the night sky, heaving a contented sigh. Beyond the treetops the stars were like a million diamonds twinkling against a velvet canvas.

As they stared up into the sky they talked about their busy weeks, catching up. The attendance at Peach Fest had exceeded previous years, setting a new record. The Peach Barn had been so busy her staff had barely managed to keep up. Especially after Granny's Perfect Peach Crisp took grand prize in the bake-off, Miss Ruby could hardly meet the demand.

Zoe told some Gracie stories that made Cruz laugh. That low chuckle still made her insides hum.

Sometime later he leaned in close, pointing overhead. "Time for your test, Miss Collins. What's that one? Right there."

"Easy. That's the Little Dipper."

His head dropped dramatically, and he gave a disappointed sigh.

"What?" She batted her lashes at him, her lips quirking of their own will.

He poked her in the side. "You're just playing me."

"It's Ursa Minor, Professor Huntley," she stated proudly. "That's Polaris, and that's Ursa Major. Draco and Cepheus and Cassiopeia—shall I go on?"

He looked down at her, his eyes shining with approval. "Well done. You're a star pupil after all." His eyes twinkled like the stars overhead.

"Ha ha. You owe me six kisses, buddy. Now pay up."

He gave her lips a quick brush, and then another. She savored the taste of him. The way his kiss was strong and gentle at the same time. The way she felt in his arms—safe and cherished and hopelessly in love. He still made her all melty inside.

By the time he backed away she'd lost count of his kisses, and so had he, judging by the look on his face. Gone were his smile and his twinkling eyes. In their place was a sober expression that was rooted as deep as the ancient oak trees around them.

She was unable to look away. Instead a confession made its way to her lips. "I used to look up at the night sky while I was away and think of you."

He blinked. "You did?"

"I missed you. I missed us."

"I missed you too. More than I can say." His voice was a low scrape. "Zoe . . ."

When he seemed to struggle with words, she touched his face, running her fingers over his freshly shaven jaw, waiting.

"Having you back in my life, having Gracie . . ." He shook his head, wonder washing over his face. "I feel like the luckiest man on the planet. In the whole universe."

She smiled. "I know the feeling."

She was at ease with Cruz. Confident of his love. She didn't have to change who she was or stuff her feelings deep inside or tiptoe around his moods. Nothing she did or said was ever going to change the way he felt about her.

It was the kind of unconditional love she experienced with her mom and with Brady. But this was different, because Cruz wasn't family. He *chose* to love her that way. She hadn't realized how much she'd wanted that, how much she'd craved it, until she finally had it.

She blinked when she realized Cruz had shifted. He was facing her now, propped on a knee. She met his eyes, questioning.

He said nothing, only extended his hand. She looked down, ready to take it. But he was holding something.

A ring.

She gasped. It sparkled in a nest of dark velvet, its diamond sparkling in the moonlight. Her hand flew to her chest where her heart had jolted to life. Her gaze shot back to his.

"I love you, Zoe. You and Gracie are everything to me. I want to wake up with you every morning. I want to do life together and raise Gracie together. And I wanted to ask you right here. Under the starry sky, where I first fell in love with you. Will you do me the greatest honor of my life and marry me?"

Her eyes burned with unshed tears, and a lump swelled in her throat as a smile stretched across her face. "Yes. Oh, Cruz, yes. I want that more than anything." She leaped into his arms, tipping him backwards.

He chuckled, low and happy, squeezing her tight. "Easy, woman, you're going to hurt yourself."

"I don't care. I'm so happy right now I can't feel a thing." She buried her nose in the cradle of his neck, breathing him in. Closing her eyes. She didn't want the moment to end.

"I love you, mi leona," he whispered into her ear. "I can't wait to spend the rest of my life with you."

"I love you too. So much."

He drew back and brushed her lips with his. His reverent touch grounded her. He was love in action. They were friendship on fire. She palmed his face, unable to get enough of him, and he obligingly deepened the kiss.

By the time he pulled away she'd almost forgotten where they were.

"So how about that ring . . ." He produced the box, pulling the ring from its nest.

It was a princess cut with a band that looked a little old-fashioned. It suited her to a T. "Oooh, it's so pretty."

"You can pick out something else if you like." He paused before he slipped it on her finger.

"Not a chance." Once the ring was on she wiggled her fingers, loving the way it shimmered in the moonlight.

Their gaze met, and his eyes held the same wonder she felt all the way down to her toes. They grinned at each other like two silly fools. Somehow, despite all the mistakes they'd made and all the wrong turns they'd taken, it had led them to this one glorious moment.

Now that was God's grace.

Eyes shining, he pulled her close and gave her a soft, lingering kiss. "Let's go tell our little girl we're going to be a family," he whispered in her ear.

Her smile stretched from ear to ear. "I can hardly wait."

Acknowledgments

Writing a book is a team effort, and I'm so grateful for the fabulous team at HarperCollins Christian Fiction, led by publisher Daisy Hutton: Amanda Bostic, Allison Carter, Paul Fisher, Karli Jackson, Kristen Golden, Kayleigh Hines, Jodi Hughes, Kristen Ingebretson, and Becky Monds.

Thanks especially to my editor, Karli Jackson, for her insight and inspiration. I'm infinitely grateful to editor LB Norton, who has saved me from countless errors and always makes me look so much better than I am.

Author Colleen Coble is my first reader. Thank you, friend! Writing wouldn't be nearly as much fun without you!

I'm grateful to my agent, Karen Solem, who's able to somehow make sense of the legal garble of contracts and, even more amazing, help me understand it.

Kevin, my husband of twenty-eight years, has been a wonderful support. Thank you, honey! I'm so glad to be doing life with you. To my kiddos, Justin and Hannah, Chad, and Trevor: You make life an adventure! It's so fun watching you step boldly into adulthood. Love you all!

Lastly, thank you, friend, for letting me share this story with you. I wouldn't be doing this without you! I enjoy connecting with friends on my Facebook page, www.facebook.com/author denisehunter. Please pop over and say hello. Visit my website at the link www.DeniseHunterBooks.com or just drop me a note at denisehunter @gmail.com. I'd love to hear from you!

Discussion Questions

1. Who was your favorite character in *Blue Ridge Sunrise*? Why? Whom did you most relate to?

2. Imagine you're moving to Copper Creek, Georgia. What would your occupation be? Where would you live? Whom would you choose for your best friend?

3. Coming back home to Copper Creek was difficult for Zoe. Explain some of the reasons why. Have you ever "gone home" again? What feelings did that inspire in you?

4. When Zoe and Cruz were young, they parted badly because of deception and miscommunication. Discuss the roles Zoe and Cruz each played.

5. What was Zoe's biggest weakness/fear that led her down a bad path? How did that play into her parting with Cruz?

6. What was Cruz's biggest weakness/fear? How did that play into their parting?

7. Being with Kyle made Zoe forget the spirited young woman she used to be. Only after getting away from him was she able to remember who she was. Have you ever experienced this or known someone who has?

8. After being under her dad's thumb, why do you think Zoe fell headlong into a controlling relationship with Kyle?

9. What are some of the things we can learn about "control" from Zoe's experiences and decisions? Have you ever relinquished control to someone else? What happened? Who should have ultimate control?

10. *Blue Ridge Sunrise* is the first book in Denise's Blue Ridge series. Who do you think will be the hero and heroine of the next book? What do you think will happen?

For Granny Nel's Peach Crisp recipe,
visit DeniseHunterBooks.com.

Center Point Large Print
600 Brooks Road / PO Box 1
Thorndike, ME 04986-0001 USA

(207) 568-3717

US & Canada:
1 800 929-9108
www.centerpointlargeprint.com